The Paranormal Detectives

The Secret of the Carter House

The Paranormal Detectives

The Secret of the Carter House

Emily Grace

For Nana and Grandad
and in memory of Nanna.
Thank you.
☺ *xxxx*

PROLOGUE

A young boy walked through a luscious green forest, the sound of flowing water and the twittering of birds filling the air around him. Streams of sunlight forced their way through gaps in the trees, creating spots of light on the forest floor, perfect for the boy to use as stepping stones. He had a light and weightless feeling as he skipped and leaped around, until he spotted a stream through an opening in the trees. Looking in wonder, he ran towards it, feeling as if he were running through clouds, then knelt down to feel the warm and pleasant water.

As he was about to sit on the edge and put his feet in, he noticed a woman standing further along the bank, looking into the water. He stood up and began to walk towards her. As he got closer, he saw that she had flaming red curls and was wearing what looked like old-fashioned clothing. As she turned to him, he noticed her startling green eyes.

She smiled warmly. "Hello, dear. I have something very important I need you to do for me. Is that alright?" she said, in a soft voice.

The boy hesitated. His parents had always told him not to talk to strangers, but the woman seemed very kind. He nodded.

"Come with me," she said, reaching her hand towards him. "Don't be scared."

Slowly, the peaceful surroundings and the kind woman all began to fade away.

The boy awoke with a gasp. He heard a loud bang coming from above, and he looked around realising he was back in his own room, lying in the top bunk of the bunk bed he shared with his older brother. His bed was quite close to the ceiling, where the noise had come from. He sat up and rubbed his eyes. Looking over the side of the bed, he noticed a few small, blurry shapes on the ground, lit up by his night light. He thought this was very odd, so found his glasses and put them on, hoping to get a better look at the objects on the floor. With his glasses on, he could see the shapes were actually his own toys, lying on the floor in a line which led out of the room and onto the landing. He knew that he had tidied his toys away before he went to bed, so was intrigued as to why they were now scattered around the floor.

Putting his cuddly *Scooby Doo* toy down on the bed, the boy descended the ladder to investigate. As he reached the bottom, he tiptoed over to his older brother, who was still fast asleep in the lower bunk. He shook him gently, but he didn't stir. Realising there was no use in trying to wake him, the boy turned back to the line of toys and began to follow the path they mapped out, picking up each toy as he went. The toys led him to the middle of the landing, where he looked around in the pitch black, clutching the pile of toys he had collected in his arms. He looked up and realised he was standing directly underneath the loft hatch.

Suddenly, there was another loud bang from above. The boy squealed and ran back into his bedroom, dropping his toys on the floor on the way. He climbed back up the ladder and into bed as quickly as he could, making sure he was completely covered by his sheets. He trembled as he hugged his cuddly toy closely, squeezing his eyes tightly shut, until sleep finally overtook him.

PART ONE

CHAPTER ONE

It was a crisp evening in early December and the residents of Teaburn were slowly starting to arrive home from work. The darkening sky prompted the turning on of Christmas lights in the village and the multicoloured lights glistened on the wet roads. A woman was walking her dog along the path, her coat wrapped tightly around her and earmuffs protecting her ears from the cold. Walking as briskly as possible so she could get back into the warmth, she passed two children playing in the street outside their house wearing big fluffy coats. The children saw the headlights of a car coming around the corner and ran onto the path giggling as it drove past, splashing through a large puddle. Inside the car, Charlie Parker was trying to give directions to Mateo Jones.

"Woah, Mat, watch out for puddles. That made me jump," Charlie said, twisting in his seat to make sure they hadn't soaked the children, who were now running around on the path looking perfectly dry.

"Oops, sorry. Which way now?" Mat asked, as he came to the end of the street.

"You go right here, then we drive along that road for a few minutes I think. Then it's another right and we're there," Charlie told him, slightly confused by the map he was trying to read on his phone.

Mat and Charlie had met when they were just six years old, when Charlie and his family had moved up north from Teaburn to Latewater-by-the-sea, a beautiful coastal town located in the North East of England. Charlie joined Mat's primary school and was instantly drawn to him on his first day as he was the only other glasses wearer in the class. He sat down next to the shy-looking boy and noticed that he had a *Scooby Doo* pencil case, so he complimented him on it. They immediately became best friends and found that they had the same taste in almost *everything*. They liked all the same books, TV shows, movies, subjects in school – it was like they shared a brain.

However, one thing they could never agree on was the matter of the supernatural. Charlie was convinced his house in Teaburn had been haunted. When they were around eleven years old, he told Mat all about the paranormal experiences he could remember having when he had lived there.

"Well, these things happen sometimes. Houses creak and bang and can be really scary in the dark, but that doesn't mean your house is haunted!" Mat had said, when Charlie told him about the bangs and crashes he would hear coming from the loft during the night.

"Are you sure that wasn't just your brother playing tricks on you?" Mat had asked, when Charlie told him how sometimes when he got up in the morning his things would be in a different place to where he had left them.

For every supernatural thing Charlie told him, Mat had a natural explanation. This really vexed Charlie. The next day he came into school with a folder full of articles he had found online about ghost hunters visiting haunted locations, detailing all the evidence they had found while they were there. The day after that, Mat came into school with a folder full of articles he had found online detailing scientific research against the existence of ghosts. This debate went on for years, until one day, Charlie had a brilliant idea.

"The only way you'll ever agree with me is if you experience some kind of paranormal activity yourself, isn't it?" he had asked Mat, feeling defeated after they'd spent half an hour debating the subject and Mat still showed no signs of budging.

"I mean, it would have to be something pretty ground-breaking, but theoretically, yes," Mat shrugged. He had always been one for facts; he would never believe in something just because there was a possibility it could be true, unlike Charlie who was very open to that kind of thinking.

"Well, why don't we put it to the test?" Charlie said mysteriously, a smile creeping onto his face.

Mat frowned at him in confusion. "What are you on about?" he asked.

"Why don't we go online right now and find somewhere close by that's haunted, then we can go and visit, and I'll prove to you that ghosts exist!" Charlie suggested, talking more rapidly as his excitement built.

Mat thought over the idea, fiddling absentmindedly with the gold ring he wore on his right hand as he did so. He knew how much this meant to Charlie.

When they were kids, Mat had wanted to be an astronaut because he was so fascinated by space, but Charlie had always wanted to be a paranormal investigator. Mat was also interested in ghosts, but he always saw it as fiction, whereas Charlie believed it was real. They would go into the woods near Charlie's house and take turns pretending to be astronauts and Ghostbusters. It was a lot of fun, and he supposed it might still be now.

He looked up at Charlie who was watching him expectantly and let out a deep sigh. "Okay, but only if you promise you'll come with me to the Kennedy Space Center at some point to return the favour."

Charlie cheered and agreed to the terms, opening up his laptop to look for some haunted sites.

They searched for a while and eventually decided on a nearby haunted quarry. Charlie spent the rest of the week researching as much as he could about the ghosts who haunted the quarry, and that weekend they got ready to go ghost hunting for the first time. Charlie suggested they film it, because if he managed to make Mat believe in ghosts then he needed it to be immortalised on video.

"I think we should make a proper intro for it. Like, sit down and explain everything. I have a load of information about the quarry's past I can read out as well. Just in case we find something amazing and we want to post it online!" Charlie suggested, his excitement bubbling over.

Mat agreed, so Charlie got out his phone and propped it up on the kitchen table, and they sat down in front of it to explain what they were doing and why they were doing it.

Charlie cleared his throat, suddenly nervous now the camera was rolling. "He– hello there everyone," he started, unsure of how to introduce a video. He glanced at Mat for some moral support, then started again. "Hey guys!" he said, more confidently this time and with a little wave. "My name is Charlie" – he pointed to himself

– "and this is my best mate, Mateo," he pointed to Mat, then looked over at him and paused to let him speak.

Mat's eyes widened, and he shifted in his chair uncomfortably. "Hi." There was a pause as he searched for something else to say. "You can call me Mat," he added eventually, giving the camera an awkward half-smile, then quickly looking away.

"I am a firm believer that ghosts exist, and Mat is the opposite," Charlie continued. "I've persuaded him to come with me to a haunted quarry, in the hope that we'll find some evidence of the paranormal and I can prove to him that I'm right."

"Not gonna happen," Mat interjected, gaining a bit of confidence, but still not looking directly into the camera. "I hope you realise I'm gonna have to look a ghost square in the eyes before I change my mind," he said to Charlie, who laughed.

"Anyway, I thought I would explain the history of the quarry before we go. Mat, are you ready for this? It gets pretty spooky," Charlie said, turning to Mat.

"I was born ready!" Mat replied, getting comfortable in his chair.

Charlie talked about the quarry's gruesome past and some of the hauntings that had been reported. Mat listened intently, laughing every so often and rolling his eyes at some of the more stupid sounding stories and theories. Then they set off to investigate the quarry with their torches to see, and their phones to film.

Unfortunately for Charlie, they didn't have much luck in finding any evidence of ghosts. The most exciting thing that happened while they were there was when the wind blew a plastic bag in front of Charlie's face. He almost jumped out of his skin, letting out a high-pitched scream.

"Oh my god!" Mat wheezed, nearly doubled over from laughing so much. "Thank god I was filming that! I can't wait to watch it back later!" Charlie couldn't help but join in with the laughter, and they spent a few minutes trying to compose themselves.

They went home having had a good time, but a little disappointed that they didn't manage to get any paranormal evidence. They decided they would have to do it more often, because they had enjoyed it so much. Mat edited together a video of their outing and it turned out really well, considering it was their first time both ghost hunting and filming themselves talking to a camera. They didn't expect much to come from their new hobby, but they decided they wanted to upload it to YouTube anyway, if only for the memories. They brainstormed some names for a channel and eventually settled on *The Paranormal Detectives*.

Their first video went down a lot better than they thought it would. People seemed to really like their dynamic and chilled approach to ghost hunting. At the time, they were both juggling university work, a part time job, and were spending all their free time running their YouTube channel from the flat they rented together near their university. They had countless late nights of Charlie researching haunted sites and Mat editing their videos and managed to get out around one video a month, sometimes less if they had a lot on at university.

Just over two years after creating their channel, they graduated and decided to have a gap year where they focused solely on YouTube to see where it would go. So, they found a new flat just outside of the city and with their new freedom put everything into their work, expanding their trips to much further afield.

Since they had more time on their hands, they could really improve the quality of their videos. Charlie delved deeper into researching the locations, so they had a lot more knowledge before they visited. Mat had always loved drawing and animation, so started doing little illustrations of the things Charlie described and animating them to add into the video when he was editing.

Their channel grew and grew, and around six months on they now found themselves having reached a milestone they never would have believed possible – one hundred thousand subscribers to their YouTube channel. To celebrate this momentous occasion, Mat had suggested they do a special episode where they visit Charlie's childhood home. Charlie had been unsure about it at first, but in the end decided that it would be good for him to revisit the house.

Charlie had always been uncertain about that chapter of his life and had a lot of unanswered questions. Although he felt pretty sure about what he had experienced as a child, there was always a tiny niggling thought in his head that maybe Mat was right, and it was all just a figment of his imagination. He needed to prove to both Mat and himself that what he remembered had been real.

They found out that the house was now used for ghost tours, so they contacted the owner, Mrs Harris, and arranged to spend a night there. Finding out that other people had also had paranormal experiences in the house gave Charlie some level of comfort, and he also found out the identity of the ghost in his research. It was strange to be able to put a name and face to his memories of lights flickering and old music playing and countless other things that had happened in that house. After they had made all of the arrangements for their trip, they drove down to Teaburn in Mat's car.

"Are you nervous, Chaz?" Mat asked now, the light from the streetlamps bouncing off his brown skin as they passed each one, turning it a warm shade of gold. He glanced at Charlie, who was staring out of the car window anxiously biting his nails, then turned his attention back to the road.

"A little," Charlie confessed, running a hand through his blonde hair. "I mean, I'm always nervous when we go to these places 'cause I don't particularly wanna be murdered by a ghost, but I'm a different kind of nervous this time. It's gonna be so weird being there again after so many years. And now I actually know stuff about the person who haunts the house! It's actually a really sad story."

"Don't tell me anything!" Mat exclaimed, trying to cover his ears with one hand, while keeping the other firmly placed on the steering wheel. "I want my initial reaction to be when we're sitting in the house and the camera is rolling."

Charlie grinned. "I won't give any spoilers, don't worry. It just feels so strange reading about the ghost who I can remember haunting my house and seeing that they were once just a normal person with their own life. It's weird reading about other people's experiences in the house as well. And when I talked to my mam and dad about it they also remembered strange things happening when we lived there!"

"Well, I think it'll be really good for you to see the house again. It might give you some closure," Mat said, smiling over at Charlie, who returned the smile.

"I think that's the turn coming up," Charlie said, checking the map on his phone. He got out the camera and turned it on to film them pulling into the driveway. "Here it is, it looks just like I remember."

Charlie craned his neck, so he could see the house properly through the windscreen. It was quite big but had a relatively plain exterior. It looked rather spooky in the darkness, but not any more so than any other house on the street. He could see a sign next to the front door that looked like it contained information about the house and contact details for the ghost tours.

"Well, I for one am very excited to see this house I've heard so much about over the years," Mat said, and Charlie turned the camera on him. "And hopefully meet the ghost!" he added sarcastically, crossing his fingers dramatically.

Charlie rolled his eyes at him and put the camera down on the dashboard, so they were both in shot. "Mat, you are going to eat your words. I've had first-hand experience of this ghost and I just know that we're gonna get something good today! You just need to open your mind before we go in."

"Of course, I always open my mind before we go hunting for ghouls!" Mat said innocently, and Charlie raised his eyebrows at him. "I do! I would love to see a ghost and find out that you aren't crazy after all. This'll be such a heart-warming video if we manage to capture you being reunited with your old mate!" he teased, and Charlie laughed.

"Right, we'd better go in. I can't put it off any longer," Charlie said, and they gathered their equipment together.

They now had a lot more than just their phones and a torch each, so they both had their hands full as they walked up to the front door. Charlie scrambled to get the keys out of his pocket, which they had collected from Mrs Harris earlier that afternoon. He opened the door and stared inside, then turned to Mat who was filming him and looking very uncomfortable because he was carrying so many things.

"Can you go first?" Charlie asked, and Mat obliged. He walked through the door and a little way up the hallway without any hesitation, then put his things down at the bottom of the stairs.

"Ooh, it's nice and toasty in here! Mrs Harris must have put the heating on for us. Makes it a bit less spooky that it has a modern heating system though," he said, taking off his beanie and ruffling his dark brown curls. He turned around and pointed the camera at Charlie who was still standing outside. "Whenever you're ready."

"Here goes nothing," Charlie said, taking a deep breath and stepping through the front door of his childhood home for the first time in fifteen years.

CHAPTER TWO

As soon as he stepped through the front door, Charlie was hit with a wave of heat. It brought back memories of going on holiday and stepping out of the plane into the heat of another country. "Whew! You weren't lying about it being toasty in here. I wonder if we can turn the heating down," he said, shrugging off his bomber jacket and smoothing out his checked button-down shirt.

"It's over here," Mat said, walking over to the thermostat which he had spotted on the wall and lowering the temperature.

Charlie looked around the hallway, noticing it looked completely different to when he had been there last. The carpet had been taken up, revealing the original wooden floors, and it had been redecorated with 1940s décor to fit the time period. He walked through the door Mat was standing next to and into the living room, where a large rug covered much of the floor.

"It's a lot smaller than I remember," Charlie said, taking it all in.

"Are you sure you haven't just gotten bigger?" Mat asked, following him through the door and pointing the camera around the room.

Charlie laughed and turned back to nod at him, then walked over to the fireplace. "I'm pretty sure this is the only thing that's still the same from when I lived here. Everything else is completely different," he said, resting a hand on the mantelpiece. "I remember my parents loved it, but I always got a weird vibe from it."

"You got a 'weird vibe'?" Mat asked, scrunching up his face, his voice dripping with scepticism. "So, you think the fireplace is haunted or something?"

"Well no, not exactly, but I believe it's one of the hotspots in the house," Charlie replied. "There's always certain places that a ghost will prefer to spend their time, and I think the fireplace is one of them."

"Hmm, I see," Mat said, nodding his head and trying to look like he was contemplating the idea, rather than immediately dismissing it.

Charlie smirked, knowing fine well that Mat had no intention of actually believing him unless there was hard evidence. "Oh, I almost forgot! I bought these EVP recorders that you can wear on your wrist," he said, pulling two wristbands out of his bag and handing one to Mat. "The recorder we normally use to capture EVP is much bigger and bulkier, so I saw these and I thought we could try them out. We just have to press this button on the side and then it'll record the whole night."

"If you're confused, remember when Charlie plays random background noises and tries to say it's the ghost talking to us? That's EVP," Mat said to the camera, resting it on a side table while he put on his wristband.

Charlie rolled his eyes. "Electronic Voice Phenomena is a real thing, actually. It's super interesting. Some of the spirit voices that people have captured are so cool."

"Isn't it funny how there are so many 'amazing' EVPs out there, but when we go to the same places they don't wanna say a word to us?" Mat said. "I mean, I'm not saying they're fake, but…" he trailed off and gave the camera a knowing look.

Charlie turned to Mat with a mock-affronted expression. "Hey! I won't take any of this slander of our fellow paranormal investigators. Maybe we're just rubbish at our jobs?" he said jokingly, making them both laugh. He started to walk back out into the hallway. "Come on, let's set everything up."

Mat turned off the camera and they dragged all of their equipment into the living room. Mat got out a bigger camera and started setting it up on a tripod, pointing it towards two armchairs which were positioned next to the fireplace. Meanwhile, Charlie dug out a folder containing all the information he had gathered about the house, including the script he had prepared to read for the episode.

"Should we do a quick Insta story first, just to tease the episode?" Charlie suggested, reaching for his phone.

"Sure," Mat replied, walking over to sit in the armchair next to Charlie, who was opening up Instagram.

Charlie fixed his hair and straightened the thick black frames of his glasses, then started recording. "Hi everyone," he said, beaming at the camera.

"Hi," Mat said, smiling and leaning into frame.

"We're currently at a secret location," Charlie said, turning the phone a little way to either side of them to tease their surroundings, while they both whispered a drawn out 'ooh' mysteriously, before turning it back to face them. "We're here filming a very special episode to celebrate a very big milestone."

"This one is very personal to our Charlie over here," Mat said, patting Charlie's shoulder. "It's kind of like his ghost hunter origin story!" He grinned, and Charlie laughed.

"Yeah, so, look out for this episode, hopefully coming in the next couple of weeks. Wish us luck!" Charlie said, crossing his fingers. Mat looked unbothered by the whole situation, like he was just having a pleasant evening out. Charlie stopped recording, watched it back, then posted it on his Instagram story.

"Right, are you ready?" Mat asked, going over to the camera to turn it on, but waiting for the go ahead from Charlie first.

"Wait, I think we left the sleeping bags in the car. Should we go and get them first?" Charlie asked, starting to get nervous.

"Charlie," Mat said kindly. "We're gonna have to start at some point. We can get them later."

Charlie nodded, and Mat pressed record on the camera. He sat down and they both prepared themselves, before starting the episode.

"Hey guys!" Charlie beamed, with a little wave. "I'm Charlie, a firm believer in the paranormal."

"And I'm Mat, a firm believer in the normal," Mat said, with a half-smile and a nod at the camera.

"I've made it my mission to convince Mat that ghosts exist, by taking him to haunted locations in the hope we'll find paranormal evidence. This episode, we're investigating the Carter house," Charlie said, finishing their introduction. "But before we start, we just wanted to take a moment to talk about something big that happened recently."

He silently signalled to Mat, and they cheered in unison, "We hit a hundred thousand subscribers!"

"Thank you from the bottom of our hearts, we really are so grateful for your continued support! We never would have dreamed that something like this was possible," Mat said, smiling widely at the camera. "It's crazy!"

"It's outrageous! If you would have told us when we were filming our first video that this was going to come from it, we never would have believed you," Charlie said. "Thank you, thank you, thank you! We love you all!"

"Since it's such a special video, I even bought a new punny t-shirt for the occasion. What do you think?" Mat asked, moving his denim jacket out of the way so Charlie could see the print on his t-shirt. It had an image of a ghost, next to round glasses that looked like they belonged to Harry Potter, with a speech bubble saying, 'I can't find my spectre-cles!'

Charlie snorted. "Nice! On brand as well. Oh look, he even has the same glasses as you!" he said, looking at Mat's big round glasses with gold metal frames and throwing his head back in laughter.

"Ha-ha, very funny," Mat said sarcastically, although Charlie could see he was suppressing a grin.

"Anyway, we wanted to do something a bit special to celebrate," Charlie said. "And Mat somehow managed to convince me to do something I always said I would never do. We've come to the place that made me believe in ghosts: my childhood home."

Mat gasped and covered his mouth dramatically.

Charlie sniggered, then continued. "But before we get into that, we're going to rewind a bit, and I'm going to tell you the story of the woman who haunts this house, Pearl Carter."

Charlie paused while he sorted out the script. He put his bottle of water somewhere easily accessible, since he knew he was about to talk for a long time, then cleared his throat.

"So, we're here at the Carter house, which is situated in Teaburn, a small village near Bletchley in Buckinghamshire, England," he began. "It is the former residence of Harold and Mary Carter, who moved here in nineteen-twenty, not long after their daughter, Pearl, was born. In nineteen-twenty-nine, Mary died when giving birth to their second daughter, Rose. Harold died in a bombing raid in nineteen-forty, leaving Pearl to look after her sister. Pearl worked away from home for most of the year, and Rose attended a boarding school.

"In December nineteen-forty-four Pearl and Rose were both back at home for the holidays. On the morning of the twenty-second of December, Rose, who was fifteen at the time, went to visit their grandparents, Raymond and Dorothy Carter. Pearl had told them that she would join them for lunch, but she never turned up at the house. Later that afternoon, Dorothy took Rose back home, but when they entered the house they found Pearl lying dead in the hallway at the bottom of the stairs. She was only twenty-four years old when she died."

"Who put a curse on this family?" Mat asked, looking horrified.

"I have no idea, but they really didn't have any luck," Charlie replied, with a hollow laugh.

"I feel so bad for Rose, she didn't have a very good childhood, did she?" Mat said sadly, and Charlie shook his head.

"I have a picture of Pearl to show you, taken a few months before she died," he said, retrieving a photograph from his folder and handing it to Mat. It was a black-and-white photo showing a young woman with short curly hair, smiling widely at the camera.

"She looks so full of life," Mat said.

"Yeah, it's really sad," Charlie agreed, and they both paused for a moment staring at the photo, before Charlie put it back in his folder and continued. "Pearl had sustained two head injuries, one on the back of her head and the other one on her forehead. They also found her handbag lying at the top of the stairs. The police ruled it an accident. They believed she had tripped over her handbag and fallen down the stairs, hitting her head on the bannister, then again on the stairs before landing face down on the floor. She would have died instantly with the impact.

"This sounds plausible at first, but there are a few things that don't add up. First of all, they found blood on the phone table, which would have no way of getting there if Pearl had died by falling down the stairs. Secondly, the blood pattern on the stairs and on the floor around her head didn't fit in with the theory of how she fell, it seemed to be more random. Thirdly, according to Dorothy Carter's statement, the front door was unlocked when they arrived at the house. She claimed that it was very unusual for Pearl to leave the door unlocked."

Mat frowned. "Wait, so the crime scene didn't exactly fit with the theory of her tripping down the stairs, but the police didn't see her death as suspicious at all? Who took the case, Inspector Mallory? Was Father Brown not around to help out?" He chuckled to himself.

Charlie laughed loudly and turned to Mat. "I don't think any of our viewers are gonna get that reference," he said with a snort.

"Don't you think?" Mat wheezed, then turned to the camera. "For those of you who don't know, I'm referencing a TV show about a Catholic priest who solves murders. If you haven't seen it, you're missing out; it's great!"

Charlie sniggered. “It’s not as good when you have to explain the joke. I appreciated it though.”

“Leave a comment down below letting us know if you’ve heard of it.” Mat smirked and pointed downwards to where the comment section would be when the video was uploaded to YouTube.

“Anyway, moving on,” Charlie continued, composing himself. “Rose said that Pearl had been acting strange the whole time she had been home. She seemed distracted and on edge, and she kept telling Rose to be careful. After her sister passed away, Rose moved out of the house to live with Raymond and Dorothy. She still firmly believes to this day that her sister’s death wasn’t an accident.”

“Oh, so she’s still alive?” Mat asked, sounding surprised.

“Yeah, she’s ninety-one years old and lives in Cambridge.”

Mat raised his eyebrows. “Really? For some reason I always just assume everyone’s dead.”

Charlie continued with the story. “The house was empty for several years after Pearl’s death, until nineteen-fifty, when Pete and Elizabeth Watson and their three young children moved in. In the December, when they had lived there for a few months, strange things started happening around the house. It started out small; lights would flicker, and they would hear noises that they couldn't explain. Then, they reported hearing faint music playing in the living room, which they couldn't find a source for. According to Pete, the song they heard was *White Christmas* by Bing Crosby."

Mat wheezed, but he didn't make a comment.

"Remember that one for later," Charlie told him. "There were many occupants of the house over the years, and a few of them reported similar happenings. One family reported that they could smell burning coming from the fireplace in the living room, despite the fact they had never lit the fire in their time living there. In all of the cases, the incidents occurred mainly in December – the same month that Pearl died." He turned to look at Mat for his reaction.

"Hmm…" Mat said thoughtfully, narrowing his eyes and nodding his head slowly, his arms crossed over his chest.

"Hmm? That's all you have to say about that?" Charlie asked, laughing.

Mat shrugged. "I mean… it was winter when all this happened, right? So, maybe it was to do with the cold weather?" he suggested.

Charlie rolled his eyes, exasperated, before continuing. "Now, this is where I come into it," he said, starting to feel nervous. His mouth had suddenly become extremely dry, so he had to take a drink of water before he could carry on. "So, my parents, Chris and

Danielle Parker, moved into this house in two-thousand-and-three, when I was four years old. We only lived here a couple of years, until two-thousand-and-five, when we moved up north."

"Did the ghost chase you out?" Mat asked jokingly, even though he knew that hadn't been the case.

"No, she didn't," Charlie replied, shooting Mat an unimpressed look before turning back to the camera, hiding a grin. "My dad's a maths teacher, and there was a position going at a school in the area where my mam was brought up. I think she'd been wanting to move back home for a while anyway, so my dad put in for it. He got the job, and that was that. We packed our bags and moved to the North East that summer. That's when I transferred to Mat's school." He gestured to Mat.

"Ahh, the day your life began. Everything started going uphill for you from that point onwards. I remember it well," Mat said, smiling serenely and looking into the middle distance.

Charlie looked over at him and laughed. "The best day of *your* life, you mean."

Mat shrugged his shoulders. "That too," he conceded, nodding his head towards Charlie in acknowledgement.

"I have a picture to show you of me, my brother, and my sister when we lived here, actually," Charlie said, opening his folder and pulling out a photograph.

Mat took it from him. “Aww, look how cute you all were!” he said, smiling down at the picture. It showed two young boys sitting together on the floor and beaming at the camera, the older one holding a baby in his arms, all of them with fair skin, blonde hair and bright blue eyes. They were sitting in the same living room Mat and Charlie were sat in now, although the room was decorated so differently that the only way Mat could tell was by looking at the fireplace they were sitting in front of.

“That’s me on the left with the glasses, I was five at the time. The other boy is my older brother, Joey, who was eight, and he’s holding my little sister, Billie, who was only a few months old,” Charlie explained for the benefit of the video, since Mat could tell them apart without help. Once Mat was finished looking at the photo, he handed it back to Charlie who put it back in his folder.

“Even though we only lived here a short time, it made quite a big impression on me,” Charlie continued. “I found it so interesting when I was researching this, that a lot of people had the same experiences as me. I was only young, so I don’t remember everything that happened, but what I do remember is very clear.

“I used to hear bangs and crashes coming from the loft during the night, and I remember hiding under the sheets ‘cause I was so scared. Sometimes, I would get up in the morning and find that things had moved around in my room. I also have a very clear memory of playing with my toys in the living room by myself, and hearing faint music, coming from that corner." He pointed into the corner on the other side of the fireplace. "I can remember going over to find out where it was coming from, and it didn't seem to be coming from anywhere. I know exactly what the song was as well, because I used to love it when I was little. It was *White Christmas* by Bing Crosby. I say I *used* to love it, because I can't listen to it anymore. It reminds me of that incident and I get chills; it's been ruined for me."

Mat frowned. "Wait, that's the song Pete said he heard as well!" he said, looking slightly unnerved.

Charlie nodded and turned to Mat in distress. "See what I mean? Some of the stuff I read about is so similar to what I remember!"

"I will admit, that is a little bit strange," Mat conceded.

"No kidding!" Charlie said. "I talked to my parents about it the other day, and it turns out they also noticed strange things happening in the house. I'd talked to them about it before, but they didn't want to worry me when I was younger. They were never convinced it was a ghost, even though they'd heard the stories about the house before we moved in.

"Apparently, the lights used to flicker quite a lot the whole time we lived here, but it would get worse around Christmas time. They always just put it down to faulty wiring. Also, when Billie was little, they would sometimes wake up to her laughing in her nursery. When they went through to check on her, they would come across the light turned on, and Billie looking at nothing, as if there was something there that she found funny. Mam told me that this happened a few times. I don't understand how they weren't more freaked out by that. I would be packing my bags and leaving first thing in the morning! No wonder you get on with them so well, Mat, you would be just like them in that situation."

Mat laughed. "I knew there was a reason I loved your family!" he said, a proud look on his face.

"This is why they've basically adopted you," Charlie said, chuckling. "Joey can't remember that much happening, but he does remember the lights flickering. So, either the ghost didn't bother with him, or he just wasn't easily frightened. Obviously, Billie was too young to remember anything – but she was really freaked out when she heard the story about her laughing at the ghost."

Mat wheezed. "That doesn't surprise me." He turned to the camera. "For everyone at home, Billie is just like Charlie when it comes to this type of thing. In fact, she's probably worse. I don't think she would ever set foot somewhere like this!"

"Definitely not," Charlie agreed. "She *hates* it when we go on our investigations; she spends the whole time worrying. In fact, I bet if I check my phone right now there'll be a worried text from her." He got his phone out and snorted when he looked at it. "Yep! She says, 'Make sure you're both careful and text me at least once an hour so I know you're not dead.' "

"Bless her!" Mat said, as they both laughed. "I feel like Joey would be okay though. We should've brought him along with us!"

"No way!" Charlie said, shaking his head. "He would probably side with you and I'd have to deal with two sceptics. I couldn't handle it. Unless we brought Lucas along with us as well; he believes in ghosts." He turned to the camera and added, "Lucas is Joey's boyfriend. Anyway, we've gone completely off topic now. Where were we up to?" He looked at his notes. "No, that was it. I don't have anything else I need to say."

"Right then – I guess it's time to start investigating," Mat said, getting up to turn off the camera.

"I guess so," Charlie said nervously.

They put away the equipment they no longer needed and prepared themselves for an evening of exploring the Carter house.

CHAPTER THREE

"I think we should start out in the hallway," Charlie said, picking up his backpack which he had filled with all of the equipment they would need around the house, so it was easily accessible. "We may as well use the main light for now. We can use our torches a bit later, but I wanted to show this part properly."

"Sounds good," Mat said, picking up his handheld camera and turning it on as they walked through the door and back out into the hallway. They made their way over to the front door and turned to face the stairs.

"This is where Dorothy and Rose found Pearl's body," Charlie said to the camera, moving closer to the stairs. "There's a picture of the crime scene, but it's not very nice, so I didn't really want to show it. It is out there though if you wanted to search online for it. But she was lying right here." He gestured to the bottom of the stairs. "Let me just find something, one second."

As Charlie rummaged through his bag, Mat took the opportunity to film around the hallway. He slowly panned around, showing the stairs, the place where Pearl was found at the bottom, the front door, the phone table and the dusty mirror that hung above it. As his eyes drifted over the mirror, he saw a pair of startling green eyes staring at him. It took him a second to process what he had seen, before his eyes snapped back to the mirror. He quickly moved towards it, but all he could see were his own dark-brown eyes looking back at him, wide and alarmed.

"…and I was thinking we could–" Charlie cut himself off as he looked up and realised Mat wasn't paying attention to anything he was saying. "Mat? Are you okay?" he asked, walking over to join him in front of the mirror.

"Yeah, I– I'm fine, it's just… never mind, I probably just imagined it," Mat said, realising he was filming the floor and lifting his arm, then turning the camera to face them both.

"What was it?" Charlie asked, sounding concerned and looking at the mirror, which Mat was still giving furtive glances. He found it very unnerving to see Mat looking scared.

"It's just… I thought I saw– well, I was looking around the hallway and– and I imagined a pair of green eyes reflected in the mirror. But it was obviously just my mind playing tricks on me, probably 'cause we're standing where she died. Nothing to worry about," Mat said, not sure who he was trying to convince, himself or Charlie.

"Oh my god… I wonder if you caught it on camera!" Charlie said excitedly.

"I won't have caught it on camera, because it wasn't real," Mat said firmly.

"Wait, that means she's probably in the hallway with us right now," Charlie said, his expression changing from excitement to fright as he looked around nervously.

"No, she's not," Mat said, rolling his eyes. "It must've just been a figment of my imagination. I shouldn't have said anything. It's just a bit spooky in here, that's all; I lost my mind for a moment. But we can review the footage if you want to."

"Yes, please."

Mat stopped recording and Charlie turned on his own camera, so he could film them watching back the footage. Mat fast forwarded through the clip until he got to the part where he had started filming the hallway. In the video, Charlie was rummaging through a bag, then the shot slowly moved over the stairs, panning down to the bottom, then past the front door and around to where the phone table stood, the dusty mirror hanging above it. The shot moved past the mirror, then jolted and quickly moved back, before dropping to a view of the floor. Mat paused the video and turned to Charlie.

"See? No green eyes. I told you I'd imagined it," he said, but he was extremely relieved all the same.

Charlie took the camera from him and rewound it to the mirror, then paused it. He looked closely and saw a slight glint of green in the reflection.

"Then what's that?" he asked. "I don't think you did imagine it!"

Mat took the camera back off him and brought it close to his face, lifting his glasses up and squinting.

"Okay, maybe I didn't *fully* imagine it… maybe there was something there, but it was just the reflection of something in the hallway," he said, turning around and inspecting the wall opposite the mirror.

Charlie turned to look as well. "There's nothing to reflect! How do you explain that?" he asked, feeling a bit scared, but also triumphant.

"It was probably just a trick of the light," Mat said, with a shrug.

"See, he doesn't even believe his own eyes," Charlie said to the camera. "He's impossible!"

"What were you gonna say before?" Mat asked, quickly changing the subject.

"I was just gonna say, we should use the thermal cam in here," Charlie said, passing the filming camera to Mat and picking up the thermal imaging camera from the floor, where he'd abandoned it earlier after he'd been distracted by Mat's possible hallucination. He hesitated. "Maybe we should switch to torches now as well."

"It's about time. Torches add to the ambiance."

Charlie found the night vision cameras in his bag and passed one to Mat. Previously, they had used handheld night vision cameras, but they had recently bought new ones that strapped onto the body.

"I think I'll put it on underneath my jacket. Do you think it'll be covered by the jacket at all? Should I keep it off?" Mat asked, starting to remove his denim jacket.

"Nah, it should be fine," Charlie said, fastening his own camera to his chest.

Mat walked over to the mirror to check his camera wasn't obscured. "It seems okay. What do you think?" he asked, turning to Charlie.

"Yeah, looks fine to me. These are gonna be so much better! Gone are the days of having to juggle two types of camera and a torch each when we're walking around the house. It's gonna make our lives so much easier."

"We look like professionals," Mat said, grinning.

Charlie laughed. "We do."

They both picked up their torches and switched them on, then Mat turned off the main light. Charlie began to point the thermal imaging camera around the hallway, watching out for hot or cold spots, which could indicate the presence of a ghost. It was hard to tell what he was looking at through the camera, as objects morphed into indistinguishable blobs, taking on a range of colours depending on their temperature. Things that looked perfectly ordinary in natural light, became intimidating when they were reduced to being just a blue silhouette on the screen.

As he pointed it towards the mirror, he shrieked, making Mat jump. The camera showed what looked like a ghostly figure standing in front of him, but when he looked up, he realised it was just his own reflection.

"Oh my god," Charlie said, breathing a sigh of relief. "I thought I saw something, but it was just me. Look!"

Mat looked at what Charlie had seen through the camera and sniggered. "It does look like a ghost, I'll give you that."

"I'm too on edge after what happened before," Charlie said, laughing. He finished examining every inch of the room with the thermal imaging camera, but didn't come across anything else that seemed unusual. "No, there's nothing. Right, I think we should do the torch experiment."

He got out a different torch and twisted the head so that the switch was between the on and off position, then placed it on the floor. This was supposed to give the ghost the ability to manipulate the torch and turn the light on and off at its own free will. Mat was always very sceptical about this though, and believed it was just a coincidence when the torch turned on or off according to their requests.

Charlie cleared his throat. "Okay, if there's someone here, can you turn on the light?" he asked, tentatively.

They waited a while, but nothing happened.

"Pearl, if you're in here, could you please turn on the light?" Charlie asked again.

The light slowly flickered and turned on.

Charlie gasped and turned to Mat. "She's here!"

"I mean, that was probably just by chance," Mat said.

"Mat saw a pair of eyes in the mirror earlier–" Charlie started, but Mat interrupted him.

"You mean I *imagined* a pair of eyes. I don't know why I bothered telling you about it when I know what you're like."

"If that was you, could you turn the light off for us, please?" Charlie requested, ignoring Mat's interruption.

They waited a while, and just when Charlie was about to ask another question, the light turned off. He turned to Mat with wide eyes.

"Oh, come on," Mat said, rolling his eyes in amusement. "That was a coincidence. It didn't even happen straight after you said it! Let me have a go." He passed the camera back to Charlie and cleared his throat. "Hi Pearl, if you aren't actually Pearl, could you turn the light on?"

They waited, but nothing happened.

Mat tried again, racking his brains for random questions he could ask. "If you're a roof thatcher from the west country, could you turn the light on?"

The light stayed firmly turned off.

Mat looked at Charlie who was starting to laugh. He suppressed a grin of his own. "Just wait, it's gotta turn on eventually. Could you turn the light on if you're an Australian ballroom dancer?"

There still wasn't even a flicker from the torch.

Charlie snorted, but Mat wasn't giving up any time soon. "If your real name is Harry Styles, turn the light on."

After a few seconds, the light flickered on.

Mat turned to Charlie with a smug expression. "Oh no, I think we must've had a mix up. It's actually Harry Styles that haunts this place, not Pearl Carter," he said. "I mean, I don't know how he's managing to haunt this house when he's still alive and well, but the light turned on, so it must be true! Your sister will be so jealous when she finds out we got to meet him."

Charlie folded his arms and held back a grin. "Well, sometimes there can be anomalies, but that doesn't mean we have to disregard all of it! She was probably just sick of you asking questions. Pearl, if the only reason you responded to Mat was 'cause he was annoying you, please could you turn the light back off again?"

The light turned off instantly.

Mat and Charlie looked at each other and burst out laughing.

"That was perfect timing!" Mat said, wheezing. "I still think it's all down to chance though. I'm not convinced. Pearl, if you want me to shut up, could you please turn the light back on?"

The light instantly turned back on, and they laughed even harder.

"Okay, I think we'll move on from the torch now, before Pearl kills Mat and there's another ghost haunting this house," Charlie said, with a snort of laughter.

"No, let her! I'd love that. It would be great for the video," Mat joked.

Charlie shook his head, chuckling. "I'd rather that didn't happen, I'd be scarred for life! Although, it would be very poetic if you were killed by something you don't even believe exists."

"You would one hundred percent be there telling me, 'I told you so,' as it killed me, then running out the front door before it got you, too," Mat said as he laughed. "No, but, in all seriousness, I'm not sure this experiment with the torch is ever gonna win me over. See, we have to twist the switch on the torch to the point where it's right on the cusp between being on and off. Now, that means it can potentially switch itself between the two. So, we stand here and ask the ghost some questions, and sometimes nothing happens, but other times the torch actually does what we've just asked the ghost to do. When that happens, Charlie gets all excited and thinks the ghost is communicating with us, and when we share it online, people think it's great evidence, and they get mad at me for not believing there's a ghost when it's just responded to our request for it to turn a light on. Surely that's brilliant and I should've changed my mind about it by now? But you have to remember, it could just be a coincidence. I just want people to bear that in mind."

Charlie thought for a moment. "Yeah, I see your point, and there are times I would agree with you on that. It *can* be random, but that doesn't mean it's *always* random. A lot of the time it consistently turns on or off in response to our questions. I just don't think it can be a coincidence every single time. I think it also depends on whether or not the ghost is in the room. If they aren't in here, then they obviously can't respond, and then we're most likely gonna find that the light will switch on randomly. But that doesn't mean there's no ghost in the house, it just means the ghost isn't in the same part of the house as us. This time however, I do believe Pearl is here with us in the hallway, responding to our requests. Or was in here just before, anyway. You might've annoyed her into moving to another room."

They agreed they should move on, so Charlie went over to his bag and pulled out another device that he wanted to use in the hallway. Mat took over filming, so Charlie could focus on what he was doing.

"This is an EMF meter. It detects electromagnetic fields," he told the camera. He walked over to the phone table. "Earlier, I told you that some of Pearl's blood was found on the phone table, with no explanation. This isn't the same one, but it's in the exact position of the original, so I thought I'd see if there are any EMF fluctuations in this area. If there are, then it could indicate the presence of a ghost."

Charlie scanned the area with the device, but there didn't seem to be anything out of the ordinary. After checking the whole hallway and finding nothing, they collected together their gear and moved to investigate the kitchen.

Charlie switched on the light as they went in. "I don't think there's been much reported about the kitchen," he said. "But we should check it anyway, just to be sure."

"She doesn't like the kitchen then," Mat commented, putting the camera down on the kitchen table, which was positioned in such a way that he could get the whole room in shot. Charlie looked at him quizzically and he elaborated. "Like you were saying earlier, about the hotspots? You said there's always certain places they prefer to float around in – or whatever ghosts get up to – and that Pearl likes to sit in the fireplace a lot."

Charlie snorted and shook his head in amusement. "I mean, there's more to it than that. But that's the gist of it, yeah."

Mat began to explore the kitchen as he continued. "Yeah, well, I think if ghosts weren't fictional and I came back as one, I would probably haunt a kitchen. It would be my room of choice."

"Would you? I'm not sure where I'd choose. I haven't really thought about it properly," Charlie said, picking up the thermal imaging camera so he could examine the room with it. "I think I might haunt a kitchen too, actually, since I like baking so much–" A loud noise suddenly cut him off and he gasped, whipping his head around to search for the source. He didn't have to look far, however, as he saw Mat had put the kettle on and was now helping himself to mugs and teabags from the cupboard. "What are you doing?" he asked, his heart beating fast.

"Making us a cuppa. Mrs Harris left us some tea making supplies. She even filled the kettle for us! We'll have to remember to thank her tomorrow," Mat said, looking through the drawers for a teaspoon.

Charlie watched him in disbelief. "We're supposed to be ghost hunting, Mat, we can't stop for a tea break."

"I know, I know. The investigation is very important. It's just I saw the kettle and it really made me want some tea," Mat said, giving Charlie an apologetic look as he spooned sugar into the mugs. "I'll be two seconds and then we can keep going."

"Honestly, I don't know how I put up with this guy," Charlie said exasperatedly to the camera.

Mat continued making the tea, while Charlie examined the room with the thermal imaging camera. He noticed a couple of hot and cold spots, but quickly realised that it wasn't anything abnormal. One of the hot spots had been the kettle heating up, and he put a cold spot by the window down to a slight draft coming through. He scanned the room with the EMF meter, but this didn't seem to show anything strange either.

"Just as I thought, there doesn't seem to be anything out of the ordinary in this room," Charlie said, putting away the devices.

Just then, Mat gasped loudly.

"What is it?" Charlie asked, spinning around to see what had happened.

"She's left us some digestives!" Mat said excitedly, showing Charlie the packet of digestive biscuits that he had just pulled out of the cupboard.

Charlie rolled his eyes at the camera.

CHAPTER FOUR

The living room felt eerily silent as Mat and Charlie made their way back through. Mat set their mugs of tea down on the side table, then found somewhere to put the camera so most of the room could be seen in the frame. They decided to switch on the table lamps, which gave out just enough light for them to see around the room without having to use their torches.

"This is one of the places I was most nervous about investigating, 'cause I'm worried about what we're gonna find in here," Charlie said, nervously running a hand through his hair. "It's one of the most active parts of the house, according to what people have reported, and one that I remember well from when I lived here."

"This is where you and that other guy – Pete, was it? – reported hearing music, isn't it?" Mat asked, dunking a digestive biscuit in his tea.

Charlie looked between Mat and the biscuit, to show that he was judging him heavily for doing this during an investigation, but he didn't comment on it. "Yeah, it was."

"I hope we hear it tonight," Mat said, with his mouth full.

Charlie grimaced. "I don't want to, but I hope we do for the sake of science. I'll tell you the full story now, actually. It's such a clear memory, although I must've only been around five years old when it happened." He walked into the middle of the room and sat cross-legged on the floor. "So, I remember I was sitting right here in the middle of the living room, and I had these *Scooby Doo* toys that I was obsessed with."

Mat grinned. "Oh yeah, I remember those! I had the same ones and we used to play with them together when we first met, didn't we?"

Charlie nodded eagerly. "Yeah, it was those ones!"

"I wonder if there's any photos of us playing with them."

"Should I text my mam? She probably has some in a photo album somewhere," Charlie suggested, getting his phone out of his pocket.

"Yeah, good idea! I bet she has loads. Your mam's always taking photos."

After Charlie had sent the text, he continued with his story. "So, anyway, I was sitting here playing with my toys. I think it might've been Boxing Day actually, and I'd got the *Scooby Doo* toys off Santa for Christmas. I was in here by myself – I'm not sure where everyone else had got to – and then, all of a sudden, I heard some music playing really quietly. I stopped playing with my toys, so I could listen properly, and I realised the music was coming from the corner over there, next to the fireplace." He pointed to the corner on the opposite side of the fireplace to the armchairs, then stood up and walked over. "So, I got up to investigate, and the music got a bit louder as I got closer. I looked around and I couldn't see where it was coming from. It was as if there was an invisible CD player sitting in that corner. I remember it was the song *White Christmas*, and I was quite happy about it at the time, 'cause I loved the song. I'm pretty sure I danced and sang along to it. But then, once I realised how creepy the whole thing was, I was a bit freaked out. I don't know how I was so brave to begin with."

Mat gave Charlie a sympathetic look, but he didn't really know what to say, so he just sipped his tea.

"I know you don't believe me," Charlie said, with a breathy laugh. "You don't need to humour me."

"It's not that I don't believe you!" Mat said quickly. "It's just, I find it so difficult to believe that something like that could actually happen. I feel like there must be a logical explanation for it."

Charlie shrugged. "It's okay, I don't mind. I already knew that you don't believe in any of this stuff. I probably wouldn't believe in it either if I hadn't experienced it myself! I mean, we both love science. In fact, you love physics so much that you did a degree in it! And the paranormal and science don't really mix when you look at it at face value. But I still believe in it."

"I am trying to open my mind to the possibility, I swear, it's just difficult for me to wrap my head around. Although, if it was real, I do love the fact that there's a ghost out there who likes to play Christmas songs. That information has improved my life, whether I believe in it or not. I just love the idea of it," Mat said, smiling to himself.

Charlie nodded in agreement and grinned. "I was thinking, I might just ask her politely if she can play the song for us, see what happens." He cleared his throat. "Pearl, do you think you could possibly play some music for us? Please?" he asked tentatively.

Nothing happened.

Mat wheezed. "It sounds like you're talking to a virtual assistant! Hey Pearl, play *White Christmas* by Bing Crosby," he requested, and Charlie laughed.

Again, nothing happened.

"Maybe I used the wrong greeting," Mat said, while Charlie sniggered. "Okay Pearl, play *White Christmas* by Bing Crosby."

For a third time, nothing happened.

"Well, that's that then. No music for us," Mat said, turning to look at Charlie.

"It's probably because you were being disrespectful," Charlie said, hiding his smile and giving Mat a disapproving look.

Mat smirked. "I mean, there's probably a few things I'd put above that on the list, but sure, that's the reason."

"Maybe if we play it for her she'll join in, or something?" Charlie suggested. He got out his phone and found the song, then prepared himself before he hit play and *White Christmas* blasted out of his phone speakers. He shuddered instantly, the memories flooding back.

Mat started to sing along and dance around the living room, as if he was dancing the waltz without a partner. "Pearl, you can join me if you'd like. All those years of watching *Strictly* are finally paying off!" he said, spinning around the room.

Charlie watched him, chuckling. "Pearl, if you like this song, go and have a dance with Mat. If you want to, that is," he said, gaining a bit of confidence in talking to her.

Mat shivered suddenly. "I just got a shiver down my spine. If that'd been you, you would be freaking out right now."

"Are you sure it was unrelated? It's not even cold in this room," Charlie asked, slightly concerned. He leant on the wall next to the fireplace and reached out his arm to rest on it. "Ow!" he cried, snatching his arm away as soon as it touched the mantelpiece. It felt as though he'd just put his arm in a scorching hot pan.

"What happened?" Mat asked, ceasing his dancing and walking over to Charlie.

"It burned me!" Charlie said, rubbing his forearm and frowning at the fireplace. He paused the music on his phone.

Mat reached out to touch the fireplace, bracing himself for the heat, but it was ice cold. "Charlie, it isn't hot. It's not even slightly warm. Are you sure it burned you?" he asked, with a confused expression. He checked Charlie's arm for any marks, but it was unblemished.

"Well… my arm feels okay now." Charlie cautiously reached out to touch the fireplace again, but it didn't burn him this time. "I could've sworn it was boiling hot when I touched it before."

Mat hesitated. "Do you think you could've imagined it?" he asked.

"I dunno… I suppose it could've just been my imagination, since I'm already feeling on edge. But I'm not ruling out any possibilities!" Charlie said, examining his arm again, just to double check there was nothing there. It felt and looked perfectly fine. He walked over to his backpack and pulled out the thermal imaging camera. "I'm gonna check it with the thermal cam, just in case," he said, walking back over to the fireplace.

The thermal imaging camera didn't seem to show anything strange when Charlie pointed it at the part of the mantelpiece where he had burned himself. But, as he panned downwards, he noticed there appeared to be a hot spot around the place where the fire pokers were stood. He snapped a picture of it.

"Mat, come and look at this."

Mat walked over and studied the image on the camera, then nodded his head and sipped his tea. "Should I touch it?" he asked, already leaning forwards, gripping his mug in one hand and stretching out the other towards the stand which held the fire pokers.

Charlie held his breath.

Mat's hand made contact with one of the fire pokers, and he jumped back with a sharp intake of breath, his tea sloshing around in his mug.

Charlie jumped and covered his mouth with one hand. "Did it burn you?" he asked worriedly, his voice slightly higher than usual.

Mat turned to him with wide eyes, then began to wheeze with laughter. "I'm just messing with you. It's not hot. Although, I did nearly spill my tea – that would've been a disaster."

Charlie let out a sigh of relief. "Oh my god, you're so annoying," he said, running a hand through his hair and laughing. He checked the rest of the room with the thermal imaging camera, but didn't find anything else unusual.

Mat drained the rest of his tea as Charlie picked up the EMF meter and scanned the fireplace.

"There's some fluctuations around the fireplace," Charlie said. "So that could be something. I suppose it could just be a coincidence that it's happening in the same place as the other things, but it is worth noting."

After he had finished scanning the whole room, Charlie put the EMF meter away and retrieved another device from his backpack. He walked closer to the camera and held it up. "I have another brand-new device for us to use. Never before seen on *The Paranormal Detectives*."

"Another one? We really blew the budget for this episode, didn't we?"

"I mean, it's not every day you hit a hundred thousand subscribers, is it? We really went all out! It's about time we updated our equipment anyway."

"Let me see," Mat said, walking over to Charlie so he could take a closer look at the device. "It looks like a little radio."

"Well done, Mat. Ten points to Ravenclaw!" Charlie said, and Mat cheered. "This is called a ghost box and it's a very cool piece of equipment. It's basically a radio with a frequency scanning function, but when it finds a station it carries on scanning. This means it keeps on jumping through different frequencies, staying on each one for only a fraction of a second. This creates white noise. Supposedly, spirits can manipulate this to communicate with us." He looked at Mat excitedly.

Mat chuckled. "I'll never understand how anyone comes up with these ideas. Do you think it was just a very bored ghost hunter? One day, he was sitting there twiddling his thumbs, waiting for a ghost to communicate with him, and he thought, 'Y'know what? Maybe they'll talk to me through a radio!' and then he started telling his friends about it?"

Charlie laughed. "I'm not sure, you could be right!" He fiddled with the ghost box until a very loud static noise started coming out of it, making them both jump. "Sorry, I forgot to warn you how loud it was gonna be," he told Mat, apologetically.

"I already hate it," Mat said, scrunching his face in discomfort.

"It's fine, we'll get used to it pretty quickly. So, I'm gonna ask some questions, and if we get a response that's a few syllables long, then it's probably a spirit voice," Charlie said, holding up the ghost box between them. "Hi Pearl, if you're here. My name is Charlie. Could you repeat that back to me please? Charlie."

They both stood listening to the static, which sounded choppy as it changed between frequencies.

There was a short noise that sounded like the beginning of a word, but they couldn't make out anything from it.

"Mat, why don't you give it a try," Charlie said, turning to Mat.

"Okay… Hi Pearl, I'm Mat. If you feel like it, could you use this little radio that my friend has brought with him, and repeat my name. Please," Mat requested.

Charlie nodded approvingly. "That was very respectful, I'm impressed."

They waited again, listening out for Mat's name.

"Any time now, whenever you're ready," Mat said.

They waited a bit longer.

"*Mah–*"

Mat and Charlie both looked at each other.

"*Mah– tay– oh–*"

Charlie's eyes widened. "That sounded like Mateo," he said, panicked.

"It did sound a bit like Mateo," Mat agreed, amused.

"But how would she even know your name is Mateo? I've only called you Mat the whole time we've been here!" Charlie started to pace around the room, white noise still blaring out of the ghost box he held in his hand.

Mat shrugged his shoulders calmly. "It's just a very freaky coincidence, don't worry about it. We probably only interpreted it that way 'cause we were listening out for my name."

Charlie let out a shaky breath. "Okay, let's carry on," he said. "Pearl, could you tell us your full name?"

They waited a while.

"*Per– erl–*"

Charlie was just about to say something else, and then–

"*Cah– tuh–*"

"Oh my god," Charlie said. "This is amazing. We're actually talking to her."

"I have to admit, I did hear, 'Pearl Carter,' but it wasn't very clear. It was quite disjointed. If I didn't know what I was listening out for I'm not sure I would've understood it," Mat said, trying to be a voice of reason.

"Yeah, it wasn't clear. But she's talking to us through a *radio*, for gods' sake! What do you expect?" Charlie said. "Pearl, your sister–"

"*Roh– zee–*"

"Yes, Rose! Your sister, Rose! Oh god. I'm freaking out, I don't know whether to be scared or excited," Charlie said, starting to pace again.

Mat laughed. "Calm down! Although, I am enjoying watching you get all worked up about it. It's quite funny."

"*Neck– liss–*"

"Necklace? What do you mean?" Charlie asked.

They waited for a while longer but didn't hear anything else apart from white noise and fragmented speech coming from the ghost box.

"Rose has always thought your death wasn't an accident. Is she right about this? Was there foul play involved?" Charlie asked.

They waited, listening to the static.

"*Yeah–*"

Charlie's eyes widened in shock as he heard the voice. "That definitely sounded like she was saying yes," he said, running a hand through his hair.

"*Cah– rut–*"

"Carrot?" Charlie said, turning to Mat with a puzzled look.

"*Av– oh–*"

"Avo? Like avocado?" Charlie said, even more confused. "Did they even have avocados back then?"

Mat wheezed. "I take back every bad word I said about the ghost box, I love it! I don't believe in it, but I love it anyway!" he said, beaming.

"*Choc–*"

Charlie sighed dramatically. "Yeah, I think we might've lost her and now we're just hearing random words."

"Or maybe she's just hungry?" Mat suggested, with a glint in his eye. "Pearl, do you want us to get you anything?"

Charlie turned to look at him, ready to give him the most unamused look he could muster, but he was stopped by another addition from the ghost box.

"*Tea–*"

They looked at each other and simultaneously dissolved into hysterics, Mat wheezing so hard he had to sit down on the armchair. Charlie dropped the ghost box on the floor as he clutched at his chest, feeling as if he might pass out from lack of oxygen. After a while, their laughter began to subside, and they managed to compose themselves.

"Okay, I think we're officially losing our minds. That really tickled me," Charlie said, picking the ghost box back up from the floor where it was still blaring white noise. "I think we should turn off the ghost box for now. We can try it again later."

Mat wiped his eyes on his jacket sleeve, still chuckling to himself quietly. "You need to drink your tea as well," he said, noticing Charlie's full mug sitting next to his empty one. "It'll be freezing by now!"

Charlie snorted. "I love how that's the only thing you care about. All this drama going on and you're just worried about my tea going cold."

"There's nothing worse than going to drink a cup of tea and finding out it's gone cold. I'm just trying to save you the heartbreak."

Charlie laughed as he turned off the ghost box, throwing the room into an eerie silence once again.

CHAPTER FIVE

Each step creaked as Mat and Charlie slowly made their way upstairs, Mat leading the way. They followed the beams of light cast by their torches, the surrounding darkness adding to the unsettling ambiance.

"Which room are we looking in first?" Mat asked, as he reached the top of the stairs.

"I'm not sure." Charlie joined him in the middle of the landing, then took a deep breath as he looked around, gripping his torch tightly in his fist. "This was my mam and dad's room… this one was mine and Joey's… this was Billie's nursery… that's the bathroom," he said, pointing the torch at each door in turn, Mat following the beam of light with the camera. Charlie paused before pointing the torch towards a hatch in the ceiling. "And this is the loft. I've never actually been in there before, but I'll be going in today." He shuddered at the thought.

"We should do the loft last. Build up to it. I'm not sure you'll be capable of going anywhere else after the loft, anyway. You'll probably have to go for a lie down," Mat said, laughing and turning the camera back to face Charlie.

"Hey!" Charlie glared at him. "Although, I can't lie. You're probably right," he added, cracking a smile. "Should we go in my parents' room first?"

"Yeah, sure," Mat agreed, and they made their way into the first bedroom.

"This room also belonged to Harold and Mary Carter, Pearl's parents. As far as I know, it was never used after they had both passed away. From my research, it doesn't seem to be very haunted either. My parents also said that they don't remember anything weird happening here," Charlie said, looking around the room.

There was some simple furniture; just a double bed, a wardrobe and two bedside tables. The owner had decorated it to recreate what it might have looked like at the time, as with the ground floor.

Charlie retrieved the EMF meter from his bag and began to scan the room with it. "I have to be honest, I'm not sure I'm one hundred percent convinced by the EMF meter."

"Really? Why not?" Mat asked.

"Because there's a lot of factors that can interfere with it, like our equipment, and the wiring in the house. All sorts of things can mess with it. And it isn't scientifically proven that ghosts can present themselves in this way at all. I dunno… it just doesn't seem to give the most concrete evidence," Charlie explained, shrugging his shoulders. "In my own personal opinion, that is," he added to the camera.

"Oh, are you coming over to the dark side?" Mat asked, adding an evil laugh at the end.

Charlie snorted. "No, I still believe in ghosts! I'm just not convinced by this method," he said.

"Why do we bother using it then?"

"Because there are a lot of other people who *do* think it gives compelling evidence. And there's a possibility they could be right, so we may as well present all our findings and people can make up their own minds."

"Yeah, that makes sense," Mat said, nodding in agreement.

Nothing showed up on the EMF meter, so Charlie moved onto the thermal imaging camera.

The room was quiet and still as he examined everywhere with the device.

Suddenly, the sound of somebody humming the tune of *White Christmas* broke through the silence.

Charlie jumped and whipped around. However, he realised straight away that it was just Mat, who was walking around the room holding the camera and humming absentmindedly.

"You okay over there?" Charlie asked, smirking over at Mat.

Mat blinked a couple of times and stopped humming. "Oh, sorry. I didn't even realise I was doing that."

Charlie chuckled. "It's fine. I'm not getting anything in this room," he said, putting the thermal imaging camera away.

"Should we move onto the next one then?" Mat suggested.

When Charlie agreed, they made their way across the landing and into the second bedroom. This room was decorated in a similar way to the first room, with a double bed, a bedside table and a wardrobe. There was also a dressing table by the window.

"This looks very different to how it looked when it belonged to me and Joey!" Charlie said, taking in the room and grinning as he reminisced. "First of all, it's so much smaller than I remember, just like the rest of the house. Secondly, we had it painted a bright yellow!" He laughed as he looked around at the beige walls.

"You already knew you were a Hufflepuff!" Mat exclaimed, grinning widely.

"I must've done! It was in my blood," Charlie said. "We had bunk beds, and I had the top bunk. I think Joey also wanted the top bunk, but he's so laidback he just let me have it."

"Yeah, that sounds like something Joey would do. He probably didn't wanna deal with you throwing a tantrum," Mat teased.

Charlie snorted. "I can't even be mad at you for saying that 'cause it's so true. I was such an annoying kid, I don't know how anyone put up with me!"

Mat laughed. "Nah, you weren't that bad."

"You didn't see me at my worst. I think I'd improved a bit before I met you," Charlie said. "Anyway, I was thinking we could try and use the ghost box again in here, since I remember her being quite active in this room. I don't have any strong memories, just quite a few mismatched ones. So, I remember hearing bangs and crashes in the middle of the night. That happened quite a lot, although Joey doesn't remember it happening at all."

"He's quite a heavy sleeper though, isn't he?" Mat asked, and Charlie nodded. "Remember that time we tried to prank him by taking it in turns to balance things on him while he was asleep, until he woke up? We were doing it for ages, but he just wouldn't wake up!" They both started laughing.

"Yeah, we ended up giving up and just leaving everything on him. He was so confused when he woke up under a pile of random things that we'd collected from around the house, and there was nobody to be seen." They laughed even harder.

"Right, we need to stop. This is supposed to be a serious investigation and we keep having laughing fits," Mat said, wheezing and wiping his eyes.

"I know, I don't know what's gotten into us," Charlie said, taking a deep breath and getting ready to carry on investigating. "So, anyway, I would hear noises coming from the loft, and I'd also wake up to find that my stuff had moved around the room. It was really scary; I used to hide under the sheets. It's good I shared a room with Joey, because I don't think I could've handled sleeping in the room by myself. Before Billie was born, I had her room, and I don't think I remember anything happening in that time, but maybe it's just 'cause I was younger then."

Charlie scanned the room with the EMF meter and the thermal imaging camera, but he didn't find anything unusual. He got the ghost box out of his bag and turned to Mat. "Right, so how do you feel about using this in here then?" he asked, holding the device up so Mat could see it.

Mat groaned. "If we really have to. I'll put myself through that torture device for the sake of the video." He put the camera down on the dressing table, making sure they were both in shot.

"That's good to hear," Charlie said, laughing. "Now, cover your ears." He turned on the ghost box, filling the room with the sound of choppy static, as the radio rapidly jumped from channel to channel.

Mat winced but didn't complain.

"Hi Pearl. We've already introduced ourselves, but in case you've forgotten, I'm Charlie and this is Mat. Could you repeat our names for us?" Charlie asked, staring at the ghost box.

They stood in silence for a short while, only hearing snippets of speech that didn't sound like words.

"We have to wait so long for a reply," Mat said, staring intensely at the radio.

"I mean, it probably takes a lot of energy to manipulate the radio frequencies and speak to us, so of course it's gonna take her a bit of time. Also, she might not be in the room with us at the moment," Charlie replied.

"What else could she possibly be doing? Washing her ghost hair?" They both sniggered.

"*Cha– lee–*"

Charlie's eyes widened. "She's here."

"*Mat–*"

Mat opened his mouth to speak, but Charlie cut him off. "You can't actually be about to deny that, Mat."

"It did sound like our names, I'll give you that. But I still think the mind is a funny thing. You hear what you expect to hear," Mat said, his voice taking on a mysterious tone.

Charlie laughed in disbelief. "You're impossible! Anyway, I'm gonna carry on talking to Pearl. Pearl, I used to live here when I was a little boy, and this was my room. Do you remember me?"

They stood for a couple of minutes, just listening to the static.

They didn't hear any distinguishable speech, so Charlie moved on. "Pearl, when I lived here, I used to hear bangs and crashes coming from the loft. Was that you?"

They waited for a reply.

"*Yeah–*"

"It was you? Okay… did you also move my things around and make the lights flicker?"

They waited a short while.

"*Yeah–*"

"Okay… this is so weird. I'm literally having a conversation with a ghost." Charlie ran a hand through his hair and then started pacing again.

Mat laughed. "You're so funny when you get like this. You aren't scared of her though, are you? If Pearl was actually a ghost, and you were actually talking to her, I don't think she'd be very scary. She seemed like a nice, normal girl. She wouldn't have any reason to hurt you."

"Yeah, but she's a *ghost*. Ghosts are always scary on principle!"

Mat laughed and shook his head at the camera, to show that he thought this was ridiculous. "You never know, they might just be misunderstood. They're just trying to live their life – or, their death – and they have people like us coming into their homes and interrogating them."

Charlie hesitated. "I know you're just taking the mick, but I hadn't thought about it like that. I feel a bit sorry for them now."

They asked Pearl a few more questions and waited for her to reply, but they didn't hear any more distinguishable speech. Charlie turned off the ghost box and they made their way through to the third and final bedroom.

Mat set the camera down on the bedside table as they entered the room. "How come we're planning on sleeping in sleeping bags in the living room when there's three perfectly good beds upstairs?" he asked, frowning as he looked around the room. Again, this room was decorated very simply, with just a single bed, bedside table and chest of drawers.

"I know, but I really don't want to sleep in my old room, and there's not much point in sleeping in either of the others. Sorry," Charlie replied. "Anyway, the living room is one of the most active parts of the house, so it's probably a good idea for us to stay in there."

"Okay, if we must," Mat said with a dramatic sigh. "I actually don't really mind, I'm used to the sleeping bag. It would've been a luxury to sleep on a bed during an investigation."

Charlie nodded his agreement, then turned to the camera. "So, this is the room that used to belong to Pearl's sister, Rose. It was also my little sister's nursery when we lived here, and my room for a bit before she was born. If you remember me saying earlier on, when we were downstairs in the living room, this is the place where my parents used to come and check on her in the middle of the night, and they'd find the light on and Billie laughing at seemingly nothing."

"Spooky stuff," Mat said from behind Charlie, where he was inspecting the room by torchlight.

"It is. It's like something you'd see in a horror movie."

Charlie went over the room with the EMF meter and the thermal imaging camera. He didn't find anything unusual, so they quickly moved on and Charlie retrieved the spare torch from his bag. "Right, we're gonna do the torch experiment in here. I thought it was appropriate since she used to turn the light on in here all the time," he said.

He twisted the head of the torch, so the switch was between the on and off positions, then set it down on the chest of drawers. He made sure it was still in view of the camera, then stood next to Mat and turned to look at it.

"Right. Pearl, if you can understand us, please could you turn the light on?"

They waited a couple of minutes, but nothing happened.

Charlie opened his mouth to say something else, but before he could the torch flickered on.

They exchanged glances with each other, then Charlie turned to ask another question. "This is the room that used to belong to your little sister, isn't it? Can you turn the light back off again if this is correct?"

They stared at the torch, willing it to turn off. After a short while, it obliged.

"Wow, I'm in shock. Ghosts really do exist," Mat said in a flat sarcastic voice, looking at the camera.

"We'll try something more difficult then. Pearl, if you believe you were murdered, can you please make the light flicker on and then back off again?"

They stood in complete silence, waiting for the torch to do something.

Just as they were losing hope, the torch flickered on, then after a couple of seconds it flickered off.

"Oh my god," Charlie said, sounding simultaneously scared and excited. He nervously ran a hand through his hair. "This is a big thing, Mat. Every time we've asked her a question relating to her death, the reply has suggested that it wasn't an accident. I don't think that can be a coincidence."

"Here, let me have another go," Mat said and cleared his throat. "If you're actually a French painter–"

"Did you hear something?" Charlie asked, cutting Mat off as he heard what sounded like a floorboard creaking.

They both paused for a few seconds, listening.

"It was probably just the wind," Mat said, but Charlie shushed him as he heard a louder creak.

"I heard it again!" he whispered.

Mat had heard it that time too.

They stood in silence, listening intently, waiting to hear it again.

Suddenly, there was a loud ringing, and they both jumped.

"Oh, it's just my *abuela* calling," Mat said, getting his phone out of his pocket, and they both laughed in relief.

"Tell her I said *hola*," Charlie said, as Mat answered the phone to his grandmother and began speaking to her in Spanish.

"*Hi, Lita. How are you? … I'm just with Charlie doing an investigation. He says hi, by the way …* She says hi, Chaz," Mat said, switching back to English and turning to Charlie. "*Thanks, glad you enjoyed it … Can I phone you back tomorrow to talk properly? … Right, talk to you then. Bye!*" Mat ended the phone call, then clutched at his heart dramatically. "I'm gonna put my phone on silent so that doesn't happen again. I nearly jumped out my skin!"

"Me too! What was she phoning for, at this time? Was it anything important?"

"No, nothing urgent. She just finished watching our last video and wanted to discuss all her theories with me."

Charlie chuckled, then turned to stare at the door onto the landing again. "I didn't hear any more creaks. Maybe you were right, and it was just the wind," he said, but he still felt uneasy about it. He turned back to face the torch and noticed that although it was still lying on the chest of drawers, it had rolled around so it was facing the other direction. "The torch has moved!" he exclaimed.

"I think there's a draught coming in through the window. It was probably the same draught that made the floorboards creak."

Charlie repositioned the torch, then walked back over to Mat and began to ask Pearl another question. "Pearl, could you–?" He stopped talking as the main light in the bedroom flickered on and dropped his torch on the ground in shock. "Oh my god."

"It's probably just faulty wiring or something," Mat said, as Charlie started to pace around the room, glancing up at the light every two seconds with wide eyes. "Calm down, it's fine!"

The light flickered off again, and Charlie quickly moved to pick up his torch from where it had landed in the middle of the floor. “I don’t like it. I just don’t like it. It’s really weird,” he whispered, looking up at Mat as he stood up.

Out of the corner of his eye, he noticed a sliver of light coming through the crack in the door, causing him to inhale sharply.

Mat turned around to see what Charlie was gaping at. He picked up the camera from the bedside table and strolled over to the door to open it, so he could investigate the source of the light.

It didn’t take much investigating though, as he saw immediately that the light next to the loft hatch on the ceiling was now turned on.

Charlie tiptoed over to join Mat in the doorway.

The light flickered off and on again as they stared at it. It was almost as if Pearl was trying to lead them there.

Mat turned to Charlie and placed an arm around his shoulders. “I think it might be time to go in the loft, Chaz.”

CHAPTER SIX

"Do you want me to go first?" Mat asked, as he watched Charlie nervously shining his torch up through the shadowy opening into the loft.

Charlie turned to look at Mat. "If you don't mind, I think I'd prefer that."

Mat nodded. "Sure, no problem." He turned the camera towards them, so they were both in shot. "We've decided we're gonna take it in turns to sit in the loft in the pitch black. Five minutes each. I'm going first. Although, I've just realised, you still have to stand down here by yourself."

"Better down here than up there. Remember, I used to hear noises coming from up there during the night," Charlie said, shuddering at the memory.

"Well, wish me luck," Mat said, handing Charlie the camera and starting to make his way up the ladder. He shone the torch into the gloomy corners of the loft as he reached the top. There were a few cardboard boxes stacked along the side, but apart from that it was completely empty. He noticed that the temperature seemed to drop dramatically as soon as he entered the loft, making him shiver. He pulled his denim jacket tighter around himself, then remembered the camera strapped to his chest and checked it was still uncovered.

"Here, take this," Charlie called up, stretching up to hand Mat a handheld night vision camera.

Mat took it from him, then sat on a small cardboard box. He set the camera down on its tripod, making sure he was in shot.

Once he was comfortable, he turned off his torch. "Ready!" he called out.

"Okay, your five minutes start… now!" Charlie replied, setting a timer on his phone. He was standing at the bottom of the ladder, shining his torch around in all directions, on high alert for any sign of movement.

Mat listened to the dead silence for a few seconds, then decided he would attempt to have a conversation with the ghost.

"Hi, Pearl," he said quietly, so Charlie wouldn't be able to hear him talking. "It's nice to finally meet you… I've heard a lot about you over the years." He paused, fidgeting with his ring absentmindedly and squinting at the obscure shapes he could see in the darkness.

"I don't actually believe that you exist, so I kinda feel a bit silly right now," he continued. "I feel like I'm just talking to air. But my best mate, Charlie, who's just down there on the landing, does think you exist. He's told me all these things that have happened to him. That you have supposedly made happen. And the thing is, he's a very clever guy. It's not like he's a crazy person – as far as I know, anyway. So… there's a possibility – albeit very, very small – that he could be right." He laughed at the absurdity of what he'd just admitted. "Don't tell him I said that, though. I'll never live it down," he added.

After a few more seconds of staring around the empty loft, Mat sighed. "I'm gonna open my mind for the few minutes I have left in here. If Charlie's right, and you do exist, please give me some sort of sign that you're in here. Feel free to whisper in my ear, or send a shiver down my spine, or pull on my hair, or… knock my glasses off. Whatever you feel like doing. Okay, I'm gonna stop talking now. I'm opening up the floor to you."

Mat sat in the darkness and waited for something to happen. Apart from the uncomfortably cold temperature, it was very calming sitting in the silence and eternal night of the loft. He found his mind drifting off, forgetting the reason he was sitting up there in the first place.

Finally, he was snapped out of his thoughts by a jingling tune coming from below. "Time's up!" Charlie called, turning off the timer.

"Well, this has been a blast, but I have to leave now so Charlie can have a turn. Be nice to him, won't you?" Mat said, starting to stand up.

However, before he reached the ladder, one of the cardboard boxes crashed to the floor. He jumped, cursing loudly.

"What was that? Is everything okay up there?" Charlie shouted worriedly.

"Yeah, I'm fine. There's a few boxes stacked up here and one of them just fell. I must've knocked it over without realising," Mat replied, his heart pounding.

He walked over to pick up the box, which was in the corner of the loft. It wasn't anywhere near the box which Mat had been sitting on, but he assumed it must have been a chain reaction from him knocking one of the other boxes. Once he had put the box back where it came from, he made his way down the ladder.

"How was it?" Charlie asked, pointing the camera at Mat as he arrived back on the landing.

"It was alright," Mat replied. "I enjoyed it actually, it was quite calming. She didn't talk to me or anything. I told her she was very welcome to, and that I wouldn't mind if she pulled my hair or something, just to let me know she was there. She didn't take me up on the offer though." He sighed and shrugged his shoulders. "But what can you do? I tried my best."

"Sometimes I think ghosts just don't like to interact with sceptics. Maybe they think there's no point in wasting their energy on people who don't believe they exist."

"Well, that's very convenient," Mat said, raising his eyebrows at the camera.

Charlie laughed. "It's only a theory."

It took a couple of minutes – and some words of encouragement from Mat – before Charlie worked up the courage to go in the loft.

"Come on, Chaz, you've got this!" Mat said, squeezing Charlie's shoulder as he put a shaky hand on the ladder and slowly started to climb up.

Once he had reached the top of the ladder, he clambered into the loft and fumbled with his torch, so he could inspect the area. He started to shiver. "It's freezing up here! I should've brought my jacket up with me."

"I can go and get it if you want?" Mat suggested, taking a couple of steps towards the stairs.

"No! You can't leave me up here alone!" Charlie exclaimed, peeking his head over the opening to the loft so he could give Mat a stern look.

"Okay, but don't blame me if you freeze to death," Mat said, holding his hands up and walking back over to the ladder.

"Just stay there and don't go anywhere," Charlie said, then he added, "please."

Mat laughed and saluted him. "Yes sir, I won't move a muscle. I have the camera set up in front of one of the boxes. Just tell me when you're ready so I can start the timer. And try not to panic, you'll be fine!"

Charlie shone the torch around until he spotted the box Mat was talking about, then walked over to sit down.

Once he was settled, he checked around the loft in the torchlight one last time, took a calming breath, and then turned off his torch. "I'm ready!" he called out, his voice a bit shaky.

"I'm starting the timer… now!" Mat replied.

The silence was deafening as Charlie sat there on the cardboard box, his eyes darting around the loft, unable to see anything through the darkness. He took another calming breath.

"Hi, Pearl," he said quietly. "Oh god, I don't know if I want to talk to her or not." He paused for a moment, running his hand through his hair nervously, then continued. "It's very strange for me being back in this house again after so many years. I sometimes wondered if I'd exaggerated my memories of this place, because I was so young when it all happened. But after coming back here, after all the things I've seen tonight, I think I have my answer. I'm pretty sure I didn't exaggerate anything. In fact, I'm positive it all happened just as I remember. I don't know whether you wanted to cause me harm or scare me, or if you were just trying to get my attention for whatever reason. Maybe you just wanted to reach out. I'm very sorry for everything you went through in your life. I can't imagine how difficult it must've been for you. Full disclosure, I'm still pretty scared of you, but I also understand you a bit more, now that I know your story. Okay… I'm gonna be quiet for a few minutes. You can do or say whatever you'd like in that time." He paused before adding, "Just please don't hurt me."

Filling the silence by talking seemed to have made Charlie feel a bit more confident, but as soon as he stopped, the fear rushed back. He instantly regretted inviting Pearl to interact with him and had to fight the urge to start talking again. He began anxiously biting his nails instead.

After a couple of minutes, Charlie felt something tug on his shirt. He gasped and jumped up, looking around him to see if there was something there, but he couldn't see anything. He sat back down, feeling even more scared, but adamant he wanted to get through the five minutes.

A few seconds later he felt a shiver down his spine. He closed his eyes and tried to ignore it, telling himself that it was probably just because it was so cold in there.

His heart beat faster and faster as he waited for Mat to tell him his time was up.

Suddenly, the opening notes of *White Christmas* broke through the silence and Charlie gasped loudly. "Mat, can you hear that?" he called down in a panic.

There was a pause, and then he heard Mat sniggering.

"It's just the timer going off. Your time's up," he called, laughing as he turned off the alarm.

Charlie let out a sigh of relief. "I hate you!" he said, but he laughed anyway.

"Sorry, I couldn't resist!" he heard Mat say as he stood up and started to move towards the hatch, but before he reached it he heard a loud crash behind him.

He screeched and spun around, then realised that one of the cardboard boxes had fallen to the floor.

"You okay, Chaz?" Mat called, sounding concerned.

"Yeah, that was another box falling!" Charlie replied, before picking up the box and putting it back where it came from.

"That's so strange!" Mat replied. "Which one was it?"

"The one in the far corner," Charlie replied, picking up the night vision camera and passing it down to Mat.

"Huh. That's the same one that fell down earlier," Mat said. "It mustn't be stacked properly. I hope there's nothing fragile in there."

"Maybe it was something to do with Pearl," Charlie said, his scared face popping over the opening to the loft.

"Nah, I don't think so," Mat replied. "It was probably something to do with gravity."

Charlie made his way out of the loft and down the ladder.

"How was that then? Were you scared?" Mat asked, handing Charlie the camera and starting to close up the loft.

"Yeah, I was. But I feel much better now I've done it. I feel like I've faced my fears," Charlie replied, smiling even though he was still a bit shaken. He turned the main light on so Mat could see what he was doing.

"You did really well, I'm proud of you!" Mat replied.

"Thanks. I'm positive I felt something tug on my shirt while I was up there though. And I felt a shiver down my spine," Charlie said. Mat opened his mouth to speak, but Charlie cut him off. "But before you say anything, I know that was probably just 'cause of how cold it was up there."

Mat laughed. "How did you know that was what I was gonna say?" he asked.

Once they had closed up the loft, they stopped filming and started to walk downstairs.

Charlie stopped midway and groaned. “Oh god, I’ve just realised I need the toilet. I’m gonna have to go back upstairs.” He turned and looked nervously into the dark abyss of the landing above.

“I mean, I can stand outside the door and be your bodyguard if you want? Stop all the ghosts from coming in,” Mat joked.

“Would you mind?” Charlie asked, looking at him with a hopeful expression.

Mat began to laugh, then realised Charlie was being serious. “Yeah, go on then.” He sighed, and they made their way back upstairs.

CHAPTER SEVEN

Mat and Charlie made their way back downstairs to settle down for the night. They removed the night vision cameras from their chests as soon as they entered the living room, as they wouldn't have any more need for them that evening.

Mat started to walk towards the door into the hallway. "I'm going out to the car to get the sleeping bags and pillows. Is there anything else you need?" he asked.

"No, I think that's it, thanks," Charlie replied.

Mat nodded and left the living room, closing the door behind him.

Once Charlie was left in the house by himself, he began to feel a familiar sense of unease, as if he were being watched. He sat down in one of the armchairs, where he had a good view of the entire room and nobody could creep up on him, then turned on the camera to give him some company.

"Mat's just gone out to the car and I'm in the living room by myself, so I'm panicking a little bit. He shouldn't be long though," he said, then he stopped talking and listened intently for any strange noises in the house.

He waited in the deafening silence for what felt like years, getting increasingly anxious by the second, and wondering what on earth was taking Mat so long.

Suddenly, the living room door banged open, and Charlie yelped.

"It's just me!" Mat said, holding his hands up as he walked in with the sleeping bags. "I come in peace."

Charlie clutched at his heart. "Don't scare me like that! I didn't hear you come in the front door."

Mat laughed lightly. "Sorry, I didn't do it on purpose."

"That's okay," Charlie said, turning off the camera and getting up to help Mat sort out the sleeping bags. "How come you took so long getting the stuff?"

"I was only a few minutes!" Mat replied. "I was just making sure we definitely had everything we need. Oh, by the way, we have so many random things in the car. We still have the Christmas lights in the boot! We definitely should've put them up in the flat already."

"Oh yeah, I completely forgot about that!" Charlie said. "So, we've ended up bringing them all the way down to Teaburn with us for no reason."

"Yep," Mat laughed. "We'll have to remember to put them up when we get home."

As soon as they were happy with the positioning of the sleeping bags, they both got changed into more comfortable clothes for sleeping in.

The first time they had stayed somewhere overnight on one of their investigations, Mat had been the only one to bring a change of clothes. Charlie hadn't wanted to get changed when there was the possibility that a ghost was in the room watching him, so had stubbornly went to bed in his jeans. He regretted it almost instantly, as he was uncomfortable and tossed and turned all night. The next morning, he told Mat he had been fine and didn't regret it at all. However, the next time they stayed over in a haunted place, and every time since, he joined Mat by bringing comfortable clothes to change into.

After getting changed, Mat walked back over to the living room door.

"Where are you going now?" Charlie asked.

"I was thinking I might get another cup of tea, and maybe a couple digestives," Mat said. "Do you want some?"

"Yeah, please. In fact, I think I'll come with you," Charlie said, not wanting to be left alone again. He picked up the camera to film, just in case anything happened while they were in the kitchen.

"I think Mat's trying to drink all the tea in the house," he said, sitting down on one of the kitchen chairs and filming Mat as he filled the kettle.

Mat grinned at him. "I feel weird being recorded when I'm making tea. People are probably gonna judge my tea making abilities!"

"For the record, Mat makes a really good cup of tea! Tell everyone how you do it, Mat. Share your expertise with our viewers."

"Okay, but just so you know, I'm definitely editing this clip out of the video unless one of us gets attacked by a ghost during my tutorial," Mat said. "So, first of all, let's go over the basics. The milk goes in last. If you do it any other way then you're wrong, and you should never be allowed to make tea–"

He stopped talking as the kitchen light began to flicker and Charlie gasped.

"Oh my god!" Charlie exhaled, nervously looking around.

Mat laughed. "Pearl obviously doesn't agree with my tea making method," he joked.

Charlie let out a short laugh, but still looked worried. "Does that mean she's in here with us?"

"Someone really needs to check the wiring in this house," Mat said, pouring boiling water into the mugs.

The light flickered again.

"No, I don't like this. I do *not* like this!" Charlie said, getting up and pacing around the kitchen while staring at the light. "Why does this keep happening?"

"It's fine, don't worry about it. Lights flicker all the time," Mat said in a breezy voice, as he finished making the tea. "Come on, let's go back through."

As soon as they were back in the living room, Charlie got into his bright yellow sleeping bag and zipped it all the way up, making sure there was no way any ghosts could come near him. Mat set up the night vision camera to film them through the night, just in case anything happened while they were sleeping. He turned off the main light, leaving them with just the dim light cast by one of the table lamps. Charlie picked up his camera and pointed it towards himself.

"We're just settling down for the night, although I don't think I'm gonna get much sleep, I'm too on edge," he said, repositioning the pillow so it was more comfortable and running a hand through his hair.

Mat was rummaging through his backpack. He pulled out a book and walked over to their makeshift sleeping area.

"What's that?" Charlie asked, staring at the book as Mat climbed into his royal blue sleeping bag.

"What?" Mat asked, then lifted his book. "Oh, this? It's *The Martian* by Andy Weir. It's really good. I'll lend you it when I'm finished," he said, before opening it and removing his bookmark.

"Why've you brought a book?" Charlie asked him.

"Because," Mat started, replacing his bookmark and closing the book, "I know I won't be able to sleep for a while anyway 'cause you're gonna keep talking to me, so I thought I may as well bring something to do while I'm here. Then at least I'm awake by choice."

"How can you be calm enough to sit and read a book after everything that's happened tonight?" Charlie asked.

Mat shrugged. "I mean, there hasn't been that much really. And there's probably a logical explanation for it all."

"Okay, I'll let you get on with it then," Charlie said. He started to talk to the camera again as Mat reopened his book. "We've agreed that we're gonna stay here until at least seven a.m. and then we're free to go."

"I would be perfectly fine staying later, but Charlie wants to get out of here as soon as possible. He originally wanted to leave at five a.m., but I managed to negotiate a couple more hours with him," Mat said, looking over at the camera.

"I'm just remembering what it used to be like sleeping in this house. I don't think I'm gonna sleep a wink."

Charlie put the camera down and got his phone out. There were a couple of worried texts from Billie, so he replied to let her know they were safe. Then he noticed that his mother had replied to his text from earlier, where he had asked about pictures of him and Mat playing with their *Scooby Doo* toys.

"Mat! My mam's sent that picture we asked for!" he said excitedly. "Actually, I think she's sent every picture she's ever taken of us," he added, scrolling through all the photos he had received.

Mat looked up. "Has she?" He put his book down, then picked up the camera and turned it on. "Charlie's mam has sent us some pictures from when we were kids. I knew we could count on Dani and her collection of photo albums! Prepare yourselves for how cute we were."

"This is the one we were on about earlier," Charlie said, turning his phone to show Mat the photo.

It showed two young boys, around six years old, both wearing glasses and smiling widely at the camera. They were in the middle of a living room floor, sitting next to a toy mansion that appeared to be half the size of them. One of the boys, who had fair skin, blonde hair, and bright blue eyes, was holding up a small figure of Scooby Doo to the camera. The other boy, who had brown skin, dark curly hair and brown eyes, was holding up a small figure of Shaggy while rolling the Mystery Machine around the floor. The rest of Mystery Inc. was strewn around them, along with some of the monsters and villains.

"Yeah, that was the haunted mansion," Mat said, smiling at the photo. "That one must've been yours since we're at your house. I think I still have mine! It'll either be at my parents' or my *abuela*'s."

"I probably still have mine too."

"Look at us! Fifteen years later and we're still playing with haunted houses," Mat said, looking at the room around them, and Charlie laughed.

They swiped through the rest of the photos Charlie's mother had sent him. There were some more of them playing with their toys, a couple of which included Joey and Billie. There were also several photos from Halloween over the years, including one where they were dressed as astronauts, and another where they were dressed as Ghostbusters.

"Aww, that must've been when you'd only just adopted Levi!" Mat said, as they looked at a picture which showed them petting a golden retriever puppy back when they were both teenagers.

"Bless him, he's so tiny!" Charlie said, zooming in on Levi, who was sitting in his lap in the picture. "For those who don't know, Levi is my family dog," he added to the camera.

"This episode has somehow turned into a trip down memory lane," Mat said, laughing.

"I mean, it was bound to happen, considering we're investigating my childhood home. We can always put some of this footage in a separate video for our second channel though."

Once they had looked through the photos, drank their tea and ate some biscuits, Mat returned to his book. Charlie lay on his back, staring at the ceiling, his eyes wide. There was silence apart from Mat laughing quietly to himself at his book every so often.

"Mat?" Charlie said quietly.

"Yep?" Mat replied, lowering his book.

"Do you feel weird? Like we're being watched?" Charlie asked, his eyes rapidly searching every inch of the room.

"I mean, we kind of are, if you count the camera we have pointing at us," Mat replied, nodding at the camera he'd put in the corner of the room.

"Oh. Yeah," Charlie said. He paused for a moment, then continued, "It's just I have this uneasy feeling; I feel all tense. I'm sure it's that fireplace, y'know."

Mat looked over at the fireplace, then back at Charlie. "I think you're just nervous about being here. And you're thinking about what happened earlier. But remember, it's just a fireplace, it can't hurt you," he said, trying to put Charlie at ease.

"Okay," Charlie replied, then continued to stare at the ceiling, listening intently for any distant noises.

After a while, Mat put his book away and his glasses on the side.

"Right, I'm gonna try and go to sleep now," he said, turning over in his sleeping bag. "You can wake me if you get scared, I won't mind."

"Really?" Charlie asked, incredulously.

"Yeah, I'm in a good mood. I think it's my book."

"Okay, we'll see if you stick to your word," Charlie said, narrowing his eyes, then laughing. "Night, Mat."

"Night, Chaz," Mat replied, then he got himself comfortable and fell asleep almost instantly.

Charlie lay there for a while, anxious and not wanting to sleep, but starting to feel tired in spite of himself.

He picked up the camera and turned it on. "Hey guys, I just thought I'd check in. Mat's gone to sleep," he whispered sleepily, turning the camera to show Mat. "I don't know how, but I'm jealous. Anyway, it's now" – he paused to check his watch – "two a.m., I've still got five hours to go. I don't know why I agreed to stay until seven." He yawned. "But yeah, I just wanted to let you know we haven't been murdered yet." He smiled and gave the camera a thumbs-up. "That's it, that's all I wanted to say." He turned off the camera and put it down next to him, then yawned again.

It had been a really long day and Charlie could do with some rest, but he was adamant that he was going to stay awake.

He snuggled down further into his pillow and thought about how comfortable he felt.

He took his glasses off as they were digging into the side of his head painfully.

He noticed that his eyes felt incredibly heavy all of a sudden.

He only had to stay awake five more hours.

Then he drifted off to sleep.

CHAPTER EIGHT

Charlie blinked his eyes against the bright light, putting his hand up to block out the sun. As his eyes slowly adjusted, he realised he was standing in a luscious green forest. There was a sense of familiarity about the place, but he couldn't quite put his finger on where he had seen it before. He slowly turned around on the spot, taking in his surroundings, hearing flowing water, and the cheerful chirping of birds. Beautiful flowers were growing all around him and he bent to pick a stunning blue one. He tried to readjust his glasses but realised he wasn't wearing any, even though he could see perfectly.

Charlie began to amble through the trees, feeling weightless, as if he were floating through the forest. He turned to stroll through an opening in the trees and realised he was on the edge of a beautiful meadow, stretching far in front of him. There was a stream not that far away from where he stood, and he felt an urge pulling him towards it.

When he had reached the stream, he looked around and noticed a woman standing further along the bank. Feeling like he should go and talk to her, he began to walk towards her. As he got closer, he felt he had seen her somewhere before, but couldn't think where or when. She turned towards him and smiled warmly, causing Charlie's eyes to widen as he realised who she was.

"Hello, dear. It's lovely to see you again after all these years," she said.

"Pearl?" Charlie asked. He had recognised her from the black-and-white photograph he and Mat had looked at, but she looked very different in full colour. Her eyes were a startling green and her curly hair was flaming red, the bright sun intensifying the colours even further.

"Yes, I'm Pearl. I really need you to help me, Charlie. It's very important." She began to nervously play with a dainty gold necklace that hung around her neck.

"Of course, what do you need me to do?" Charlie asked. Feeling unnaturally calm, he took another step towards her.

"Come with me, and I'll show you," Pearl said. She beckoned for Charlie to follow her, then turned to continue walking along beside the stream.

Slowly, Pearl and her peaceful surroundings all began to fade away.

CHAPTER NINE

Charlie was awakened abruptly by a loud bang coming from upstairs. All thoughts of his dream slipping from his mind, he swiftly sat up in his sleeping bag and scrambled to put his glasses back on.

He turned to Mat and began to shake him. "Mat!" he said in an urgent whisper. "Wake up!"

"What is it?" Mat mumbled into his pillow.

"I heard a noise from upstairs," Charlie said, looking at the ceiling apprehensively and shuffling his sleeping bag closer to Mat's one.

Mat slowly started to stretch and turn over. "It was probably just the heating turning on or something," he said, with a yawn.

"No, it was definitely something upstairs. It sounded like what I used to hear when I lived here," Charlie said, turning to look at Mat.

Mat fumbled to find his phone, then squinted at the screen so he could read the time. "Charlie, it's twenty to three in the morning."

"Listen!" Charlie whispered. He sat there quietly, Mat still lying down, the only noise the pattering of rain on the window.

"That's just the rain, Chaz," Mat said, yawning again and turning over in his sleeping bag. "Go back to sleep."

Charlie anxiously scanned the whole room and noticed one of his shoes lying next to the door into the hallway. He looked around frantically and found that he couldn't see the other one anywhere.

"Mat, my Converse have moved! They were right here when I went to sleep, and now ones over there and I don't know where the other one is," he whispered, getting himself worked up.

"Okay, okay, calm down," Mat said, sighing and then sitting up. He put on his glasses and looked around. "Mine've disappeared too. Should we go and have a look?"

Charlie picked up the camera and turned it on, then followed Mat to the door, both of them clutching their torches. Mat picked up Charlie's shoe and inspected it, then opened the door. They crept through and looked around the hallway.

"Is that one of yours?" Charlie whispered, pointing his torch at the bottom of the stairs.

Mat walked over to check and saw his own Converse trainer sitting on the bottom step. "Stay behind me and get ready to call the police," he whispered. "I think somebody must've broken into the house."

They slowly started to creep up the stairs, Mat picking up another one of Charlie's shoes at the top. He raised his left arm, holding the shoes like a weapon, then checked all of the rooms.

"All clear," he called, as if he were a police officer clearing a property on one of the murder mystery shows he and Charlie watched. He held up the shoes that were still in his hand. "I don't know what I was planning on doing with these if I'd actually come across an intruder." He laughed, then turned to the camera. "By the way, I'm not normally this brave. I don't know what's come over me."

Charlie spotted Mat's other shoe, lying directly underneath the hatch into the loft. As he bent down to pick it up, there was another loud bang from above. He jumped back and exchanged a frightened look with Mat. "Do you think we should go up there and check?" he asked nervously.

Mat nodded, and they both put on their shoes, then took a deep breath and opened the loft hatch.

"Hello? Is anyone up there?" Mat called, shining his torch through the opening. When there was no reply, he pulled the ladders down and started to climb up.

"Be careful," Charlie whispered, filming him from the landing.

Mat reached the top of the ladder and shone his torch all around the loft. "There's nothing here. It looks exactly the same as it did earlier."

"I think Pearl wants us to go up there for some reason," Charlie called up.

"It's more likely someone found out we were here tonight and broke in somehow, so they could mess with us," Mat said, with a nervous laugh. "They must've gone now, though."

"I'm coming up," Charlie said, starting to climb the ladder. Reluctantly, Mat moved from the ladder into the loft to make way for him. "Wait, can you take the camera off me first?"

"We'll have to ask Mrs Harris if she's ever had problems with people breaking in before," Mat said, reaching down to take the camera from Charlie. "It's a scary thought, but it's the only explanation."

"I mean, it isn't the only explanation," Charlie said, as he reached the top of the ladder and clambered into the loft. "It could also have been Pearl."

Mat rolled his eyes at the camera but didn't respond.

"Only problem is, I don't know why she wants us to come up here so desperately," Charlie said, frowning and shining the torch around the loft, trying to see if he could notice anything different from earlier that night.

"I mean, I'm not entirely sure how we've both ended up in the loft. I don't know what we're gonna achieve by this."

"Well, there must be a reason we keep being led up here," Charlie said, turning around and shining the torch at Mat, who shielded his eyes. "Like earlier when the lights were flickering. Maybe we should get the ghost box and see if she'll talk to us through that."

Mat sighed. He knew there was no use fighting the situation; it would be easier to just go along with it. "Sure, I'll go get it."

"No!" Charlie said quickly. "I'll get it. I still don't fancy sitting up here by myself. I won't be long."

Charlie climbed down the ladder as quickly as he could and rushed to the living room, leaving Mat alone in the loft with the camera.

Mat decided to sit down on the cardboard box again while he waited for Charlie to return. "I didn't think this was what I'd be doing at nearly three in the morning, but here we are," he said to the camera, with a yawn. "But I suppose it's our duty as ghost hunters to check everything–" he was cut off by a loud crash, coming from the corner of the loft.

Mat jumped, cursing as he clasped a hand to his heart. "I swear to god, if that was that box falling again–" He got up and looked in the corner of the loft.

"It was! Who stacked these boxes? I really hope there's nothing fragile in there."

He stood up and positioned the camera on the box he had just vacated, then picked up the fallen box and restacked it very carefully, hoping to prevent it from falling again.

As he cautiously backed away from it, checking it over to make sure it looked sturdy, he heard Charlie's voice from below. "I'm back!"

Mat moved over to the hatch to help him.

"I got our night vision cameras for us to put back on as well," Charlie said, handing everything to Mat and then making his way back up the ladder and into the loft.

"That cardboard box fell over again. I nearly died," Mat told Charlie, as they strapped their cameras back around their chests. "It's even worse when you're half asleep."

"That's so weird!" Charlie said, frowning. "This'll probably be worse when you're half asleep as well, so prepare yourself."

Mat groaned and covered his ears as Charlie turned on the ghost box, the loud noise echoing around the loft.

"Hello again, Pearl," Charlie started. "It's Mat and Charlie again. Were you trying to lead us up here into the loft?"

They listened to the choppy static and waited to hear anything that sounded like a voice.

After nearly a minute of waiting patiently – or not so patiently in Mat's case – they finally heard something.

"*Yeah–*"

They glanced at each other, then Charlie carried on. "You were? Why did you want us to come up here?"

They stared at the ghost box for a while again.

Just as they were about to give up, they heard something.

"*Hell–*"

They frowned at each other, but just as Charlie opened his mouth to speak, they heard more.

"*Help– me–*"

"Help me?" Charlie repeated, looking scared.

"That's what I heard," Mat agreed. "I don't wanna keep harping on about this, but I'm gonna say it anyway. I still think it's just random sounds that our brains take in and manipulate into words, because that's what they're trained to do." He shrugged.

"Pearl, why do you want our help?" Charlie asked.

They waited a short while, staring at the ghost box.

"*Luk–*"

"Luck? She needs our help for luck? Are we lucky or is she lucky? You might need to expand on that, Pearl," Mat said, smirking.

"*No–*"

"No? This is so confusing," Charlie said, running a hand through his hair.

"*No– book–*"

"No book?" Charlie said, turning to look at Mat, who mirrored his look of bewilderment. He turned back to the ghost box. "What does that mean, Pearl?"

"It's just a load of gibberish that doesn't connect."

They waited for a while, feeling more and more perplexed by the second.

"*Hid–*"

They looked at each other with quizzical expressions.

"*Hih– den–*"

"Hidden?" Charlie repeated.

"So, let's review," Mat said, turning to look at the camera. "So far, we've had, 'help me,' 'luck,' 'no book,' and 'hidden,' " he listed, counting each one on his fingers. "I may not believe in ghosts, but I love a good mystery."

They pondered for some time, Charlie pacing the loft.

The loud static was still blaring out of the ghost box, unintelligible speech interspersed throughout it.

Suddenly, Charlie gasped. "Maybe she meant 'look,' as in, 'looking for something.' Then she would've said 'look,' 'no book,' and 'hidden.' Maybe there's a hidden book!"

"Normally, this is where I would make a sarcastic comment. But this is actually quite fun, so I'm just gonna go along with it," Mat said, nodding his head.

Charlie laughed. "Great! Glad to have you on board!"

"Although, why would she say, 'no book,' if there is a book?" Mat questioned.

"I dunno," Charlie said, frowning and starting to pace again.

"Can we turn the ghost box off now? It's grating on me, I can't think properly."

Charlie turned off the ghost box and the loft became silent once again.

"That's better," Mat said, massaging his temples.

"Maybe we misinterpreted what she said?" Charlie suggested. He began repeating the phrase they had heard using different inflections. "No book… *no* book… no *book*… no… book… no-book…"

"That sounded a bit like 'notebook,' " Mat suggested.

"Yeah, you could be right! Or she was trying to throw us off for some reason," Charlie said, and Mat nodded. "So, where do you think it is?"

Just as he finished asking the question, there was another loud crash and they both jumped.

"Oh my god, I'm gonna nail that box to the wall so it can't fall off again. That's four times now!" Mat said, walking over to put it back again.

"Wait, what if that's where the book is hidden?" Charlie suggested, starting to get excited.

"I don't wanna burst your bubble, but I don't think it can be," Mat said, turning back to Charlie. "These are just boxes that Mrs Harris is storing in here. There won't be a connection to Pearl or anything. I think it's just badly stacked."

"Oh," Charlie said, feeling a bit deflated. "I don't even know where to start then."

They stood in silence, trying to think of places somebody could hide a book in a house, but they were both flummoxed.

"I'm stumped," Mat said after a short while, throwing his hands in the air.

"I mean, it must be in the loft somewhere, 'cause why else would she keep leading us up here?"

Mat yawned. "Yeah, I suppose," he said, picking up the camera from the cardboard box to make a space for him to sit down.

"Hang on! I've got an idea. What if we set up a load of lights around the loft and ask her to turn on the one nearest to the hiding place? We know she's capable of that 'cause she's been turning on lights all night," Charlie said, talking rapidly and already making his way to the opening so he could go and get the lights he needed for his plan.

"Like when Joyce put those fairy lights all over her house in *Stranger Things*?" Mat said, laughing. "Do we even have enough lights to put around the loft? We only brought a few torches with us."

Charlie stopped for a moment, deep in thought, then his eyes lit up. "Exactly! Just like Joyce in *Stranger Things*! Mat, you're a genius!"

He began to descend the ladder as fast as he could, leaving Mat alone in the loft again, feeling completely baffled.

CHAPTER TEN

Mat yawned as he looked around the silent, gloomy loft, waiting for Charlie to return once again. He sighed and turned the camera around to face him.

"I think Charlie might've gone a bit mad. This is what happens when he's sleep deprived," he said. "But it's okay 'cause I'm having a good time, y'know? It feels like we're on a treasure hunt. But I don't think there's actually gonna be any treasure at the end of it. We'll see, though. This old house might hold some secrets, you never know."

A couple of minutes later Charlie returned and shouted for Mat to take the few boxes he was holding, so he could climb back up the ladder. Mat put down the camera again and rushed over to help. As Charlie handed the boxes to him, Mat realised they were the battery-operated fairy lights he had spotted in the boot of the car earlier that night, when he had gone out to get the sleeping bags.

"I remembered you saying earlier that you'd seen these in the car," Charlie explained, as he started opening boxes and getting lights out. He turned to look at the camera. "Please don't judge us for not having our Christmas decorations up yet! I promise we'll put them up as soon as we get home. I mean, it's a good thing we forgot really, because we needed them for this."

Mat picked up a box and joined in, even though he didn't think there was any chance of it actually working. "When you were down there, did you notice anything wrong with the front door?"

"What do you mean?" Charlie asked.

"I'm wondering how people managed to get in the house. Did it look like anyone had tampered with the lock, or anything?"

"Oh, right. I should've guessed," Charlie said, rolling his eyes at the camera. "No, I didn't notice anything strange. I had to unlock the door to go out to the car. But I thought we'd already decided it was Pearl?"

"No, *you* decided it was Pearl. It seems like the person must've had a key. I don't wanna start making accusations, but I wonder if it could've been an inside job? Some sort of publicity stunt for the ghost tours," Mat suggested, raising his eyebrows.

Charlie laughed. "Okay, Detective Jones. I think we should just focus on this theory for now, then we can start on the conspiracy theories later."

Mat rolled his eyes and smirked. "Y'know, most people would consider *ghosts* as the conspiracy theory, but okay. Where should we put the lights then?" He put his hands on his hips and surveyed the loft. "Are we hanging them on the beams?"

"We've only got five sets of lights, so we need to use them wisely. I think we should just lay them out on the floor."

They both started to put the lights around, trying to cover as much of the loft as possible so if their plan worked, they would only have a small area to search.

Once they were finished, they looked around at their handiwork. The floor was now covered in fairy lights.

Mat began to laugh. "We've gone properly mad now," he said, with a wheeze.

Charlie snorted. "I know, I do feel a bit crazy. But it's for science!"

They decided to try and turn the switches of the lights between the on and off position, in an attempt to replicate twisting the head of the torch for the torch experiment.

Mat picked up the camera, so he could film the action from a better angle than the cardboard box would give, and they prepared themselves for what was to come.

"Hopefully this'll work," Charlie said, then cleared his throat. "Pearl, please could you turn on the lights closest to where the book is hidden?"

They stared at the fairy lights, but nothing seemed to be happening.

Then, one of the sets of lights began to glow faintly. It was the set that was placed closest to the cardboard boxes.

"Oh my god, it actually worked! What do we do now?" Charlie said. "Should we narrow the search area?"

Mat agreed, amused by how seriously Charlie was taking their hunt. They placed each set of lights in a small pile, arranged along the area next to the boxes where the lights had lit up.

Before Charlie had even made the request, the set of lights by the boxes in the corner glowed brightly for a couple of seconds, then turned off.

"I would just like to point out for the record: that's the same set of lights that lit up the first time, as well," Mat said. "Just saying."

"Oh my god, it's the lights next to the box that keeps falling over!" Charlie said, ignoring Mat. "I was right! It must be hidden inside this box."

Charlie picked up the box and moved to start opening it, but Mat stopped him.

"Charlie! We can't just start rooting through Mrs Harris' stuff!" he said. "Why don't you put the lights on top of it or something, just to check?"

Charlie agreed that this was the best approach. They pulled out the boxes that were stacked in the corner and placed a set of lights on top of each of them, then placed one on the floor, underneath where the boxes had been stacked.

They stared at the lights, feeling more and more restless as they waited for something to happen.

After a couple of minutes, one of the sets of lights began to glow.

Charlie nudged Mat, who had zoned out, almost falling asleep standing up.

They moved closer to the lights, and Charlie knelt down to pick them up from where they were glowing on the floor.

He breathed out slowly. "So, it wasn't the boxes themselves Pearl was trying to lead us to, it was the section of the floor where the boxes were stacked."

Mat knelt down to film the wooden floor more closely while Charlie inspected the area.

"Be careful you don't get any splinters," Mat said, moving the torch closer to the floor so Charlie could see what he was doing.

As Charlie moved his hand around the floor, he noticed that one of the floorboards felt a bit loose.

On closer inspection, he realised that there was a small notch in the side of the floorboard. It was a perfect semicircle, as if it had been made on purpose so the floorboard could be easily removed.

He managed to get a grip on it, then prised the board upwards, revealing a hole in the floor.

They turned to each other excitedly as Charlie moved the floorboard out of the way.

Mat shone the torch into the gap and they both peered inside.

"There's something in there," Charlie said, his voice shaking with excitement.

He reached in and pulled out a small, leather-bound notebook, covered in dust. He blew the dust away, sending it into a cloud around them, which made them both cough.

"Sorry, I couldn't resist," Charlie said, waving his hand around to get rid of the dust cloud. "They always do that in films."

Mat looked over Charlie's shoulder as he opened the notebook, so they could both read what was written inside. Charlie furrowed his brow in confusion as he flicked through the pages. He turned to Mat, who also looked puzzled.

"I think it's written in code."

PART TWO

CHAPTER ELEVEN

The winter sun was just beginning to rise, the bright rays appearing over the tops of the buildings, lighting up the morning frost which lightly coated the pavement below. Pearl Carter hurried along the path, the wind whipping her ginger hair around her face as she pulled her coat tightly around her. She had been running late for work that morning, so had told her friend to go on without her, leaving Pearl to walk by herself. She checked her watch. She still had a few minutes. She could make it if she quickened her pace a little bit more.

Throughout her life, Pearl had always felt as if she were racing to catch up with a world that was turning too fast for her. She had been given a great start to life, with two loving parents, Harold and Mary Carter, who would do anything for their little girl. Her father had a well-paid job, and they were able to afford to live in a rather large house in the beautiful English village of

Teaburn. Her parents were fortunate enough to have the means to give Pearl everything she wanted in life. She only knew love and happiness, never having to want for anything, until her perfect world began to crumble down around her.

Pearl had always been followed by tragedy. When she was only eight years old, her mother died while giving birth to her sister, Rose. It was an incredibly difficult time for the family and very confusing for young Pearl; she had lost her mother, but at the same time had gained a little sister. She decided she would do everything she possibly could to ensure Rose only ever felt love and happiness in the same way she would have done if their mother was still with them. The world could be cruel, and she wanted to protect Rose as best as she could.

On Rose's tenth birthday, Pearl gave her a delicate gold necklace with an angel wing pendant. She had bought two linking pendants and gave the right angel wing to Rose, keeping the left for herself. Pearl put the necklace around Rose's neck, then got her own and connected the pendants together.

"Oh! They link together!" Rose exclaimed, looking at the necklaces in wonder.

"Yes, Rosie. They are two halves of a whole, just like us. No matter what happens to us in life, we will always have each other. And no matter how far apart we are, as long as we have our angel wings we will always be connected," Pearl said, smiling at Rose, who was beaming back at her.

"Thank you, Pearl. I love you," Rose replied, engulfing Pearl in a hug.

"I love you too, Rosie, always and forever."

When the Second World War started, Pearl tried to take all of the emotional burden on her own shoulders, protecting Rose from the reality of the situation as best as she could. Their father suffered from an injury which prevented him from fighting in the war, so he became an air raid warden. The family managed to get by like this for a while, finding their own bubble of happiness despite the terrible circumstances, and without experiencing anymore personal trauma.

Pearl had always been bright. Her father had paid for her to have the best education she could possibly have, as she had shown from a young age that she was surely going to take the academic route in her life. Pearl was top of most of her classes, but as her studies progressed, she found she had a particular affinity for mathematics. Whenever she had a free moment, Pearl could be found with her head in a book, doing further research into the subject. After she had completed her high school education, Pearl went on to study a mathematics course at Newnham College in Cambridge. Her head was full of plans for her future and she was determined not to let any obstacles get in the way of her accomplishing everything she wanted to in life.

However, before she had the chance to properly go out into the world and start following her dreams, she was summoned for an interview. It was very secretive, and Pearl could not find out any information about the job beforehand. All she was told was when and where she was to be interviewed, and she was asked not to disclose where she was going to anyone, even her family, as it was top secret. Pearl was very intrigued by the mystery, especially as the interview was to be held so close to where she lived.

So, when the day finally arrived, Pearl told her father and sister that she was going for an interview, but she refrained from telling them where it was. She made her way to the railway station and then the main house at Bletchley Park, as she had been directed. Once there, she assumed she would be filled in on all the details of the job, and why it had to be so secret. But to her surprise, she was taken into a room where a plain dressed, unsmiling woman asked her many different questions, confusing her no end, as she tried to figure out how everything connected.

After the woman had deemed her suitable to be hired, Pearl was given a very vague explanation of the nature of the work. She discovered that she was being recruited by the Government Code and Cypher School, as they needed people with Pearl's mathematical knowledge to help in the war effort. She was told that she would need to go home and pack her things right away, as she would be required to start work at Bletchley Park as soon as possible.

Pearl had always been good at keeping secrets. When she was at school, she was the person who all of her friends would confide even their deepest, darkest secrets to, as they knew she was trustworthy. So, when she was asked to sign the Official Secrets Act and told she could never breathe a word of her work to *anyone* under *any* circumstances, she didn't hesitate. The only problem she could possibly encounter with this order was if Rose asked her about her work, as they were so close and told each other everything. But Pearl knew she could manage it as long as she avoided the subject as much as possible. She hoped that there would be a day in the future where she would be free to explain everything to Rose, but until then she would have to settle for a cover story based on some truth, which she could use whenever Rose asked about her work.

Pearl moved into the provided accommodation soon after, telling her family that she had been offered a job doing clerical work, where she needed to work away from home. She was very ambiguous and didn't let on where she was going to be staying or what she would be doing, as she was scared she would say too much. The country house where she was staying housed other women who worked on the site, and Pearl quickly became friends with two of the women who lived there.

On the day she arrived at the house, Pearl had been attempting to drag her heavy case up the stairs to her new bedroom, when it slipped out of her hands and began to fall back down again. She watched helplessly as it banged down each step and landed with a crash at the bottom, causing the case to snap open and her clothes to spill out onto the floor.

"Oh, for goodness' sake," Pearl muttered to herself, letting out a frustrated sigh as she made her way back down the stairs and knelt next to the case, throwing her possessions back inside haphazardly.

"What on earth is going on down–? Oh, hello," a voice called from the top of the stairs.

Pearl looked up and saw a young woman peering down at her from above.

"Hello, my name is Pearl Carter. I'm just moving in," Pearl said, smiling at the woman who was now running down the stairs towards her.

"Nice to meet you, Pearl. I'm Betty Wright." She smiled, kneeling down and helping Pearl as she closed up her case.

Now that she could see her more clearly, Pearl observed that Betty looked quite young and decided she must be a couple of years younger than her. She had short black hair that was pinned back in waves and was wearing bright red lipstick. As they stood up, Pearl noticed that Betty was wearing a pretty green dress that fell just below the knee.

"I love your dress. It's beautiful!"

"Oh, thank you! I've had it for years," Betty replied, her face stretching into a wide smile. She gestured to the case. "I'll help you take this up to your room."

Pearl and Betty worked together to heave the case up the stairs, then collapsed at the top, out of breath.

"What have you got in there?" Betty asked, wiping her brow.

"Well, we are going to be here a while," Pearl replied, laughing as she stood up and pulled Betty to her feet.

"You are able to wash your clothes while you're here, you know!" Betty joked.

They picked up the case again and carried it into Pearl's bedroom, which was a much easier task as it wasn't far from the stairs.

"Wait here, I want to introduce you to Ruth Clarke. Her bedroom is just across the hall from yours," Betty said, beaming as she hurried out of the room.

Pearl heard the sound of Betty rapping loudly on a door, and within a minute she had returned with another woman in tow.

"Ruth, this is Pearl Carter," Betty said, moving out of the way so Pearl could take a proper look at Ruth.

Pearl thought Ruth must be a few years older than her. She had short brown hair that was pinned into rolls on her head and was wearing a blouse tucked into a neutral skirt. She smiled as she walked into the room, and Pearl noticed she had very kind eyes.

"Hello, it's lovely to meet you," Ruth said politely, reaching out to shake Pearl's hand.

"It's lovely to meet you, too," Pearl replied, smiling widely.

Pearl knew straight away that she was going to get on with Ruth and Betty, and from that moment on they became good friends. She learned that Ruth was a mathematician, the same as her, and Betty was a linguist, specialising in French and German.

Pearl was sent to work in Hut 6, along with Ruth, where they were tasked with deciphering intercepted German messages, which had been encrypted using the Enigma code. They did this by finding the key to the code, which changed daily. This was a massive task which was very difficult, and took many mathematicians putting their heads together to complete. As the years went on, the task of finding the key was made a lot simpler by the addition of the Bombe machines, which were used to partially establish the daily code. The information could then be sent back to Hut 6, where they would be able to find the key much more easily. Once they had cracked the code, they could input the encrypted messages into a Typex machine, and if they had the correct key, it would output plain German text. The message was then sent through a chute which connected the hut to Hut 3, where Betty worked, presumably to be translated into English.

Truth be told, there wasn't much Pearl could have told Rose about her work even if she was allowed to. The majority of the operation in Bletchley Park was kept secret even to those working there. She knew her own job very well, but she didn't know the underlying purpose or wider implications. She had her ideas about what they could be doing, as she knew they were deciphering German messages. She guessed that it could have been German military correspondence, which had the possibility of containing very valuable information. But, since she couldn't read what the messages said, it was just as likely that they only contained insignificant civilian communication. She learned not to be too nosey, and to just get on with her job. All she knew for certain was that she was helping the war effort in some way and was doing some good for her country, and that was good enough for her. She was a small cog in the giant machine that was the codebreaking operation at Bletchley Park.

Three years into the war, when Pearl was twenty-two years old, she faced her second massive tragedy. Her father was killed in a bombing raid. She was devastated by this loss but tried to remain strong for Rose, who was only thirteen years old. Pearl took on responsibility to care for Rose, trying to make life feel as normal as possible for her. It was very difficult though, as Pearl had to spend most of her time working at Bletchley Park, so couldn't stay home with her. Rose attended a boarding school, so Pearl always tried to schedule her leave to align with the school holidays, so she would always be there whenever Rose needed her.

This particular year, Pearl had managed to arrange a couple of weeks leave around Christmas. She grinned to herself as she rushed along the pavement, realising there was only a week left until she would be at home to take part in the festivities. She was terribly excited to be able to spend Christmas with Rose and their grandparents, but she reminded herself that she needed to contain her eagerness while she was still at work.

Slightly out of breath, Pearl arrived at work perfectly on time and hurried to her desk to start the day, completely unaware of how eventful it would turn out to be.

CHAPTER TWELVE

It was nearing midday and Pearl's stomach had begun to rumble. She was just wondering how long it would be before she could go for her lunch, when Kenneth Johnson walked into the room.

He stopped by the doorway and cleared his throat. "Miss Carter, can I see you in my office for a moment?" he said unsmilingly.

"Of course, Mr Johnson," Pearl replied, then stood up and followed him through, sharing a quizzical look with Ruth as she walked past.

As soon as Pearl entered the room, the door closed behind her and she was swiftly pulled in for a kiss.

"Kenny! We're at work," Pearl whispered, giggling and looking around to make sure nobody could see into the office. Luckily, the blinds were closed.

"I'm sorry, I just couldn't wait until our date this evening," Kenneth replied in a low voice, moving away and taking her hands in his.

Not long after they had moved into the same building as each other, Kenneth had made a habit of calling Pearl into his office to ask her to run errands for him. Pearl had been a little irritated by this, but he was very courteous and charming, and it didn't take up too much of her time, so she agreed. As time went on, Kenneth appeared to get more comfortable with asking Pearl to carry out tasks for him, until it got to the point where it had started to affect her work, as she was leaving her desk a few times throughout the day.

One day, Pearl had been in the middle of some very important work when Kenneth had popped his head through the door and asked her to follow him into his office. Exasperated, she followed him through and made polite conversation, waiting to find out what errand he wanted her to run this time.

"What can I help you with?" Pearl had asked, with a sweet smile.

"Would you be able to take this to Eugene Smith, please? I would happily take it myself, but I'm extraordinarily busy right now and I promised I would get it to him before lunch." He held out a file for Pearl to take and smiled at her expectantly.

Pearl stared at the solitary file in Kenneth's outstretched hand. She decided she couldn't carry on like this. She had to stand up for herself. She took a deep breath, then let out everything she had been thinking about the situation. "Mr Johnson, forgive me for saying this, but I am not your assistant. I don't mind running the odd errand for you, but frankly, it is becoming quite ridiculous! I understand that your job is very important, but so is mine, and I don't have the time to be leaving my desk a few times per day to assist you."

Pearl instantly regretted speaking her mind as soon as she closed her mouth. She turned her eyes to the ground. Kenneth sighed deeply, and Pearl wondered briefly whether he had the power to fire her.

"I apologise, Miss Carter, I hadn't realised you felt that way. It was never my intention to cause you any offence."

Pearl looked up quickly. "That's quite alright, Mr Johnson," she said, slightly caught off guard by his sincere look of apology.

"Only, I would like to make it clear that I do not think of you as my assistant. The reason I request your help so often is because… well, to be quite plain, it gives me a chance to spend some time with you."

Pearl frowned, thinking she must have misheard what he had said. "I'm afraid I don't quite understand."

"Well, forgive me if this is entirely inappropriate, but what I'm trying to convey is… I would like to take you out on a date, Pearl."

Pearl gaped at Kenneth for a few moments, not knowing what to say in response to his proposition.

Kenneth cleared his throat and began rustling papers on his desk to busy himself. “However, if the offer doesn’t appeal to you then I understand completely. I will stop bothering you and leave you to get on with your work, as you wish.”

“No, it’s not that it doesn’t appeal to me. I’m just surprised, is all,” Pearl replied. She made up her mind and smiled widely. “I would love to accompany you on a date.”

“Oh, splendid!” Kenneth grinned. “Don’t worry about taking the file, I can take it myself. You were right, it was unfair of me to ask.”

“I’ll take it, but this will be the last time!”

One date had led to more, and they were now a few months into their relationship. Kenneth had asked Pearl if she minded not telling anyone that they were together, at least for the time being. Pearl had to think about this for a while, as she knew it would be difficult to keep their relationship a secret from Ruth and Betty, since she lived with them and they were very intuitive, especially Betty.

Eventually, Pearl had agreed not to tell anyone. She was already keeping so many secrets, so what harm could one more do?

“Are you still able to come for dinner this evening?” Kenneth asked now, with a charming smile that made butterflies erupt in Pearl’s stomach.

“Yes, I’m very much looking forward to it.”

"Wonderful," Kenneth said, lifting Pearl's hand up to his lips and kissing it lightly. "I was just about to leave for my lunch. I thought I would use the time to go home and sort out a few things for later."

Pearl smiled. "That sounds like a grand idea. I had better get back to my desk soon, Kenny. We don't want to start rumours."

"Yes, of course. But before you go, I'll give you these files to take to Jonathan Hughes, otherwise people will wonder why I asked you into my office," Kenneth said, walking swiftly over to his desk and reaching above it to a pile of documents resting on a shelf.

As he reached up, his suit jacket caught on the edge of the desk and a file fell out from underneath it, dropping to the ground.

"Oh, I'll get that for you," Pearl said, rushing over to help. As she bent down to pick it up, she paused for a moment, staring at the words written in large font on the front of the file.

TOP SECRET

Pearl blinked at it, drawing in a sharp breath, which she managed to disguise as a cough.

She quickly came to her senses, picking up the file and setting it on Kenneth's desk.

She turned to Kenneth, who was standing right next to her, holding the pile of documents and looking very flustered.

Pearl decided it was best to pretend she hadn't noticed anything out of the ordinary. She plastered a smile on her face and took the documents from Kenneth. "Will that be all?"

Kenneth cleared his throat and straightened out his suit jacket, returning to his usual demeanour. "Yes, thank you, Pearl. I'll see you later this evening."

Pearl smiled and nodded her head, before scurrying out of the office and swiftly closing the door behind her.

As she walked past the door leading into her own work area, she caught Ruth's eye. She had obviously been waiting for Pearl to come out of Kenneth's office.

Ruth frowned at Pearl and mouthed, "What did he want?"

Pearl gestured to the pile of documents in her arms and rolled her eyes. Ruth responded with an affronted look and glared in the direction of Kenneth's office, even though it was out of her eyesight.

Pearl smirked to herself as she carried the documents to their destination, but the smirk quickly slipped away as she remembered the incident with the top-secret file. She simply could not understand why Kenneth would need to carry around a classified file inside his suit jacket. The thoughts distracted her for the rest of the day, and she had to remind herself how important it was for her to properly focus on her work.

At the end of her shift, she quickly packed away her things and followed Ruth out of the building, throwing on her coat as she left.

"I cannot believe Kenneth Johnson had the nerve to ask you to carry out a menial task that he could have easily done himself! And not for the first time, either," Ruth said crossly, as they walked briskly back to the house.

"I know, it's rather terrible," Pearl agreed, feeling slightly guilty for being unable to tell Ruth the full truth.

"It's disgraceful. He seems to think his time is worth more than ours, and we're only there to be of assistance to him."

"Well… I'm sure that isn't *entirely* true," Pearl mumbled.

"Pearl, you have to stand up to him! It's been going on for far too long. You have enough work to be getting on with, without having to do his as well," Ruth said, starting to fling her arms around as she spoke.

"I don't particularly mind doing small errands for him," Pearl said, biting her lip. "But I will stand up to him if it happens again," she added hurriedly, noticing the look on Ruth's face.

Ruth smiled, satisfied with Pearl's agreement. "Just be careful of that man, Pearl. He gives me a bad feeling."

Pearl made a mental note to ask Kenneth to stop coming up with reasons to invite her into his office. At this rate he was going to end up as Ruth's most hated person, if he hadn't been given the top spot already.

As soon as they arrived back at the house, Pearl made some vague excuses to Ruth that she would be going out later to run some errands, which Ruth seemed to believe. She went up to her room as quickly as possible and started to get ready for her date. She looked in her wardrobe for something a bit fancier than her usual attire, and ended up settling on a rather pretty dress that she had owned for years.

As Pearl sat down in front of the mirror to touch up her makeup, there was a knock on the door.

"Come in!" she called, not bothering to turn around. She knew instantly that the visitor would be Betty, having just finished her own shift.

"Hello, lovely. So, Ruth tells me you're running errands later."

Pearl nodded, not wanting to say too much, as she knew Betty could see right through her. She busied herself with readjusting the pins in her hair which held her curls back from her face.

"Do you want some company?"

"Thank you for offering, but no. I was quite looking forward to having some time to myself. I'm only going to the post office and then for a walk, but I might be gone a while."

"You're getting awfully dolled up to go and post some letters," Betty said, a sarcastic tone to her voice.

Pearl hesitated for a moment. "I just felt like getting a bit dressed up this evening. Is that a crime?" She glanced at Betty in the mirror, who was giving her a rather sceptical look.

"No, it's not," Betty responded. "So… are you ever going to tell me anything about him?" she added, sitting on the edge of the bed and watching Pearl with a smirk on her face.

"About who?" Pearl asked innocently, as she carefully applied her bright red lipstick in the mirror.

"Your secret boyfriend."

"I'm afraid I have absolutely no idea what you're talking about," Pearl replied breezily, with a laugh.

"Oh, come on, Pearl. I'm not stupid. You've been acting different recently, disappearing more than usual. Ruth and I have both noticed," Betty said, lying down on the bed and making herself comfortable. "So, who is it?"

"It's nobody!" Pearl replied, avoiding eye contact and rummaging through her things.

"Pearl, you may be a brilliant secret keeper, but you're a terrible liar," Betty said, raising her eyebrows at Pearl's reflection in the mirror.

"That doesn't make any sense," Pearl retorted, hoping to steer the conversation down a different path.

"Yes, it does make sense if you think about it. But back to the matter at hand, if you're so stubborn about keeping it a secret then I assume it must be someone quite high up." Suddenly, Betty gasped and sat bolt upright. "It's not Alan Turing, is it?"

Pearl laughed and turned to look at Betty. "Of course not! Don't be so ridiculous."

"Ah, so it is someone, just not him. I see," Betty said, nodding thoughtfully.

"Stop twisting my words!" Pearl laughed, picking up a pillow and hitting Betty with it lightly.

Betty laughed, then stood up and began to walk towards the door. "Okay, I'll leave you to it. Have fun on your date – I mean, at the post office," she said with a wink, before exiting swiftly and closing the door behind her.

Pearl chuckled to herself, then retrieved her handbag and began to pack her things into it.

Her mind started to drift to her interaction with Kenneth earlier that day. The image of the top-secret document falling out of the inside pocket of his suit jacket played in her head. She tried to push it out of her mind, but it was difficult when she was going to see him again that evening, without yet having the chance to process what she had witnessed.

Surely, Kenneth must have a good reason to hide a top-secret document in his jacket pocket?

Yes, it sounded somewhat dubious when it was phrased in that way, but Kenneth wouldn't have any need to steal documents, as he was high up with high security clearance already, as far as Pearl knew.

Although, the more she thought about it, Pearl realised how little she actually knew about Kenneth's role at Bletchley Park. All she knew for certain was that he had an office in the same building as her, where the work was focused around decrypting coded messages. Kenneth certainly always acted as if he held a lot of power in their department, at least.

However, where Pearl worked it was quite normal not to know much about someone's job, as everyone working there had signed the Official Secrets Act. This meant people rarely talked about their work, and if they did, they would be very vague about it.

Pearl realised she had been dawdling in her room, packing and unpacking her handbag. She sighed deeply and prepared herself for her date with Kenneth, trying to push the thoughts out of her mind for the time being. Kenneth had probably been innocently trying to conceal the document from Pearl for reasons of confidentiality. Instead though, he had sowed a seed of doubt in her mind.

She put her coat on and made her way out of the house, shining a dimly lit handheld torch in front of her. The sky was slowly getting darker and darker, causing Pearl to walk as quickly as she could, and it wasn't long before she arrived outside of Kenneth's house.

She paused for a moment on the front porch, gathering her thoughts together.

She decided she was going to let herself have a nice evening and worry about the incident in the office another time.

Taking a deep breath, Pearl knocked on the front door.

CHAPTER THIRTEEN

"Pearl! You look beautiful," Kenneth said as he opened the front door. He was wearing a shirt and tie with suit trousers and the sleeves of his shirt were rolled up. He looked rather dishevelled, with his usually pristine hair falling forward into his face and his glasses slightly askew.

Pearl smiled and pecked him on the lips as she entered the house. "Why, thank you."

"Please excuse my appearance, I'm still not used to working in the kitchen. I'll freshen up before we eat," Kenneth said, taking Pearl's coat and hanging it on the coat stand.

"You look handsome as you are," Pearl reassured him, straightening his glasses before she was led into the living room.

"Thank you, my darling. I'll still freshen up, though," Kenneth replied, with a wink. He turned and began to walk back out of the room. "I'd better go and check on the food. Make yourself comfortable, I'll be back in a jiffy."

Pearl sat down on the edge of the sofa and looked around the room in silence, fiddling with her necklace nervously. She realised she was sitting very stiffly, so tried to relax herself. She took another deep breath, not wanting Kenneth to recognise that she was at all tense, or uncomfortable in his presence.

She reminded herself that there was no real need to be wary of him. There was most likely a perfectly good explanation for the earlier occurrence, so it was best for her to just push it out of her mind, as she had already decided to do before she arrived.

Noticing a few photographs in handsome gold frames on the mantelpiece, Pearl stood up and walked over to peruse them, hoping to distract her mind. There were a couple of black-and-white photographs of Kenneth with his mother and father. Pearl smiled at them, picking one up to have a closer look. She put it back and picked up another black-and-white photograph, which she assumed showed Kenneth and a group of friends from university. They all wore suits and had large smiles on their faces, Oxford University visible in the backdrop.

Out of the corner of her eye, Pearl spotted an unsealed envelope on a side table next to an armchair. Her curiosity sparked, she placed the photograph back on the mantelpiece and walked over to pick up the envelope.

She hesitated before looking inside. She knew that it was wrong, and Kenneth would be angry if he caught her snooping through his possessions. She decided just to have a quick peek, then she would put it straight back where she had found it.

Pearl opened the envelope cautiously and peeked inside. All that was in there was a roll of camera film. She frowned, wondering why Kenneth would need to send camera film in the post. As she put the envelope back on the side table, she supposed that he was most likely planning to send the film back home to his mother.

Deciding that she had done enough prying around for one evening, and feeling incredibly guilty for invading Kenneth's privacy, Pearl walked back over to the sofa.

Only a moment after she had sat back down, Kenneth appeared in the doorway, making her jump. "Oh, my goodness! You gave me such a fright."

"Sorry, my darling," Kenneth replied, chortling as Pearl clasped a hand over her heart.

Pearl observed that he was now wearing his suit jacket and had fixed his hair, putting it back to his usual style – smartly slicked over, with a crisp side parting.

"Dinner is served, if you would like to make your way through to the dining room," he said, standing to the side and gesturing through the door for Pearl to lead the way.

Once they were in the dining room, Kenneth pulled out a chair for her, pushing it in behind her as she sat down.

"Oh, this looks delightful!" Pearl said, looking down at her plate, filled with meat and vegetables. She hadn't seen so much food on one plate in a long time.

"There wasn't much choice left at the butchers by the time I went to get my rations, so I had to make do with what they had."

"This is perfect," Pearl said, smiling at Kenneth over the table as they began to eat their meal.

As they ate, Kenneth acted like his usual, charming self, which made Pearl feel a lot more relaxed. He obviously wasn't concerned about what had happened earlier, so it can't have been anything too serious.

Either that, or Kenneth was just an extremely good actor.

Pearl preferred to believe the former.

"Your friend, Ruth, gave me a particularly frightening glare when I passed her in the corridor earlier today. She hasn't found out about us, has she?"

Pearl chuckled. "No, you can rest assured she doesn't suspect a thing. I had been going to talk to you about that, actually. Ruth believes that you are taking advantage of me and treating me as if I were your assistant."

"Oh… so she isn't too fond of me?"

"No, I'm afraid not. But if you smile and greet her politely when you pass her, there is still a chance she might warm up to you. I think you should stop inviting me into your office, as well. We shall have to find another, more inconspicuous way to meet up."

"How about meeting at lunch? I'm sure there must be a private place in the grounds where nobody will be able to see us," Kenneth suggested, and Pearl agreed.

The telephone began to ring in the hallway, causing Pearl to jump. She glanced up at Kenneth and saw a spark of apprehension in his eyes. "Aren't you going to answer the telephone? It might be important."

Kenneth glanced at Pearl and cleared his throat. "Yes. Yes, of course. Please excuse me for a moment." He stood up and slowly made his way through to the hallway.

Pearl narrowed her eyes as she watched Kenneth leave, wondering why he was so nervous about answering the telephone.

Who was he expecting to receive a call from?

She stood up quietly and crept over to the door to listen in on what was being said.

"Kenneth Johnson speaking … Yes, I have it … So soon? Are you sure?" Pearl heard the sound of Kenneth writing something down, followed by a ripping noise, which she assumed must have been a page being ripped out of a notepad. "Yes, that will be manageable … Goodbye."

Hearing the receiver being put down, Pearl quickly sneaked back to the table and sat down just before Kenneth entered the room.

"Is everything alright?" Pearl asked, watching as Kenneth tucked a folded sheet of paper into the front pocket of his suit jacket.

"Yes. It was just one of my colleagues," Kenneth replied, sitting down at the table and carrying on with his meal.

Pearl noticed that Kenneth was considerably quieter for the rest of the evening and seemed uncharacteristically subdued. She had to try a lot harder to make conversation with him, which was very unusual as it was normally Kenneth who did most of the talking.

Not long after they had finished their meal, as they were sitting on the sofa in the living room, Kenneth yawned loudly.

"My apologies, Pearl. I'm very tired," he said, covering his mouth with a hand.

Pearl watched him with a concerned expression. "I think it might be time for me to leave. We both need to get up early for work tomorrow."

"Are you sure? You don't have to leave on my account," Kenneth said, but Pearl could tell that he was only saying it so as not to come across as rude.

"I should probably be heading back anyway. I don't want Ruth and Betty to start worrying about me," Pearl replied, smiling as she stood up and gathered her things together.

She made her way into the hallway, closely followed by Kenneth. He retrieved her coat from the coat stand and helped her into it. She subtly looked towards the telephone table, where she could see a notepad and pen lying next to the telephone. She wished she could find out what Kenneth had written down on that sheet of paper. It was within arm's reach, tormenting her as it stuck up out of the top of Kenneth's jacket pocket.

Then, an idea occurred to Pearl. What if the pressure of the pen had left an imprint on the paper below it? There was only one way to find out.

She needed to get that sheet of paper.

Pearl opened her handbag and began rooting around inside it. She slowly moved towards the telephone table, resting her bag on the edge.

"What's the matter?" Kenneth asked, following her over.

"I seem to have misplaced my lipstick! I think I might have left it in the living room."

"I'll go and check for you," Kenneth said, briskly walking towards the entrance to the living room.

As soon as he disappeared through the door, Pearl ripped the top sheet of paper from the notepad, trying to do so in a way that didn't make too much noise. She quickly stashed it in her handbag, just as Kenneth returned to the hallway, empty handed.

"I can't see it in there. Are you sure you brought it with you?"

"Oh, here it is! I couldn't see for looking," Pearl said, pulling her lipstick out of her handbag.

"Panic over!" Kenneth said, laughing and walking over to Pearl. He pulled her in for a kiss, before enfolding her in a warm embrace.

"Thank you for this evening, Kenny," Pearl said, as they separated.

"And you, my darling. I had a wonderful time." Kenneth raised her hand to his lips and kissed it lightly.

"See you in the morning," Pearl said, opening the front door and walking outside into the cold night air. It was pitch black now, with only the moonlight lighting the pavements.

"Farewell, Pearl." Kenneth stood at the door and waved as Pearl walked along the path, flicking on her torch so she could see where she was going more clearly.

Pearl quickened her pace as she heard Kenneth close the door, feeling very vulnerable in the darkness. There was an eerie silence pressing in around her, the only sound the rushing of the freezing cold wind in her ears. She was eager to get back to the safety of her house.

Another reason she was eager to get back, was to inspect the sheet of paper she had taken from Kenneth's house. She felt slightly guilty for being so suspicious of him, but it was better to be safe than sorry.

When Pearl arrived back at the house, she found Ruth and Betty sitting together in the living room, music blaring from the wireless radio.

Betty smirked, glancing over at Pearl as she stood in the doorway. "Did you have a nice time?" she asked.

"Yes, lovely, thank you. I think I'm going to head up to bed now, I'm rather tired." Pearl yawned loudly to prove her point.

"You won't get out of it that easily, I'll be questioning you tomorrow," Betty said, and Pearl laughed.

"Goodnight, Pearl. Sleep well," Ruth called, blowing her a kiss.

Pearl blew them both a kiss, then made her way up to her room. Once there, she retrieved the sheet of paper from her handbag. She held it up to the light and looked for any noticeable indentations.

Looking closely at the paper, Pearl could see impressions, but no matter how hard she squinted she couldn't read what it said. She lowered the paper and racked her brains for what to do next.

Suddenly, an idea struck her, and she began to look through her bedside cabinet. Eventually, she found what she was looking for, and pulled a pencil out of the drawer.

She sat down at her dressing table and began to lightly colour over the indentations in the sheet of paper with the side of the pencil, making sure not to press too hard. Excitement flooded over her as she realised it seemed to be working.

Once she had finished, Pearl held up the sheet of paper and read the words that were now clearly visible, written in white against a grey background.

Friday, 3 p.m.

Pearl stared at the words on the paper, written in Kenneth's messy scrawl.

What did it mean?

She had so many questions flying through her head. Finding out what he had written down seemed to have brought her more confusion than clarity.

It had to be a meeting time, but who was he planning on meeting?

And why had he not needed to write down a location?

She thought it all over, trying to think of any viable reason for Kenneth to be planning to meet up with someone in such a secretive way.

He hadn't seemed entirely pleased to be speaking with the mystery caller, so he couldn't have been arranging to meet with family or friends.

Why would he have reacted in such a way if it had truly been a call from one his colleagues, as he had told her?

Deciding she should keep a written record of everything that had happened so far, Pearl stood up from her desk and began searching through her bedside cabinet for an empty notebook. She came across one in the bottom drawer and sighed as she pulled it out. She stared at it for a moment, running her hand over the beautiful leather exterior. It had been a gift from her father on the last birthday she had celebrated with him before he passed away. She had been saving it to use for something special, but supposed this was as good a time as any.

Pearl walked back over to the dressing table and opened up the notebook, then hovered the pen above the paper, trying to decide exactly how to phrase what she wanted to write. She didn't want to write in plain English, in case anybody came across the notebook who shouldn't. It needed to be written in a more obscure way, so only she would be able to read it.

She gasped as an idea came to her. If she encrypted the notebook, then only those who knew the key would be able to read it. Of course, those who worked with her at Bletchley Park would most likely be able to crack the code if they were given the chance, but at least it would prevent any prying eyes from accidentally reading about her suspicions.

Pearl thought for a moment about how to approach the encryption. She needed to use a cipher which offered security, but which wasn't so complicated that it would take her too long to encrypt if she was in a hurry. She had to remember that she would be doing it all by hand, without the help of the machines she had grown used to using at work.

Eventually, she settled on the Vigenère cipher, with which she would only need to come up with a single phrase that she could use as the key for her code.

She sat back in her chair and closed her eyes, trying to think of a suitable phrase to use. She needed something that was easy for her to remember, but which was also secure. It needed to be something that people wouldn't be able to guess very easily.

Her eyes snapped open and she sat up in her chair as the perfect phrase popped into her head.

White Christmas.

Pearl's favourite song was *White Christmas* by Bing Crosby, but the only person who knew this was her younger sister, Rose, as it was a song that was very special to both of them.

It was the perfect phrase to use, as the only person who would have any chance of guessing the key was the person she trusted most in the world.

She pulled her chair closer to the dressing table and bent over the notebook, setting to work on encrypting an initial sample phrase, so as to test out her key. She checked to make sure she could decrypt the message to give the same phrase she had started with.

PROPERTY OF PEARL CARTER

Perfect.

She hesitated before adding a small musical note next to the encryption, to allude to the phrase she had used as the key. Pearl hoped that there would never be a scenario where Rose would need to be given a clue to work out the key, but she wanted to cover all her bases. It seemed silly not to prepare for every outcome, especially after everything that had been thrown at her in life so far.

As she flicked through the notebook, Pearl noticed a small pocket in the back inside cover. She retrieved the sheet of paper she had taken from Kenneth's house and tucked it away in the pocket for safe-keeping, then flicked back to the first page of the notebook and set to work on encrypting her journal entry. She recorded everything that had happened that day, from the top-secret document in Kenneth's office that morning, to the suspicious phone call at his house.

Just as she had finished writing down everything she could remember, Pearl let out a loud yawn and decided it might be time for her to finish sleuthing for the night.

She stowed the notebook away in her bedside cabinet and thought about what her next steps should be, coming to the conclusion that she needed to somehow find out where Kenneth was planning on going on Friday afternoon.

But for now, she needed to get some sleep.

CHAPTER FOURTEEN

The next morning, Pearl woke up feeling tired, but filled with determination to get to the bottom of this mystery she had found herself wrapped up in. She got dressed quickly and made her way downstairs, wanting to get into work as soon as possible in the hope that she would bump into Kenneth before their shift started.

As she grabbed something quick to eat for her breakfast, her mind raced, thinking of how she could go about questioning Kenneth without raising any suspicion. She was so lost in her own thoughts that she didn't hear Ruth trying to get her attention.

"Pearl!" Ruth called, lightly touching Pearl's shoulder. "A penny for your thoughts?"

"Oh, sorry! I'm just tired," Pearl said, laughing lightly as she turned to look at Ruth. "I wanted to try and get into work a bit earlier today, so I don't end up rushing around like usual."

"If you give me a chance to eat something, then I'll join you," Ruth suggested, making her way to the larder.

"Oh, no, that won't be necessary. You can just leave at the normal time," Pearl said, shaking her head and waving Ruth off.

Ruth looked surprised. "Oh, okay. I'll see you at work, then."

"Goodbye, see you soon," Pearl said, waving as she quickly made her way out of the front door and began the freezing cold journey to work. She hoped she hadn't been too rude or dismissive in her rejection of Ruth's offer, but she needed to walk on her own in case she happened to come across Kenneth.

But, as it turned out, she didn't see Kenneth on her walk to work. Thinking he must already be there, she sneaked a look into his office, only to see that it was empty.

Disappointed, Pearl made her way to her desk and set herself up for the day. She switched her mind into work mode, deciding she would try to find Kenneth again later on when she took her break.

The morning passed over rather quickly for Pearl, but there was still no sign of Kenneth. She assumed she must have missed him arriving, as she was so engrossed in her work, but when she walked past his office she noticed it was still empty. Thinking this was very odd, Pearl frowned as she left the building and made her way to the catering building for lunch. As she was walking, she thought she heard a hissing noise. She stopped in her tracks and listened intently.

"Psst!"

Startled, Pearl spun around, trying to work out where the noise was coming from. "Who's there?" she called, her voice wavering slightly.

"Psst! Pearl, over here!"

Pearl whipped her head around in the direction of the voice and saw a dark figure lurking between two of the surrounding buildings. She looked more closely and realised it was Kenneth, glancing all around and gesturing for her to come over.

Pearl sighed with relief and scuttled over to join him. "Kenny! You scared me half to death! What are you doing down here?"

"Well, you said we weren't to meet in my office anymore," Kenneth replied in a low voice, frowning as if he thought hiding down a dark alley between buildings was the obvious solution to that problem.

"Oh, right, I see. I wish you would have warned me! How long have you been waiting here?" Pearl whispered back.

"Oh, only about ten minutes. I tried to time it around when you normally leave for your lunch," Kenneth said, smiling proudly.

"That explains why I couldn't find you in your office," Pearl muttered, smiling as she began to calm down from the shock of Kenneth's surprise.

"Oh, were you looking for me?" he asked.

Pearl nodded. "Yes. I tried this morning as well, but you were nowhere to be seen."

"I was most likely in a meeting."

Pearl felt silly for being so suspicious of Kenneth for even the simplest of things.

"So, why were you looking for me?" Kenneth asked, leaning against the side of one of the buildings and lighting a cigarette.

Pearl moved slightly to one side, trying to get out of range of the smoke. She had never been able to stomach the smell of it. "I just wanted to ask if you'll be free on Friday afternoon. Only, I have the afternoon off work, and I'll be leaving the next day to go home for Christmas, so I thought it might be nice for us to go to the pictures and see a film?"

"Oh, um…" Kenneth scratched his head, looking slightly uncomfortable as he thought over the offer.

Pearl hoped she hadn't been too obvious with her question. It was all true though; she really did have the afternoon off, and it would probably be her last chance to see Kenneth before her scheduled leave. "It's perfectly okay if you can't. We can just see each other when I get back."

Kenneth sighed. "I really wish I could, my darling, but I have some… errands to run on Friday afternoon, so I'm afraid I won't be able to make it." He gave Pearl an apologetic look.

Pearl noted how unsure he sounded when saying he was running errands. She smiled widely. "Don't worry about it. I need to go and have some lunch before my break is over. I hope you have a wonderful Christmas, Kenny. I'll see you when I get back."

She stepped forward and gave him a peck on the cheek, before hurrying away, leaving a bewildered Kenneth standing alone in the dark shade of the buildings.

* * *

When Friday finally came, Pearl spent most of the morning preparing herself for her mission that afternoon. She hoped that nothing would come of it, but she couldn't deny the fact that Kenneth had been acting awfully out of character recently.

She went over her rather vague plan for the day in her head. She was going to hide somewhere in Kenneth's street and wait for him to leave the house, then follow him to find out where he was going. She had already dug out her camera and a fresh roll of film, to take photographs of the meeting in case she saw anything incriminating. She was also going to disguise herself, so it would be easier to follow Kenneth without him recognising her.

Since she didn't know how far Kenneth would be going, and therefore what time he would need to leave the house, she opted to go over early in the afternoon and hope that he was still there.

After she had eaten a light lunch, Pearl carried out a last-minute check of her handbag to make sure she had everything she needed, before pulling on her coat and shoes. She checked her hair in the mirror before she left the house, making sure it was still neatly tucked away under her headscarf. The last thing she wanted was for Kenneth to spot her bright ginger hair and recognise her.

She made her way to Kenneth's street and stood in a back alley, where she had a good view of his house. She could see a light on in the front room, confirming the fact that he hadn't left yet.

Thank goodness.

All that was left to do was cross her fingers and hope that everything panned out the way she hoped it would.

Pearl waited for what felt like hours, but there was still no sign of Kenneth. She was just starting to wish she had left the house later, or at least brought a chair with her, when she heard the sound of a front door opening. She ducked down to make herself less noticeable as she peeked out from behind the wall, then watched as Kenneth locked the door and walked to the path, swinging a briefcase by his side.

He turned right and began walking along the path in the opposite direction to where Pearl was hiding. She crept out from her hiding place and began to trail him from far enough away that he wouldn't be able to sense her following him, but close enough so she could keep track of where he was.

They walked for a while, winding through numerous different streets, until Kenneth came to a halt near the end of one and entered a corner shop. Pearl stopped and leaned against a wall, trying not to look suspicious while she waited for him to reappear in the doorway. She worried that the corner shop might actually turn out to be the meeting place, but didn't want to risk getting any closer to check in case she was seen.

Kenneth emerged from the shop not long after, with a newspaper tucked under his arm. Pearl breathed a sigh of relief, knowing she had been right to go with her instincts and keep her distance. She hurried to follow him as he turned and carried on walking briskly down the street, rounding the corner at the end.

She followed him until they arrived at an open grassy area, surrounded by shops. Kenneth walked over to a park bench positioned on the edge of the grass and sat down, placing his briefcase on the floor by his feet. He unrolled his newspaper and opened it out, then began to read.

Pearl stared at him. It was a much more public area than she had expected for the meeting to take place in. She presumed he must have bought the newspaper to pass the time while he waited for the arrival of the person he was meeting. She checked her watch and saw that it was almost 3 o'clock, meaning there wasn't long left to wait.

She looked around for a good place to hide, where she would be able to have a good view of what was happening, without being seen herself. Spotting a well-placed post box near the end of the street she skulked over and hid behind it, then got out her camera and snapped a few photographs of Kenneth on the bench, even though his face wasn't visible behind the newspaper.

Several minutes passed and Pearl began to grow impatient, starting to wonder if anybody else was going to make an appearance. She didn't want to witness anything terrible, but she did wonder why Kenneth would possibly have come all this way just to sit on a park bench and read a newspaper.

However, her wish for something to happen was granted only moments later, as a rather tall man approached the bench and sat down next to Kenneth.

Pearl snapped some photographs as she took in his appearance.

The mystery man wore a long, grey trench coat and a fedora, which he had angled down over his forehead. Due to the shadow cast by his hat, paired with the dark glasses he was wearing, it was difficult to see his face. Pearl wondered if the man could actually see anything through the dark glasses, as it wasn't a particularly sunny day.

Then, she gasped as she noticed something else. The man had put a briefcase on the floor by his feet as he sat down, right next to Kenneth's briefcase. Pearl squinted her eyes as she looked at the two briefcases, trying to confirm what she thought she had seen. Her eyes widened as she realised she had been correct.

The briefcases were identical.

Her eyes flickered up to the man, who was now reaching inside his trench coat. Pearl held her breath, her heart rate quickening, imagining him pulling all sorts of dangerous things out of his pocket. She held up the camera, getting ready to capture whatever it was that he was retrieving. He removed his arm from inside his coat, and Pearl took a photograph, trying to figure out what he was holding. The man placed it down on his lap, and she realised it was a brown paper bag. He reached inside, then pulled out a sandwich from within and began to eat it.

Pearl lowered her camera, frowning at the scene before her in confusion. It was beginning to look as if Kenneth was on a very innocent outing and the mystery man had only sat on the bench to eat his lunch. It was probably only a coincidence that they had matching briefcases. She started to feel rather guilty for suspecting Kenneth, then having taken it upon herself to follow him around with a camera, trying to find evidence to prove her misgivings.

Pearl sat watching the two men for a few minutes, feeling increasingly guilt-ridden as they continued with their completely innocent activities. As she waited for them to finish, she came to the decision that if she didn't find anything suspicious while following Kenneth around, then she would stop snooping. It was starting to look as if it might have all been her overactive imagination.

Pearl drew her full attention back to the bench, raising her camera as she noticed that the man had finished his sandwich and was crumpling up the paper bag. She took a few photographs as he stood up, picked up the briefcase and threw his rubbish in a bin, striding away purposefully.

Suddenly, something clicked in Pearl's brain and she gasped as she realised the man had picked up the wrong briefcase. He had surreptitiously taken the one which was closer to Kenneth. The error most likely wouldn't have been noticeable to any passers-by, but Pearl had been so focused on taking photographs of him that she had been able to pick up on the switch.

Thinking it might have been an accident, or a theft, Pearl considered going over and saying something, but then she remembered where she was and what she was doing. It would be very foolish for her to expose herself now. She carried on watching Kenneth, who was still reading his newspaper on the bench, and felt dreadful for only watching and not doing anything when there was a possibility he may have just had his belongings stolen.

Only a few minutes later, Kenneth folded away his newspaper and slipped it inside his coat pocket, then picked up the briefcase from the floor and placed it on the bench beside him.

Pearl raised her camera again and took some photographs, wondering for a moment whether he realised the briefcase was an imposter. She hoped she was right about it being a misunderstanding and the other man had only mistakenly picked up the wrong briefcase. Hopefully he would realise his mistake and return the briefcase shortly.

But then, her mouth fell open as her worst fears were confirmed.

Kenneth subtly opened the briefcase a small amount and peered inside, then quickly closed it again, seemingly unphased by the contents within.

Pearl snapped a few more photographs and then lowered the camera slowly, staring at Kenneth in utter bewilderment.

She was so stunned, it took her a few moments to realise Kenneth had stood up and was beginning to walk in her direction.

Snapping back to her senses, Pearl inhaled sharply, quickly spinning around and dashing in the opposite direction.

She ducked into the nearest shop and stood out of view of the window, breathing heavily as she waited for Kenneth to pass.

Only a few seconds later, he strode past the shop window, with the impostor briefcase swinging by his side and a frown creasing his forehead.

"Can I help you at all, love?"

Pearl jumped and whirled around to search for the source of the voice. Her eyes came to rest on the woman behind the counter, who was smiling at her expectantly.

Pearl relaxed. She had forgotten she was in a public place.

"No, thank you," she replied, forcing a smile, and the woman nodded at her politely.

Pearl walked over to the window, craning her neck to see Kenneth's retreating figure striding down the road.

She closed her eyes, trying to process what she had just witnessed.

Try as she might, she couldn't think of an explanation for Kenneth exchanging briefcases with a mystery man that didn't point to him being involved in something illegal.

She opened her eyes, her heart sinking into her stomach.

There was no denying it any longer, the evidence was clear.

Kenneth was a spy.

CHAPTER FIFTEEN

"Oh Pearl, I hope you have a wonderful Christmas with your family!" Ruth said, beaming and pulling Pearl in for a hug.

"Group hug!" Betty squealed, throwing her arms around the two of them.

Pearl laughed and squeezed them both tightly. "I'll miss you both while I'm gone. I hope you have a wonderful Christmas, even if you can't be at home with your families."

Betty waved her off. "Oh, don't worry about us. We'll have a jolly good time! We'll probably be served a better Christmas dinner here than we would be able to buy with our rations anyway."

Pearl laughed. "I hope you enjoy the party this evening. I'm sad I won't be able to join you."

Ruth groaned. "Don't remind me."

There was a Christmas party being thrown that evening, organised by some of the women who worked on the site. They would often arrange parties for special occasions, as well as purely to raise morale in the workforce. It could be quite exhausting doing their jobs day in and day out, so it was nice to have something to look forward to every so often. Pearl and Betty loved going to these parties, but Ruth loathed them, only going because the others dragged her along.

"We'll have a great time, Ruth. It'll be such fun!" Betty said, smiling widely at Ruth, who still didn't look convinced.

Pearl chuckled to herself, then said her final goodbyes before leaving the house and making her way to the bus stop.

It wasn't long before the bus arrived, which was lucky as Pearl felt as if her nose was about to freeze off with the bitterly cold wind. She paid her fare and chose a seat near the back, squeezing her case in beside her and settling in for the relatively short journey.

As she stared out of the bus window, she began to think over the events of the previous day. She had hurried up to her room as soon as she had arrived back at the house after trailing Kenneth, immediately rooting through her bedside table for her notebook. Then she had sat down at the dressing table and written down everything that had happened on her outing, while it was still fresh in her mind. Although, she needn't have worried about forgetting any important details, as she could still remember everything just as vividly as if it were happening that very moment. She didn't think she would be able to forget it even if she wanted to, she had been so shocked by Kenneth's actions.

She reached her hand out to her case and gripped it protectively, remembering the contents hidden within. She had buried her notebook and the camera film between the piles of clothes in her case, not wanting to leave any of the evidence she had collected unattended back at the house. She found herself feeling very uneasy on the bus, suspecting every one of her fellow passengers of wanting to steal the valuable information hidden in her case, even though they had no way of knowing it was in there. She felt rather relieved when the bus reached her stop and bustled off as quickly as possible.

It wasn't long before Pearl reached the front door of her family home, and she instantly felt more relaxed as she opened it and entered the hallway. It was obvious that her grandparents had been visiting to take care of the empty property, as they usually did almost daily when both Pearl and Rose were away. She felt a wave of affection for them as she walked into the living room and saw that the fire had been lit ready for her return. They had also left a basket of fresh fruit and vegetables on the bench in the kitchen, alongside a note written in her grandmother's elegant handwriting.

Dear Pearl and Rose,
Welcome home! We are overjoyed to be able to spend the Christmas holidays together this year. We have been counting down the days and are eager to see you both once you have settled in.
In the meantime, please enjoy this basket of fruit and vegetables that have been freshly picked from our garden.
Lots of love,
Grandma and Grandpa.

Pearl smiled as she read the note, then closed her eyes and held it close to her chest. She made a mental note to thank them for everything as soon as she saw them next.

She walked back into the hallway and noticed her case still lying abandoned at the bottom of the stairs. Her heart sank. The warmth and calmness of being home meant she had almost forgotten about the evidence she had brought with her. She walked over and began to heave the case up the stairs and towards her bedroom.

It took a lot of effort, but she was soon puffing and panting in her room as she swung the case up onto her bed. She dug through her clothes to retrieve the notebook and roll of film, then sat on the edge of her bed as she decided what she should do with them.

She felt the weight of responsibility resting on her shoulders as she stared at the two items in her hands.

She had a duty to her country to let the authorities know what Kenneth was using his position at Bletchley Park for. However, she still worried that there could have been a misunderstanding, and if given the chance Kenneth may have a rational explanation for his actions.

Pearl bit her lip as she thought through her options. She could either hand in the evidence she had collected, and Kenneth would be investigated for the crime of espionage, possibly ending up in prison, or she could confront him and find out for herself whether he was a traitor or not. If it turned out that he was, then she would have the chance to convince him to hand himself in, which would be better than being reported by someone else.

She considered confiding in someone she trusted, but quickly dismissed that idea. She couldn't bring herself to knowingly pass so much responsibility onto any of her loved ones, and anyway, she wasn't entirely sure she was ready to tell anyone about her suspicions. There were so many secrets involved that she wouldn't even know where to start.

She shook her head and stood up, deciding it would be best to wait until after the Christmas holidays before doing anything. This would give her time to think everything over and make sure she was making the right decision, but it would also give her an opportunity to gather more evidence to support her case, if the opportunity was to present itself.

She began to pace around the room, staring at the objects in her hands. She needed to find a place to hide them for the time being, until she had decided what to do. She walked out of her room and into the middle of the landing, then slowly turned around on the spot, taking in the rooms around her. Her eyes hovered for a moment on the door to her parents' room, then quickly shot away.

Her parents' room would probably be the best place to hide the evidence, as nobody went in there. It was still in the same condition as it had been when her father passed away a couple of years earlier. With a big sigh, Pearl walked over to the door and steeled herself to go in, her hand hovering over the doorknob. She closed her eyes for a moment and grabbed the doorknob, but she couldn't bring herself to turn it. Her shoulders slumped as she let go, her arm dropping down to her side as she turned away from the room.

It was no good; she was going to have to find another hiding place.

She racked her brains for anywhere in the house that was a good place to hide small objects. Any sort of removable panel or loose floorboard…

She gasped as it came to her, smacking her palm to her forehead. She felt foolish for not thinking of it earlier.

When the war had started, her father had worried about the prospect of the country being invaded by the Nazis. One of his concerns was the possibility of homes being looted and possessions taken. So, he had made a small hiding place in the loft where they could easily conceal their most treasured possessions if it was needed. It hadn't been however, until this very moment.

Pearl rushed to find the rickety ladders her father had always used to climb into the loft, then carried them over to the entrance. She climbed up and pushed her way through the hatch, only to realise there was no light source in the space; it was pitch black.

She huffed with annoyance, wanting to hide the evidence as quickly as possible, then made her way back down the ladder to search for a lamp. She found one sitting on a shelf in her bedroom and quickly rushed back onto the landing, ascending the ladder for a second time.

In her haste to climb up, Pearl started to lose her grip on the lamp and nearly dropped it onto the landing, causing her foot to slip as she tried to steady it. She grabbed the ladder tightly and managed to catch herself, before taking a moment to breathe and calm herself down, deciding she needed to be more patient.

As she climbed into the loft, Pearl realised her hands were shaking. She squeezed them into tight fists in an attempt to control them, then made her way over to the corner where she knew the loose floorboard was.

She held the lamp out in front of her and scanned the floor, until her eyes came to rest on a rounded notch carved into the edge of one of the floorboards. She kneeled down next to it, putting the lamp down beside her and the evidence by her feet. She reached towards the floorboard, placing her finger in the notch and pulling upwards. A small amount of dust clouded the air, and she waved it away with her hand.

Pearl peered into the hole, using the lamp to see if there was anything occupying the space. The thought occurred to her that her father could have stashed something in there before he had passed, meaning it would have been left there to gather dust. Her heart sank. She hadn't realised she had been hoping to find anything hidden in there until she saw it was empty.

Pearl pushed her disappointment to the back of her mind and returned to the task at hand. She picked up the roll of film, wrapping it in a handkerchief for protection, before placing it carefully in the space. She sighed as she picked up the notebook and gently stroked the cover, before placing it next to the camera film.

She stared at the two very ordinary looking objects, which she knew were of much more importance than they appeared to be at first glance. She wondered whether she was doing the right thing by not telling anyone about what she had discovered.

Pearl sighed – something she realised she had been doing an awful lot lately – and placed the floorboard back over the gap in the floor. As she stood up, she placed her hands on her hips and surveyed the area. The evidence would be safely hidden in the loft, where there was no chance of anyone stumbling across it. Even if someone was searching for it, they would find it difficult to discover the hiding place.

Feeling satisfied with her choice of hiding place, Pearl descended the ladder, closed up the hatch, smoothed down her skirt and began the hefty task of preparing the house for Rose's return.

CHAPTER SIXTEEN

The next few hours passed in a whirlwind of activity, and before she knew it Pearl was standing on the platform at Bletchley railway station waiting for Rose's train to arrive. As she stood there shivering in the cold, she thought over their plans for the next couple of weeks. She was determined to act as if everything was fine in front of Rose, as she didn't want to give her any unnecessary stress. Rose deserved to have as normal a Christmas holiday as was possible under the circumstances, and Pearl intended to give her that.

A few minutes later, the train pulled into the station and Pearl spotted her sister's round, smiling face through a window. She readied herself and plastered on a smile as Rose emerged from the train dragging her case behind her, before abandoning it so she could reach Pearl more quickly. Rose was a miniature version of Pearl, with the same startling green eyes and flaming red curls. Her hair bounced as she swerved through a group of people and ran into Pearl's outstretched arms, squealing excitedly.

Pearl laughed. "Oh, how I've missed you!" she cried, hugging her sister tightly. Her smile became genuine as her worries began to melt away. She released her sister from her embrace and held her at arm's length, taking in her appearance. She noticed Rose appeared to be almost the same height as her now. "Have you grown?"

Rose nodded. "I've grown one and three-quarter inches!" she announced proudly.

"How marvellous!"

They retrieved Rose's case before making their way out of the railway station, Rose chattering enthusiastically all the way to the bus stop.

"I cannot wait to change out of this skirt and into my dungarees," she told Pearl, tugging at the fabric of her skirt and looking at her school uniform with great disgust. "I'll never understand why they force us to wear these wretched things. Once I've finished school I'm refusing to wear a skirt ever again!"

Pearl laughed as she watched her sister, seeing her own stubbornness reflected back at her. "No need to worry, Rosie. I've already sorted out your favourite blouse and dungarees for you and set them out nicely on your bed. You can go upstairs and change into them straight away."

"Thank you, Pearl. You're the best!"

It wasn't long before they arrived home, Rose sprinting upstairs to get changed before Pearl had even closed the front door, leaving her case lying discarded at the bottom of the stairs and shouting, "I'll take that up later!"

Pearl chuckled to herself and shook her head. She dragged the case to the side of the hallway where it didn't get in the way, then walked into the kitchen to make a pot of tea.

Being alone in the kitchen gave Pearl time to think again, and she began to doubt whether she had made the right decision by hiding the notebook away in the loft. She shook her head impatiently. She was tired of her mind going around in circles, making a decision on what she should do and then changing course two minutes later. She needed to come to a decision and stick with it.

However, the sound of Rose's footsteps bounding down the stairs interrupted her thoughts and she resolved to think it over another time.

She turned around and smiled as Rose walked into the kitchen, carrying a large sketchbook under her arm. She was wearing her favourite orange blouse underneath her blue dungarees, which seemed to be showing more ankle than they usually did. Pearl made a mental note to check if she had enough clothing tokens to buy Rose some new ones.

Rose inhaled deeply and breathed out a relaxed sigh, a serene smile on her face. "It's so nice to be home and in my regular clothes."

Pearl grinned. "You look much more like yourself now, I have to say. I'm just making us a pot of tea. We can have a proper cuppa to celebrate us being home together, Rosie. I'll use some of our milk rations instead of condensed milk, for a treat," she said, pouring milk into the teacups as she waited for the tea to brew in the teapot.

"Ooh, that sounds wonderful. Tea isn't often served at school, I've missed it terribly!" Rose said as she sat down at the kitchen table and opened her sketchbook to a half-finished drawing. She removed a pencil from behind her ear and bent over the table, immediately setting to work on completing her illustration.

Pearl smiled and looked over Rose's shoulder, where she could see that she was carefully sketching an image of a rose. She was always in awe when she saw Rose's artwork. Pearl couldn't draw for the life of her, but it came so naturally to her sister. It reminded her of being a little girl and watching her mother painting for hours on a canvas she had propped up in the living room. Most of Pearl's memories of her mother involved watching her paint, as this was when she had looked her happiest.

She felt the same way as she watched Rose sketching, her tongue sticking out of the side of her mouth as she concentrated.

"That's brilliant, Rosie. People are going to be lining up to buy your artwork when you're older," Pearl said, placing a hand on Rose's shoulder.

Rose chuckled and glanced up momentarily. "Thank you, Pearl, that means a lot. I'm not sure I'll ever sell any of my pieces though."

Pearl frowned. "But I thought that was your dream?"

"Yes, it is, but Matron says it's unrealistic. She says I need to focus on more practical things like learning how to run a household and mend clothing and cook meals. It all sounds like a real bore to me, but I suppose I'll have to learn." Rose shrugged, continuing with her sketch, each stroke of the pencil carefully thought out and perfectly placed on the page.

Pearl huffed, feeling outraged at the thought of Rose having her dreams crushed by her school matron. "How ridiculous! I've never heard such nonsense! I can't believe that school is teaching young girls they will only amount to being housewives and nothing more. I've half a mind to phone that woman right now and tell her what I think of her advice. Of course, it is important to learn how to do those things, but it doesn't have to be *instead* of following your dreams. You can do anything you set your mind to, Rosie, don't let anybody tell you different.

One day, you'll have your own exhibition in a fancy art gallery and people all around the world will know your name, you mark my words."

Rose grinned from ear to ear, putting her pencil down and turning in her chair. "Do you really think so?"

Pearl relaxed and smiled at her sister. "Of course I do. You're a very talented artist."

"Thank you, Pearl," Rose said, sheepishly. "I was thinking I might try and do some more painting over the holidays, as well."

Pearl smiled fondly. Rose loved painting, but it was quite difficult to buy art supplies while things were being rationed, so she always had to be careful and use her paint sparingly. For this reason, she usually only painted on special occasions, choosing to draw with just a pencil in her sketchbook the rest of the time.

"That sounds like a wonderful idea! I'll get everything sorted for you tomorrow," Pearl said, turning to walk back over to the bench.

"Would you mind if I attempted to paint a portrait of you?" Rose asked tentatively.

Pearl turned back to her sister and grinned. "I would be positively honoured. Right, I'll pour the tea and we can have some sweets as a treat. I bought some sherbet lemons for you, and some pear drops for me." She produced two paper bags from the cupboard and handed one of them to Rose.

Rose's eyes widened. "Wow! Thank you! I assume they mustn't have had any KitKats in the sweet shop?"

Pearl shook her head and gave Rose a forlorn look. KitKat's were Pearl's usual treat of choice, but while the war was on she had found they were extremely difficult to come across, and she hadn't been able to have one in a long time. "I cannot wait until rationing is over!"

They spent the next few hours chatting in the living room, filling each other in on everything that had happened since the last time they had been together. It was mainly Rose doing the talking, as Pearl didn't have much to say. Although there had been a lot of things happening in her life recently, there wasn't much she was able to tell Rose. Instead, she decided to update Rose on everything that was going on in the personal lives of her friends from work.

"Betty has recently become an aunt, so that was very exciting news. Her sister sent some photographs of the new baby, but Betty hasn't been able to meet her yet. She's hoping to meet her early next year. Ruth, however, had some not so great news, bless her heart. Her younger brother was called up a few months ago, so she's been quite worried about him, understandably. We've been trying to keep her mind off it by distracting her. Forcing her to go to parties with us and that sort of thing."

Rose laughed, then sighed unhappily.

"What's wrong?" Pearl asked, her brow knitting together.

"Nothing. I was just thinking that I would love to meet your friends, they sound lovely. But it isn't likely to happen any time soon, seeing as we don't even get to see each other as often as we'd like! I wish we could just stay here and not go back to school or work at the end of the holidays." Rose stared at the ground miserably.

Pearl moved over to perch on the arm of Rose's chair, putting an arm around her shoulders. "I wish we didn't have to leave either. It would be lovely to be able to spend more time together. But it won't be long until we can both move back into this house permanently and be together all the time. We'll spend so much time together that we'll be sick of the sight of each other!" Pearl said, and Rose laughed. Pearl reached for her angel wing pendant and held it up. "But remember, Rosie, no matter how far apart we are–"

"–as long as we have our angel wings we will always be connected," Rose joined in, holding her own necklace up and connecting it to Pearl's one.

"That's right," Pearl grinned, reaching down to hug her sister. "Now come on, let's listen to some music to cheer you up."

Rose's eyes brightened instantaneously. "Can we dance, like we used to do?" she asked, jumping up from the seat and moving into the middle of the floor, where there was an open space.

"Of course we can! I've missed dancing with you, Rosie," Pearl said, looking through her collection of records which were stacked next to the gramophone. "What about this one?" she asked, as she pulled one out.

"Yes, our favourite song! And it's the right time of year for it, too," Rose said excitedly.

Pearl set the record on the gramophone and the opening notes of *White Christmas* by Bing Crosby filled the room.

Beaming, Pearl joined Rose in the middle of the floor and began to waltz around the room with her. They sang along loudly, not caring that they were both very out of tune.

As they danced, Pearl managed to push her concerns about Kenneth to the back of her mind.

She decided it was best for her to try and forget about the whole ordeal, at least for the time being.

CHAPTER SEVENTEEN

Over the next few days, Pearl tried her best to enjoy the festivities and make her time with Rose as special as possible. They visited their grandparents as soon as they had the chance and had a wonderful reunion with them. They picked fruit and vegetables in the garden, which their grandmother used to cook them a delicious meal. Afterwards, they all dressed in their nicest clothes and took a trip to the pictures to see a film, which was always a grand occasion for the family.

Another day, Pearl dragged all the Christmas decorations down from the loft – being careful not to disturb her secret hiding place – and they spent a delightful afternoon listening to Christmas music on the gramophone and putting up the tree in the living room. Rose had the marvellous idea to make paper garlands to hang around the house, and a wreath to hang on the front door. Pearl let Rose take the lead on these activities and made sure she followed her instructions to the letter.

When Rose decided she felt ready to paint the portrait of Pearl, they brought her painting supplies into the living room and set up her canvas and easel where natural light flooded through the window. Rose asked Pearl to sit in the armchair, then staged the scene around her to make the perfect setting for her painting. She set to work, and they spent most of the day in this way, only stopping to eat and drink. The sun had set by the time Rose announced she was finished.

"It isn't perfect, but I think it captures you nicely," Rose said, looking between the painting and her sister, comparing the two.

"Can I see it?" Pearl asked, smiling widely at Rose, who looked rather nervous.

"Yes, you can. But please don't expect too much from it!" she replied, worry creasing her face.

Pearl hopped up from the armchair and walked over to Rose, then turned to look at the painting. She gasped and covered her mouth with her hands, tears immediately springing to her eyes. In the painting, Pearl was sitting on the armchair with a serene smile on her face, her green eyes sparkling and alive and not a ginger curl out of place on her head. Pearl noticed small details in the scene around her, which she knew Rose had put a lot of thought into, but which looked very natural on the canvas. The crackling fire was glowing brightly next to the armchair, and there was a pile of books placed carefully by her feet. She was holding a teacup and saucer delicately in her hands, and the pleats of her skirt fell perfectly around her knees. It was beautiful, and Pearl felt so proud that her little sister had painted it.

"It's breathtaking," she whispered, turning to Rose and hugging her tightly. "You really are very talented!"

Rose let out a sigh of relief and laughed. "Thank you, Pearl. I'm glad you like it."

"We're going to have to hang it somewhere in the house!" Pearl said brightly, turning back to the painting and gazing at it intently.

They spent the rest of the evening searching the house for a good place to hang the painting, but in the absence of the perfect place presenting itself to them, they agreed to leave the decision for another day and retired to bed instead.

However, despite all the fun they were having, Pearl still found herself getting distracted and feeling on edge. Her mind kept wandering, thinking over every possible scenario and worrying endlessly. Sometimes, she was so lost in her thoughts that she was concerned Rose might notice there was something wrong. She hadn't said anything to her outright, but Pearl had caught her sister looking at her worriedly one evening as they ate dinner. It turned out Rose had been trying to have a conversation with her, but Pearl hadn't heard a word she had said. She had laughed it off and told Rose how tired she was, but she wasn't sure she had believed her. It was true that Pearl was extremely tired, though, as she had been finding it difficult to fall asleep.

One morning, after a particularly restless night spent tossing and turning and thinking about Kenneth and what she should do about him, Pearl sat on an armchair in the living room, slowly drinking a cup of tea. Rose was upstairs getting ready for the day, although they hadn't planned what they were going to do yet. Pearl was running out of festive activities and her mind was too full to think of any more. She closed her eyes and contemplated the situation she found herself in. The more she thought about it, she realised she didn't actually have much information about what exactly it was Kenneth was doing. It was obvious he was passing information to somewhere he shouldn't, but to what country or organisation? And what type of information was he passing to them? Pearl realised she needed to talk to him, so she could try and get to the bottom of it and understand exactly how serious a crime he was committing. She decided that she was going to confront him about it as soon as she saw him next. Just the thought of it made her heart beat faster and her palms become slick with sweat, but it had to be done.

A loud rapping on the front door dragged Pearl out of her thoughts, making her jump and almost spill her tea. She gently placed the teacup down on the side table and paused for a moment to compose herself, before making her way over to the door and opening it. She was greeted by a scrawny young boy with dark skin and short black curly hair, who was holding his bicycle by his side and beaming up at her.

"Bernard! It's lovely to see you. How are you, my dear?" Pearl asked, surprised by the unexpected arrival of Rose's friend.

"Morning, Miss Carter! I'm well, thank you. Is Rose back from school yet, by any chance?" Bernard asked, looking past Pearl and into the hallway.

"Yes, she is. She's upstairs, I'll just call for her," Pearl said, moving over to the stairs. "Rose, darling, Bernard Lawson is here to see you!"

Not a moment later Rose was bounding down the stairs. "Bernard!" she shouted excitedly, engulfing him in a bear hug once she had reached the front door.

"I'll just be in the living room," Pearl said, smiling and backing out of the hallway, closing the door after herself. She could still hear their excited chatter as she made her way over to her usual armchair, picking up a book on the way.

A few minutes later, Rose popped her head around the door. "Is it okay if I go out with Bernard? We were going to ride our bicycles around the village."

"Yes, of course! Just make sure you're back in time for lunch," Pearl said over the top of her book.

Rose smiled widely, then disappeared in a flash, shouting, "Thank you, bye!" as she went.

Pearl heard the front door close, then watched through the window as Rose and Bernard set off cycling down the road. She tittered to herself in amusement, then sighed happily. She loved seeing Rose look so happy. Even though they had been through so much as a family, Rose always managed to keep a positive outlook on life. Pearl often worried about Rose when she could see that she was feeling down, but it was never long before the sparkle was back in her eyes and her bright smile was back on her face. This was a trait Pearl had always admired in her younger sister. She secretly thought that Rose was much more capable of looking after herself than she gave her credit for, but this wouldn't make an ounce of difference in the grand scheme of things. No matter what, Pearl knew she would always protect her sister to the best of her abilities; after all, that is what big sisters are for.

Pearl turned back to her book and sat in silence for a while, before she realised she wasn't taking in any of the words on the page. She had been rereading the same paragraph for ten minutes when she decided it was a lost cause; her mind was too busy for reading. She replaced her bookmark and sighed. It was much more difficult to stop herself from worrying when she was by herself, silence pressing in from all around her. She looked around the room and searched for something else which could grab her attention and occupy her mind for a while. Her eyes landed on the wireless radio, and she immediately stood up and walked over to turn it on. She turned the dial to the station that broadcasted light entertainment, as she thought this would be a better distraction than worrying herself further by listening to news about how the war was progressing. She returned to her seat and made herself comfortable, closing her eyes so she could concentrate better on what was being said.

Pearl sat like this for a while, willing her mind to listen to the broadcast and dragging it back every time it wandered off. She grew increasingly annoyed as her mind continued with its inner monologue, the wireless not appearing to make any impact on it. It simply refused to think of anything other than Kenneth. She opened her eyes and let out a frustrated sigh, then stood up and walked over to the wireless, twisting the dial rather roughly to turn it off. She put her head in her hands and tried to quieten her mind, which was being so loud that she could feel a headache starting to develop. No matter how many times she thought everything through and made a final decision, she kept finding herself back at square one. She began to pace around the living room and debate the possibilities with herself.

On one hand, she had already made the decision to wait until after Christmas to confront Kenneth. It would be good for her to have time to process the overload of information which had been thrown at her over what was only a short period of time. It was a lot for one person to take in, and she needed to think about what she wanted to say to Kenneth when she saw him next. Anyway, for all she knew, he could have already seen the error of his ways and hung up his spy gadgets for good (Pearl suspected he must have a cabinet full of various contraptions, which she may have been able to find if she'd had longer to snoop around his house), pledging full allegiance to his country and vowing never to betray it again. She sighed, knowing that this was wishful thinking and most likely wouldn't be the case. She didn't know how long the whole operation had been going on for, but if it had been a while, then it was unlikely he would stop of his own accord. Pearl hoped that if she had the chance to talk to him and push him in the right direction, then she might be able to persuade him to quit.

On the other hand, it would be much easier to get the whole thing over and done with as soon as possible. If she was able to resolve the situation sooner rather than later, then she would be free to have a relaxed and enjoyable Christmas with her family, safe in the knowledge that Kenneth was no longer sharing government secrets with an unknown party. Or, she would discover that the whole thing had been a misunderstanding and she had been mistaken about him being a spy. However, this outcome was looking less likely the more Pearl thought about the facts.

One thing she knew for certain was that she was never going to be truly at ease until she spoke to Kenneth and heard his side of the story.

She considered using the telephone and confronting him right there and then, but she knew this was something she needed to do in person.

She sighed and stopped pacing around the room.

There was only one thing for it; she was going to have to arrange a face-to-face meeting with him.

Before she could change her mind, Pearl strode into the hallway and right up to the telephone table. She picked up the handset, then hesitated before beginning to input Kenneth's telephone number. She felt her nerves building as she waited for the wheel to reset itself with a click each time she entered a number. Once she had dialled the number, she listened to it ringing and waited for Kenneth to answer the call.

"Kenneth Johnson speaking."

Pearl took a deep breath. "Hello, Kenny. It's Pearl."

"Oh, Pearl! It's good to hear your voice. How are you, my darling?" Kenneth asked, sounding surprised.

"Fine, thank you. I was just wondering whether you would be free to meet with me tomorrow morning?" Pearl grimaced, realising she might have been too hasty to get to the point.

There was a pause. "Whatever for? Is everything alright?" Kenneth asked tentatively.

Pearl racked her brains trying to think of a plausible reason. She inwardly scolded herself for not thinking of a story before making the phone call. "Oh… I just miss you, is all. I would quite like to see you again before Christmas."

"I've missed you as well, Pearl."

Pearl sighed with relief. Kenneth didn't sound suspicious. "So, would you like to come over to my house tomorrow morning? Say, ten o'clock?"

"Yes, I believe I'm free until the afternoon. It's a date!"

"Splendid! I'll see you tomorrow, then. Goodbye!"

"Oh! Goodbye, Pearl," Kenneth replied, sounding slightly thrown by the sudden end to their conversation.

Pearl put down the handset and took a deep breath. She closed her eyes and reached up to her neck, so she could hold onto the angel wing pendant that hung there.

She wasn't quite sure what to expect from their meeting the next morning, but she hoped Kenneth would be regretful of what he was doing once she confronted him about it.

No matter what happened, she knew she could not allow him to continue with his shady endeavours.

The outcome would either be Kenneth handing himself in, or Pearl doing it for him.

Tomorrow, she was going to put an end to the whole ordeal.

CHAPTER EIGHTEEN

After her spur of the moment decision to arrange a meeting with Kenneth, Pearl began building a strategy for how she should go about the confrontation the next morning. She wished that she had taken some time to think of a plan before picking up the telephone, but she knew that if she hadn't done it straight away, then she would have talked herself out of it and she wouldn't be any further forward.

One of the most prominent challenges was that she had invited Kenneth to her house, the fact that Rose lived there as well appearing to have completely slipped her mind in the moment. She needed to come up with a way to get Rose out of the house in the morning without raising her suspicions or making her at all worried, as she didn't want to involve Rose in the situation at all. It was something that Pearl needed to deal with alone, and she didn't think it was worth dragging anybody else into it, at least for the time being.

After her eventful telephone call, Pearl went straight up to the loft and recorded the latest development in her notebook. She tried to encrypt and write as quickly as she could, while also putting in as much detail as possible. She knew Rose could arrive home at any moment, and she didn't fancy having to come up with an explanation for sitting in the loft while she was alone in the house. Luckily, she had just put the ladder away when the front door opened downstairs.

"I'm home!" Rose shouted in a tinkling melodic tone.

Pearl quickly looked in the mirror, checking her appearance for any signs that she had been clambering around in the loft only moments earlier. She fixed her hair and tucked her blouse back into her skirt where it had started to come loose, then made her way downstairs to greet her sister. "Did you have a nice time?" she asked, smiling brightly.

Rose nodded enthusiastically. "We had a wonderful time! I'm sorry I'm back a bit later than I said I would be. I lost track of time."

Pearl hadn't even noticed the time, to be quite truthful, but she smiled and waved away Rose's apology anyway. "Oh, that's fine, you haven't missed anything exciting. I'll go through to the kitchen and prepare us some lunch."

As she prepared their food, Pearl decided this would be the perfect time to put her plan into action. So, when they had sat down at the table and were beginning to eat, she posed a question to Rose. "I was wondering if you wanted to go with Grandma to buy some new clothes tomorrow morning, Rosie? Only, I had been planning to take you, but I have a few errands I need to run."

Rose looked up from her plate. "Oh, have you? What do you need to do? I don't mind coming along with you."

"Oh, I would love for you to join me, but it's work-related, so I wouldn't be allowed to bring you," Pearl said, knowing that Rose wouldn't ask any more questions if she knew it was related to her work.

"Ah." Rose nodded. "Yes, it will be good to go with Grandma. Although, she'll probably try to persuade me to buy a dress." Rose stuck her tongue out and pulled a face, showing her disgust at that prospect.

Pearl laughed. "Don't worry, I'll give her strict instructions to let you buy whatever clothing you feel most comfortable in. There is no point in forcing you to wear skirts and dresses at home, when you already have to wear them enough at school. You could have a look for some smart trousers, however, that would be nice."

Rose thought about it, then nodded. "Yes, I think that's a grand idea. Do we have enough tokens?" she asked.

"Yes, you should be able to get some dungarees and trousers, and maybe a couple of blouses. I'll give them to Grandma when she picks you up in the morning." It was at this moment that Pearl realised she had missed out a vital part of the plan – she hadn't actually asked their grandmother if she would be able to take Rose to buy new clothes in the morning. She smiled at Rose and carried on eating, deciding to telephone her as soon as she had the chance.

Fortunately for Pearl, it turned out that their grandmother was more than happy to take a trip out with her youngest granddaughter, and she turned up at the house the following morning at precisely 9:30 a.m., exactly as agreed upon.

"Lovely to see you, Grandma," Pearl said, hugging her grandmother tightly.

"You as well, my dear. We'll go back to my house and have a spot of lunch after the clothes shop, I think. Will you be free to join us, Pearl?" their grandmother asked, as she and Rose stood by the front door with their coats on.

"I'll come along as soon as I'm finished with my errands. Hopefully I won't be too long," Pearl replied.

Her grandmother smiled and nodded. "Jolly good, then. We'd best be off!"

"Bye, Pearl. See you later!" Rose said, reaching up to give Pearl a hug.

Pearl held on a little longer than was necessary. "You just make sure you're careful," she said sincerely.

Rose laughed. "We're only going to buy clothes!"

Pearl waved at them from the front door as they made their way down the path, turning around to wave back at her as they went.

"Goodbye!" Pearl called after them.

As she stepped back into the house and closed the door behind her, everything began to properly sink in. She had been so concerned about making sure Rose wasn't in the house, that she had almost forgotten she was going to be confronting Kenneth in half an hour's time. Her heart began to beat furiously in her chest and she felt too hot all of a sudden. She was extremely nervous, as she didn't know how Kenneth was going to respond to her questioning.

Would he be forthcoming, or would he try to deny it?

Pearl began to pace, and before she knew it, there was a loud knock on the front door. She turned and stared at it, her heart stopping for a moment.

She walked towards the door, then took a deep breath and opened it, plastering a smile on her face. As expected, Kenneth was standing on the other side. "Hello, Kenny! Oh, do come in," she said brightly, standing to the side to allow him to enter the house.

He winked at her as he walked in. "Hello, darling," he said, before leaning in to kiss her. Pearl turned her head at the last moment, so he kissed her on the cheek instead, then busied herself with closing the door.

"You have a lovely house," Kenneth said, looking around the hallway. "Very quaint."

"Thank you. Why don't we sit down in the living room?" Pearl said, already starting to walk through. Kenneth quickly took his coat off and hung it over the bannister, before following behind her.

Pearl sat down in her usual armchair, then glanced up at Kenneth who was looking slightly awkward, as if he wasn't quite sure what to do. "Take a seat," she told him, gesturing to an armchair. She realised it had sounded more like an order than an invitation, so she added, "make yourself comfortable."

Kenneth quickly sat down on the armchair and pushed his glasses up his nose where they had slid down. He smiled at Pearl. "How are you? Have you had a nice holiday so far?"

"Yes, thank you. It's been rather nice being back home," Pearl said, trying her best to have a normal conversation with him. She wasn't sure exactly how long was an appropriate length of time to make light conversation with somebody before accusing them of being a spy.

Kenneth smirked. "But it would have been better if I had been here with you, no?"

Pearl smiled, then dropped her eyes to the ground. Deciding it was time to confront him, she looked up and met Kenneth's eyes. "Kenny, I'm sorry for deceiving you, but the real reason I asked you to come here this morning was because I need to talk to you about something important... I know that you have been leaking classified documents from Bletchley Park."

There was a long pause where Kenneth didn't say anything. Pearl could see the cogs turning in his brain, and she had just started to think that he wasn't going to respond, when he let out a long sigh. Pearl couldn't tell if it was due to frustration or sadness. "How long have you known?" he asked, sounding defeated.

"Only a couple of weeks," Pearl replied, wiping her sweaty hands on her skirt.

Kenneth stood up and paced the room, a frown creasing his forehead. "I don't understand. I thought I'd been really careful," he muttered to himself. He whipped around to face Pearl. "How did you find out?"

"Well... where to start. There were a few things that raised my suspicions." Pearl thought through her response carefully. She didn't want to show her entire hand this early on. "The first thing that really put doubt in my mind, was when I was in your office and I saw a top-secret document fall out of your suit jacket."

Kenneth groaned. "So, you did see it? I thought you hadn't realised what it was; I thought I was safe."

"I wasn't sure, but it did make me a bit more wary of what you were doing. I had to do a little bit of investigative work, but it became clear to me that you were passing on government documents to… someone. This is why I wanted to talk to you, because I don't know much more than that." Pearl watched Kenneth as he walked around the room, seemingly deep in thought.

He sighed and looked at Pearl. "Okay, I'll tell you it from the beginning. There's no point denying it now. Just so you know, I've never said any of this out loud before, so I may forget some of the details." He sat back down on the armchair and began to tell his story. "It all started when I was studying at Oxford University. I was young and easily persuaded, I must admit, and I became involved with a group of people who supported the communist regime and ideologies. You have to understand, around this time, fascism was gaining popularity in Europe, and it was starting to become more concerning. We became increasingly worried of what might happen in the future, and Communism seemed the strongest way to fight it. I was approached by a Soviet Intelligence Officer one day–"

"A Soviet Intelligence Officer?" Pearl asked, furrowing her brow in confusion.

"Yes, a spy handler for the Soviet Union. They find people with communist beliefs and recruit them to work as government spies. I was approached by one of their handlers and recruited while I was still at university. Ever since then, as I've worked my way up to where I am now at Bletchley Park, I've been passing information to my handler that could prove valuable to the Soviets. And the rest, as they say, is history." Kenneth shrugged, as if this revelation was not a big deal.

Pearl stared at him. "So, to sum it up, you are a Soviet spy, and you are betraying Great Britain?"

"No, you misunderstand," Kenneth said, shaking his head. "I would never pass information that would damage Great Britain. My only aim is to assist the communist regime."

"But you don't know that for certain. There may be more to the documents than you fully understand. There's a reason they're labelled as 'top secret'!" Pearl replied, with a frustrated sigh. As he had been recruited at Oxford, she wondered how he had managed to evade discovery for so long. "How do you pass over the information to your handler without being seen?" she asked, failing to mention what she already knew from trailing him the previous week.

Kenneth stood up and began to pace again. "Well, I smuggle out the documents and take them home, like you witnessed when you were in my office. Then I take photographs of them before I smuggle them back in. I place the roll of film in a briefcase and go to the agreed location, where I pass the information over to my handler, Frank."

"Frank?" Pearl asked, frowning at the ordinary sounding name; it wasn't a name she would expect for a Soviet spy handler.

"It isn't his real name, just his codename. I only know him as Agent Frank," Kenneth explained.

"Oh, right. How do you communicate with Frank?" Pearl asked, folding her arms over her chest and leaning back in her chair. She wanted to find out as much information as possible, both to satisfy her own curiosity and so she could write it all down in her notebook later on.

"Mostly through encrypted messages. When we meet, it's always in public and we never speak to each other. He switches our briefcases and there's always an encrypted message in the one I take home, telling me when the next meeting will be. Occasionally, I'll get a telephone call at home, but he only makes contact using that method if there's a last-minute change of plans, since it isn't as secure."

Pearl stared at Kenneth as he spoke. He was talking so casually about the whole thing, as if they were only having a light conversation about what they'd eaten for dinner the night before. "Kenny… you know what you're doing is wrong? It is against the law. You can be sent to prison for espionage," Pearl said slowly, hoping that this might help the seriousness of the situation sink in for him.

Kenneth nodded. "Well, yes, of course. I know that is what the law states, but I don't have to agree with it. I'm just following my beliefs. And I can't be prosecuted unless I'm found out."

Pearl shook her head disbelievingly. "But Kenny, your actions are helping another country instead of your own. It's *treason*," she said, emphatically. "You need to confess what you've done before it's taken out of your hands and it's too late. You can't carry on like this."

"Pearl, I think you're overreacting a bit here. I mean, I could understand if I was a spy for the Nazis, but the Soviets are on our side," Kenneth said, his voice remaining calm and controlled.

Pearl frowned at Kenneth. "They might be on our side at the moment, but you never know what the future holds. Your loyalty should lie with Great Britain. No matter how you dress it up, it is still an act of treason!" She stood up and walked over to the fireplace, feeling frustrated by Kenneth's inability to see what was wrong with his actions. She stared at the flames as they danced in the hearth and thought over everything he had told her so far. She didn't understand how he could think his behaviour was okay. She turned to look at him. "Can't you just… hand in your resignation, or whatever the spy equivalent is?" she asked, desperate to find an easy solution to the problem.

Kenneth chuckled darkly. "I can't just stop, Pearl. That isn't how this sort of thing works. I made a commitment. I couldn't leave even if I wanted to."

Pearl closed her eyes for a moment, then looked at Kenneth sadly. "Well, if you refuse to give it up, and you won't hand yourself in, then I'm going to have to report you myself. It isn't what I want to do, Kenny, but it's the only option. I can't just stand by and watch as you betray our country."

Pearl immediately saw Kenneth put his guard up, his expression becoming emotionless and unreadable. "I mean no disrespect by this, but nobody would believe you. It would be your word against mine, and they would be much more inclined to believe my version of the story."

Pearl was taken aback by his sudden change of mood. "It isn't just my word, I have evidence to prove it!" she said, then immediately regretted it. She hadn't been planning to tell Kenneth about the evidence if she could help it. However, she knew there was no way he would be able to find it and destroy it, as she had hidden it well.

"Evidence?" Kenneth said sharply, looking surprised. He obviously hadn't considered the fact Pearl might have physical proof of his guilt. He seemed to change tactic again, a charming smile crossing over his face and his stance becoming more relaxed. "Listen, Pearl, there's no need to take such drastic action. I can see why you would be upset about this, but it's nothing for you to worry your little head over," he said. His voice was silky smooth, as if he thought he was going to be able to charm his way out of the situation.

Pearl couldn't believe the nerve of him. "Excuse me?" she said, incredulously.

Kenneth continued, his tone becoming increasingly patronising. "Some people just don't have the… *capacity*, to understand such complex situations. It isn't your fault. Hopefully, one day you'll come to understand." He smiled and walked towards Pearl, snaking his arms around her waist. "In a way, I'm pleased you found out, because now I can teach you everything that makes Communism great. In fact, why don't you join me? I'm sure I would be able to put in a good word for you."

Pearl stood frozen on the spot for a moment, trying to compute what Kenneth was saying to her. She blinked and came to her senses, then used all her strength to push him away from her. He stumbled backwards, and Pearl saw confusion flash across his face for a moment, before he cleared his throat and composed himself, his face turning neutral again.

There was a long moment of silence as Pearl stared at Kenneth, seeing him in a completely different light.

As she looked at him, all she saw now was a man with questionable morals and a flawed belief system, who constantly had to put on a calm and composed front to try and cover the desperation that was clearly visible in his eyes.

Pearl thought the desperation must have always been there, but the crack she had made in his façade had only made it more obvious.

Finally, Pearl dropped her eyes to the ground and sighed. "You would do well to hand yourself in; it would be much better for you," she said. She still wanted to give Kenneth one last chance to do the right thing.

"It isn't as simple as that, my darling. Like I say, you don't understand," Kenneth said, speaking in a soothing voice.

"Don't call me that!" Pearl narrowed her eyes at him, the sliver of her last hope diminished into nothingness. "If you refuse to hand yourself in, then I'm afraid I'll have to telephone the police myself!" she said furiously, spinning around and starting to walk briskly towards the hallway.

Kenneth lunged forwards and grabbed Pearl's arm. She staggered for a moment, almost losing her footing with the sudden force of being pulled back.

"Please, Pearl, I'm begging you," Kenneth pleaded, all calmness gone from his voice. Pearl could sense his eyes trying to find hers, but she couldn't bring herself to look at him.

"I'm sorry, Kenneth, but you leave me no choice," Pearl replied coldly, yanking her arm out of his grasp and striding towards the telephone in the hallway.

"No!" she heard Kenneth call desperately from behind, but she paid him no attention. She had already given him plenty of chances to redeem himself, and he hadn't taken any of them.

Suddenly, she felt a heavy impact on the back of her head.

There was a searing pain and she felt herself falling towards the telephone table.

There was another impact, this time on her forehead.

Then, everything went black.

CHAPTER NINETEEN

Pearl opened her eyes drowsily, but immediately closed them again as she was blinded by a bright light. She covered her eyes with a hand, then opened them again cautiously. Squinting through her fingers, she realised she was looking at the light hanging from the ceiling in the hallway.

Feeling groggy, Pearl sat up and tried to remember how she had ended up lying on the floor. The last thing she remembered was arguing with Kenneth and telling him she was going to have to telephone the police.

She glanced up and realised that Kenneth was standing in front of her, looking extremely pale and holding what looked like a metal pole. When she looked more closely, she realised it was a fire poker he must have taken from the fireplace, and it appeared to be covered in blood.

"What happened? Where did that blood come from?" she asked Kenneth, feeling extremely confused.

However, Kenneth appeared to be looking straight through her at the floor, with an expression of great shock. "Oh god, what have I done?" he said, looking at the fire poker in his hand and dropping it on the floor in repulsion.

"What do you mean? What did you do?" Pearl asked, her head foggy as she tried to piece together what had happened.

Kenneth didn't reply. He didn't even seem to hear what she was saying. He put his head in his hands and began to sob loudly, his whole body shaking.

Pearl stood up and walked towards him to try and comfort him. Despite everything, she still cared about Kenneth and hated seeing him so distressed, which was most unusual for him. However, when she tried to put her arms around him they passed straight through his body, as if she were trying to grasp at thin air.

Pearl stepped back in shock, noticing Kenneth shiver as she did so. He took his hands away from his face and started to walk straight towards Pearl, who jumped out of the way just in time.

"Kenneth! Why aren't you answering my questions?" Pearl asked, starting to get frustrated.

She followed him with her eyes, a heavy feeling of dread pressing on her chest.

As she turned around to face the direction she had come from, she gasped at the scene she saw before her.

A body was lying on the floor in the space she had just vacated.

Her own lifeless body.

She watched in complete shock as Kenneth knelt down next to her body and gently brushed her hair out of her eyes.

Unable to look any longer, Pearl closed her eyes and tried to concentrate on what she could remember.

She had confronted Kenneth and tried to give him a chance to hand himself in, but he refused.

She decided she would have to take matters into her own hands and started to make her way into the hallway.

A heavy impact.

A searing pain.

Another impact.

Blackness.

Her eyes snapped open and she looked down at Kenneth, who was now holding her body while he cried.

Looking around at the bloody scene she saw before her, it started to dawn on her what must have happened.

As Pearl was walking over to the telephone, Kenneth must have grabbed a fire poker out of desperation and hit her with it, to stop her from telephoning the police. Then she must have fallen forward and hit her head on the telephone table, knocking her out.

She didn't want to believe it, but looking at the facts presented to her, there was no other explanation.

She reached her hand behind her head to feel around and see if there was any damage, but she couldn't feel anything, and when she looked at her hand there was no blood.

Then, she remembered the other her lying on the floor, and felt very silly for forgetting that vital piece of information. That must be why she couldn't feel any injury on her own head.

Not wanting to believe the worst had happened, her mind whirred trying to think of scenarios that could explain what was happening.

Maybe she was dreaming? That seemed plausible. Yes, maybe this was all a dream and she would wake up at any moment, safely tucked up in her bed.

Although, she had been sure that the last memory she had was of her arguing with Kenneth…

Perhaps she was having an out of body experience? She had heard of that happening before, although she had always thought it was a work of fiction.

Maybe this was something that happened when you had a close shave with death, and all she needed to do was get back into her body, so she could wake up again, whole.

Deciding this seemed the best solution, Pearl smoothed down her skirt and calmly walked over to where her body lay. She knelt down and tried to get into the exact same position on the floor. It was very difficult as Kenneth was holding and swaying her.

"I'm so sorry, Pearl. I didn't mean to do it. I only wanted to stop you reaching the telephone. I just wanted you to understand!" he whispered to her lifeless form.

"Put me down, you great buffoon! It's your fault this is happening in the first place and you aren't even allowing me to fix the situation!" Pearl said crossly, even though she knew Kenneth couldn't hear her.

However, as she passed through the place where Kenneth's hands were, he shivered and put her down on the floor, bringing his hands up and rubbing them together, as if he were trying to warm them up.

"Thank you!" Pearl huffed. She managed to place herself back into her body, then lay there for a few seconds.

Nothing seemed to happen.

Pearl started to grow impatient, not knowing how long this sort of thing would take. She lay there for a few minutes, beginning to feel as if the whole thing was ridiculous, but not wanting to accept the alternative. She waited stubbornly, hoping that at any moment she would be reconnected to her solid body.

As she lay there, she watched Kenneth, who had now started to pace around the hallway. He seemed to be growing more and more panicked and was muttering to himself anxiously.

Finally, he seemed to have reached an unappealing conclusion, and he turned to look at Pearl sadly.

"I'm so sorry, my darling, but I can't let anyone find out what I've done," he said, before his expression hardened and he purposefully walked over to her body.

Avoiding looking directly at her, he began to drag Pearl's body towards the stairs.

"What are you doing?" Pearl exclaimed, jumping up off the floor and watching in horror as Kenneth dragged her body across the hallway. She ran over and tried to stop him, to tackle her body away from him, but her hands went straight through his body, making him shiver again.

Unable to do anything to stop him, Pearl was forced to watch as he began to heave her body up the stairs. It felt so surreal for Pearl to watch herself being dragged around from an outside point of view.

When he had hauled her body up a few steps, Kenneth seemed to struggle to pull her any further and had to stop. Pearl's body appeared to be caught on something on the stairs, and he had to tug rather roughly to pry her free. As he did so, Pearl caught a glint of gold in the light as something fell from around her neck. She gasped as she realised it was her angel wing pendant.

"No!" Pearl called out as the necklace fell between the wooden spindles of the bannister and onto the floor. She ran over to the side of the stairs and realised the dainty necklace had begun to slip between the floorboards. She tried to grasp at it, but she couldn't do anything to prevent it from falling through the crack.

Pearl felt around her own neck, and realised she was still wearing the necklace. She wondered briefly how she could still have the necklace when her body didn't, but immediately pushed these thoughts to the back of her mind.

Trying to forget about her lost necklace, Pearl turned her attention back to Kenneth, who had now reached the top of the stairs with her body.

He began to lift her body up, so she was hanging limply in his arms with her feet brushing the floor.

"Forgive me, Pearl," he said, closing his eyes.

Realising what he was about to do, Pearl swiftly turned around to face the other direction. She felt a wave of nausea come over her as she heard the unmistakable noise of her body falling down the stairs and landing with a thud at the bottom.

As she listened, she braced herself to feel the pain, but it didn't come.

She began to realise that she must no longer have a connection with her body.

As much as she didn't want to accept it, there was no other conclusion she could come to.

She must be dead.

But if that was the case, why was she still here?

She paused to prepare herself for what she was about to see, then turned around. In her peripheral vision she could see her body lying in a heap at the bottom of the stairs, but she tried to avoid looking at it directly.

She watched in disdain as Kenneth came down the stairs and carefully stepped over her dead body. He looked around at the hallway, and Pearl saw the realisation come over his face as he looked at the scene properly and saw the blood on the floor where he had dragged her body.

Kenneth ran past Pearl and into the kitchen, returning soon after with a wet towel. He began to clean the blood off the floor, wherever it looked out of place. Once he had finished cleaning the floor, he picked up the fire poker and removed all the blood from it, before putting it back in its place next to the fireplace.

Pearl watched as he walked around the living room, seeming to ponder over what he should do next. He spotted Pearl's handbag next to an armchair. He picked it up, then made his way back into the hallway and up the stairs.

Pearl moved next to the stairs and watched numbly as he placed her handbag at the top, lying on its side as if she had tripped over it and fallen down the stairs. Even in his panicked state, he seemed to have thought of everything.

Pearl worried that the police would immediately rule her death an accident and wouldn't bother looking any further into it. She watched nervously, hoping that he would miss something which could be traced back to him.

Kenneth ran down the stairs and jumped over Pearl's body. He picked up the bloody towel from the floor and hesitated as he decided what to do with it, then opted to shove it down his shirt.

He threw his coat on and took one last look around the hallway, then looked out of the window cautiously before swiftly making his way out of the front door.

"Kenneth! You won't get away with this!" Pearl called out desperately, running after him. But when she reached the front door, she hit a solid wall and was thrown back. She ran back towards it and began hitting the door with her fists, but it was as if there was an invisible barrier stopping her.

She was unable to leave the house.

Pearl stood in the silence and took a deep breath, trying to take in the events of the past hour or so.

She looked around the hallway and noticed a glistening patch on the edge of the telephone table. On closer inspection, she realised there was a patch of blood from where she had hit her head as she fell, which Kenneth must have missed in his panic. She breathed a sigh of relief, hoping that this one mistake would be his downfall. With any luck, the police would notice it and begin a full enquiry into her death. However, she couldn't rely on that alone, as there were so many more layers to everything that had happened.

She thought of her friends, Ruth and Betty, and wished she had confided in them about her relationship with Kenneth. As it was, the only connection that could be established between her and Kenneth was the fact they worked in the same building, which didn't give him a very strong motive for murder.

She thought of her notebook, neatly hidden away in the loft, and berated herself for not thinking to give any clues about the hiding place to Rose as a precautionary measure.

Although, she had given her sister clues for other pieces of the puzzle. She hoped Rose would be able to fit everything together and fill in the blanks, or if she spoke to the police, they would be able to figure it out.

Pearl was starting to wish she hadn't been quite so secretive about everything in her life. She realised now that her recklessness had ended up having the opposite effect to what she had intended. Instead of *protecting* Rose from further harm, she had actually *caused* more harm, as her actions meant their grandparents were the only family Rose had left in the world. If she had confided in just one other person, it might not have ended this way.

Pearl held her necklace and closed her eyes as she thought of her sister.

No matter how far apart we are, as long as we have our angel wings we will always be connected.

She thought the words as strongly as she could, hoping that Rose could feel the love she was sending her. She was thankful that Rose was currently with their grandparents, blissfully unaware of what she would find when she returned home.

Pearl found herself hoping that moment would never come, as she couldn't bear to witness it.

She thought of her necklace, sitting beneath the floorboards, and resolved to make sure it was retrieved and given to Rose. It held too much sentimental value for it to sit under the floor gathering dust for the rest of time.

Now there was more time to think, she began to question why she was still there, and wondered if her spirit would ever move on.

Perhaps it was because she had too much unfinished business.

Maybe she would be forced to stay there, a prisoner in her own house, until somebody found her notebook and learned the information she had discovered.

Kenneth couldn't get away with everything he had done, she wouldn't let him.

No matter how long it took her, she was going to bring him to justice.

PART THREE

CHAPTER TWENTY

Mat and Charlie were kneeling in the loft of the Carter house, staring at the coded notebook in Charlie's hands with expressions of shock on their faces. They had never expected they would ever find something like this in any of their investigations, especially not in such strange circumstances.

Charlie twisted around to look at Mat. "What do we do? We've never been in this situation before. Do we need to inform the authorities or something?" he asked, running a hand through his hair.

Mat furrowed his brow, deep in thought. After a few seconds, he looked up at Charlie. "I reckon we should go back to bed and try to get a few more hours of sleep. Maybe sleep a bit later than we'd planned if you feel up to it. Then we can look at it with fresh eyes in the morning and assess the situation properly. What do you think?"

Charlie nodded. "Yeah, I think that's a good plan. I feel a little more comfortable here now, 'cause I think Pearl was just trying to get us to find her notebook. We just need to figure out what it means, and how it connects to her death," Charlie said, standing up and starting to pace around the loft.

"Is that all? Should be a piece of cake," Mat joked. He stood up and turned the camera around to face him. "We thought we'd reached the end of this investigation, but it turns out there's a lot more to this mystery than we first thought."

"And I think there's even more still to discover," Charlie added.

Mat nodded solemnly. "Come on, we'd better go back downstairs."

Charlie made to replace the floorboard over the hole in the floor, but as he did so, the beam of Mat's torch passed over something hidden within, lighting it up for a moment. "Wait! There's something else in here."

Mat quickly stood up from where he had been collecting the fairy lights on the floor and walked over with the camera to film Charlie.

Charlie reached his hand between the floorboards for the second time that evening and felt around for the mysterious object. When he had grasped it, he pulled it out and held it up to the torchlight. Realising it was something that had been wrapped up in an old-fashioned handkerchief, he carefully removed the cloth and let the object roll into his other hand.

"What is it?" Mat asked, moving closer.

Charlie looked up at him excitedly. "I think it's an old roll of film."

"Oh my god. I wonder what's on there?" Mat said, his eyes widening.

"I don't know, but I hope it hasn't been damaged. If it was put here at the same time as the notebook, then it's probably been sitting here for seventy-six years."

"That's if we're right about the notebook belonging to Pearl," Mat reminded Charlie.

"True. But it has to though, surely? Why else would she have led us here?"

Mat shrugged and raised his eyebrows at the camera.

"We'd better go back down. I don't think there's anything else hidden in there," Charlie said, passing the roll of film over to Mat and covering up the hiding place with the floorboard.

They collected their things together and silently made their way back down the ladder.

Once they were back in their sleeping bags Mat fell asleep almost instantly. It took Charlie a little bit longer, but he was soon asleep, his head filled with muddled dreams of secret notebooks and encrypted messages, with a distant tune playing in the background which he couldn't quite make out. A red-headed woman was desperately calling out to him, trying to talk to him through the chaos, but to no avail.

* * *

The next morning, Charlie woke up before Mat with the sunlight streaming through a gap in the curtains and straight into his eyes. He blinked rapidly at his unfamiliar surroundings, confused about where he was for a moment. But as he reached for his glasses, he spotted Pearl's notebook on the floor and the events of the night before began to flood back to him.

He let out a deep sigh and picked up the notebook, flicking through the pages of code written in neat capitals. "What was so secret that you had to go to all this effort to hide it?" he whispered.

His question was met with silence, only disturbed by the roaring of the wind outside.

He sighed again and flicked through the notebook one last time, ready to discard it to the side until Mat had woken up. But as he reached the back of the notebook, Charlie noticed a small pocket on the inside of the back cover. He frowned and opened it to see if there was anything in there. His eyes widened as he realised it wasn't empty. He retrieved the item from the pocket and found that it was a folded-up piece of paper.

Feeling his excitement building, Charlie turned to Mat and shook him gently. "Mat! Wake up! I've found something in the notebook!"

Mat stirred and mumbled, "What?"

"I was looking through the notebook and I found something hidden in a little pocket at the back!"

"What is it?" Mat asked, his speech muffled as he spoke into his pillow, reluctant to get up.

Charlie rolled his eyes. "Get up and I'll show you!"

"Okay, okay, I'm up," Mat said, yawning and slowly moving into a sitting position. He squinted at the paper in Charlie's hands, not wanting to put his glasses on so he could see properly. Realising it was no use, he gave in and found his glasses. "Ooh, do you know what it is?"

Charlie shook his head. "No, I thought we'd better look at it together. And we'd better film it too."

Mat nodded and reached for the camera.

"Right. I'll have to be delicate. It's a very old piece of paper by the looks of it," Charlie said. He unfolded the paper carefully and inspected what was written on it. The writing was an old-fashioned scrawl, written in white with an uneven grey background.

Friday, 3 p.m.

"Friday, three p.m.," Mat read out, filming the paper and frowning at Charlie. "I wonder what that means?"

"Beats me." Charlie shrugged. "What's been used to write this? It reminds me of when we used to go on nature walks in first school, and we'd trace over things."

"Like when we used to put paper on tree bark, or whatever, then colour over it with crayons to get the texture of the tree?"

"Yeah, but with pencil." Charlie looked more closely and frowned. "Do you think she's scribbled over impressions in the paper to find out a secret message, or something?"

"Let me have a look." Mat passed the camera to Charlie, swapping it for the note so he could take a closer look. He lifted his glasses and squinted at both sides of the paper. "I think you could be right, y'know. The white writing looks like it could be made from indentations. Like, what would be left on the piece of paper below the one that'd been written on."

"I've seen them do stuff like that in films, but I didn't think they did it in real life!" Charlie said, looking at the paper in awe.

"She was like a proper little Nancy Drew, wasn't she?" Mat said, taking the camera back from Charlie and setting it down in front of them on its tripod. "I wonder where she got this note from?"

"I dunno, but it must be important for her to go to all this effort to keep it secret."

They looked at the piece of paper for a bit longer, then put it aside to come back to later. They needed to figure out what was in the notebook before they could find out the significance of the piece of paper.

Once they were up and ready for the day, they regrouped and decided what their next steps should be.

Mat set up the camera on the kitchen table and they both sat down in front of it to lay out their plan.

"So, let's discuss what we've found so far," Mat started, raising his left hand so he could count on his fingers as he recounted the list, "a notebook that's written in code, so we can't read it; a note saying, 'Friday, three p.m.,' acquired by sleuthing methods most commonly used by Nancy Drew and the like; and an old roll of film with unknown contents."

"We have quite a bit, we just don't understand any of it." Charlie grimaced. "But luckily, we know two people that may be able to help us with this. My older brother, Joey Parker, is a Detective Constable in the police, so I was thinking we could call him and ask his opinion on the whole situation. I don't really know where we stand with all this, legally, but I'm hoping he'll have more of an idea. And as an added bonus, his boyfriend, Lucas Thompson, is a photographer, so I'm hoping he might have an idea about what we can do with this." Charlie held up the old roll of film to the camera.

"I'm just hoping it isn't knackered. I'm not sure if film has an expiration date," Mat said, taking the film from Charlie and inspecting it.

"Yeah, me too. Let's hope not." Charlie crossed his fingers, then got his phone out and texted Joey to ask if he was free to video call, and if he wouldn't mind acting as a consultant for their investigation. "Do we have the screen-recording equipment with us?" he asked Mat.

"Yeah, I definitely packed it. Give me a second. We might have to use the laptop rather than the phone."

Just as Mat had finished setting up the equipment on the table, Joey replied to say he was free.

"Perfect timing!" Charlie said, starting to video call him.

Two seconds later, a portrait-oriented video of Joey's face popped up on the laptop screen.

"Charlie! Matty!" he exclaimed, waving at them both.

Mat and Charlie returned the greeting and waved back at him through the screen.

"Would you be able to turn your phone landscape, please, Joey? It just looks better for the video," Mat asked, checking the equipment to make sure it was recording the image and sound properly. The last thing they needed was to find that the footage was unusable when Mat went to edit the video later.

"No problem," Joey said, turning his phone around and filling the laptop screen with a landscape-oriented video. "Is that better?"

"Perfect!" Mat replied, giving him a thumbs-up.

"So, how's the investigation going?"

"It's going well, actually. We've had a bit of a breakthrough," Mat said, nodding his head.

"We found a secret hiding place in the loft, and there was a notebook stashed away in there!" Charlie said, lifting the notebook up so Joey could see it. "We even found a piece of paper in the back with 'Friday, three p.m.' written on it."

"Ooh, that's exciting! That must've been there the whole time we lived in that house, and we had no idea!"

"I know! Mad, isn't it? The problem is, the notebook's been written in some sort of code, so we can't read it."

"Charlie, didn't you used to do that sort of thing when you were at uni? Can't you decode it or something?"

"Yeah, I did a cryptography module and I loved it. But I don't know what type of code was used, and I don't know the key," Charlie said, flicking through the notebook sadly. "I can have a go, but I can't promise I'll be able to decipher it."

"We also weren't sure what the law is for this type of thing, that's why we wanted to talk to you about it. Do we need to hand it into the police?" Mat asked.

Mat and Charlie both looked at Joey's image on the screen helplessly, hoping he would be able to give them some advice.

Joey's brow creased as he thought over the situation. "I'm not sure on the proper procedure for this exact scenario, so don't quote me on this. But, I would say that at the moment the notebook still belongs to the owner of the house. Is it just the notebook?"

"No, we found an old roll of film in there as well," Charlie said, holding up the film for Joey to see.

"Okay, well I think both items will belong to the owner, unless you find something that proves they're evidence in the woman's death."

Mat turned to Charlie. "Okay, so we can look over the notebook today and you can try to decipher it, but if we can't do anything with it then we'll have to give it to Mrs Harris."

"Is that legal, Joey? We're not gonna be sent to prison?" Charlie asked.

Joey laughed. "No, you won't be sent to prison."

"Okay," Charlie said, relieved. "Thanks, Joey. We owe you one!"

"Thanks, mate," Mat added.

"No problem. Keep me updated on any developments."

Charlie nodded. "We will."

"We wanted to talk to Lucas as well. Is he there?" Mat asked.

"Hey, I heard my name!" Lucas called distantly, in his distinctive American accent. There was the sound of footsteps and then his head popped into frame and he took the phone from Joey. "What's up?"

"Woah, Lucas! Since when do you have blue hair?" Charlie asked, momentarily distracted by the bright turquoise blue that had replaced what used to be brown hair.

"Since yesterday. Your sister wanted to practise colouring with bright hair dye, so I volunteered," Lucas replied, ruffling his hair to show off the bright colour in the light.

Charlie nodded in understanding. Billie had finished high school earlier that year and was now working as an apprentice hairdresser in their mother's hair salon. She had been helping out at the salon for years and had always shown an interest in the profession, so it hadn't been a shock when she had decided to follow in their mother's footsteps. However, she had recently decided that she wanted to try out new hairstyling techniques, and she kept trying to use the family as guinea pigs. Mat and Charlie had managed to avoid anything drastic so far, but she had obviously managed to convince Lucas to be her first victim.

"What do you think?" Lucas asked.

"I love it! You really suit it," Mat said, smiling widely at the laptop screen.

"It looks so cool! Billie did a good job of it as well," Charlie agreed, nodding enthusiastically.

They heard Joey's voice come from just out of frame. "It looks great, doesn't it? It somehow makes his eyes look greener."

Lucas waved them away. "Oh, stop it, guys. You're making me blush," he said, although they all knew fine well he was secretly loving the compliments. "Anyway, what did you wanna talk to me about?"

"Oh yeah, I almost forgot the reason we called," Charlie said. He held up the roll of film for Lucas to look at. "We were investigating the house, and we came across this old roll of film in the loft. We think it must've been hidden away in there for around seventy-six years, so we're a little bit concerned that it might be no good now, since it's been sitting there for so long."

"We thought, since you're a photographer, you might have more of an idea," Mat added.

"Wow, that's awesome! A seventy-six-year-old roll of film? I wish I could look at it in person," Lucas said excitedly, squinting at the film as Charlie held it up to the camera. "But to answer your question, it's hard to say for sure when I'm not looking straight at it. Sometimes film can be damaged if it's been exposed to extreme temperatures or moisture. If that's the case, then the photos might not develop properly. Was it protected, or was it just lying there?"

"It was wrapped up in a handkerchief under the floorboards," Mat said, his hope diminishing rapidly.

"Okay, okay…" Lucas said, trying to hide a grimace. "What are the conditions like up there?"

"Freezing cold," Charlie replied.

Lucas raised his eyebrows as he considered this. "I mean, cold is better for film than heat, at least, so it might've survived. I think it's probably best for you to take it to a specialist, so they can take a look and give their opinion. There's still a few places that develop that sort of film. I'm pretty sure I remember visiting one in Cambridge back when I was travelling the UK. I'll do a quick search online for the website and send you the details ASAP."

"Thanks, Lucas. That would help a lot," Charlie said, feeling slightly more optimistic after their chat.

"No sweat, guys. I hope it all works out for you!" Lucas said, crossing his fingers.

They said their goodbyes and ended the video call, then turned to look at each other.

Mat let out a sigh of relief. "Thank god we have Joey and Lucas. We wouldn't have a clue what to do next without them. We'd be screwed."

Charlie laughed. "Definitely. We'd be wandering into the local police station by now trying to hand in the notebook, without even knowing whether it's important or not."

Mat hesitated. "Do you think you'll be able to decipher it?"

Charlie puffed out his cheeks and blew the air out. "I'll try, but I can't promise anything. Hopefully she used one of the ciphers I learnt about at uni. I might have to do some research to refresh my memory, but I'd have more chance of being able to decipher it then. I really think this notebook's gonna be the key to solving the mystery of what really happened to Pearl."

Mat nodded. "Yeah, me too. I can feel it in my bones."

They both stared at the notebook on the table in front of them, as if it was going to suddenly spring to life and tell them everything. But it lay there motionless, all of Pearl's secrets still hidden within its pages.

Charlie sighed. "Why did you have to go and make it so difficult for us, Pearl?"

CHAPTER TWENTY-ONE

As soon as Lucas sent over the details, Charlie contacted the specialist photography shop in Cambridge to find out whether it was worth driving all the way there, or if it would just be a waste of their time. The upshot of the phone call was that they couldn't know for sure whether there was any damage until they inspected the film in person. If there was no damage, then the pictures could be developed within a couple of hours.

"What are we gonna do in Cambridge while we wait?" Mat asked when Charlie told him the news. They were still sitting at the kitchen table, as Mat found this was the best place to set up the camera.

"I dunno, we could work on figuring out the notebook?" Charlie suggested.

"It's gonna eat up a lot of our day. It's an hour and a half drive each way. We'll have to make the trip worth our while," Mat said, having gone straight to Google maps to find out the distance.

Charlie twisted his face. "Really? I thought we were way closer than that," he said, running a hand through his hair as he thought it over. "Wait a minute! You know who lives in Cambridge? Someone who it would *definitely* be worth our while visiting?"

Mat frowned, before realisation slowly dawned on his face. "Rose Carter."

Charlie nodded eagerly. "Yep. She lives in Cambridge with her husband."

"But how would we contact her? And would she even want to meet with us?"

"I'm not sure. We could ask Mrs Harris? We need to phone her anyway to see if there's any chance of her letting us stay here an extra night."

Mat nodded. "Yeah, that's a good idea."

"I'll phone her now. There's no time like the present." Charlie got his phone out of his pocket and dialled the number, putting the phone on loud speaker so Mat could listen in.

After a few rings, Mrs Harris picked up. "Hello, Bletchley Ghost Tours. This is Allison Harris speaking. How can I help?"

"Hi, Mrs Harris. It's Charlie Parker."

"Oh, hello, love. I hope you and your friend enjoyed your night at the Carter house?"

Mat mimed drinking tea at Charlie.

Charlie nodded to show he had understood. "Yes, thank you. We wanted to thank you for the tea and biscuits you left for us. It was very thoughtful of you. Mat enjoyed them, especially."

"You're very welcome. It's the least I could do for two lovely young men such as yourselves. Did you find anything interesting in your investigation?"

Charlie hesitated. "You could say that, yes. Actually, we were wondering if you wouldn't mind us staying here another night? We feel like we didn't get everything we wanted; there's still more for us to investigate."

"Yes, of course! I have some ghost tours going in the afternoon until late evening, but it'll be free from around nine p.m., if you wanted to come back later?"

"That sounds perfect! We were planning on going out during the day, anyway. This might be a weird question, but do you have any contact details for Rose Carter?"

"Yes, I have a phone number for her granddaughter. But beware, she might not want to meet with you. She isn't very keen on being hassled by the media with questions about her sister."

"That's okay. It's worth a try, anyway."

"I'll send you a text message with her details."

"Thank you, Mrs Harris. That would be great!"

They said goodbye and Charlie ended the call. It wasn't long before he received a message with Rose's contact information.

"What does it say?" Mat asked impatiently, as Charlie read through the text in his head.

"She's just sent the phone number of Rose's granddaughter, Joanne Williams. I think we should think about this one before I phone her. We only have one chance to persuade her to arrange a meeting with Rose. We don't wanna mess it up."

"Yeah, that makes sense. We don't want them to think we're nosey reporters or anything. We need to make it clear that we actually just wanna help them."

Charlie nodded. "Okay, so what do we know about Rose?"

Mat shrugged. "I don't know anything, apart from the fact she's Pearl's younger sister."

"I found out a bit about her in my research. She kept her surname when she got married – which was quite unusual for the time – so she's known as Rose Carter-Lawson now. She was a successful artist, although she isn't as active on that front anymore."

"Really? I wonder if I've ever seen any of her work," Mat said, his interest piqued.

"You never know, it could've been in your art syllabus at school. I don't really know much else, she's quite a private person, I think. Should I just call Joanne now?"

"You may as well, we'll have to do it at some point."

Charlie dialled the number and put his phone on loud speaker again. They waited apprehensively, willing her to answer.

Eventually, a woman's voice came through from the other end of the phone. "Hello?"

"Hi, is this Joanne Williams?"

"With whom am I speaking?" she asked, her voice guarded.

"Oh sorry, I should've started with that. My name is Charlie Parker and I'm here with my friend Mateo Jones."

"Hi," Mat said in the background.

"We're from the YouTube channel, *The Paranormal Detectives*, and we were wondering–"

The woman cut Charlie off with a loud gasp. "You're kidding! Is this some sort of prank?"

Charlie blinked, taken aback by the woman's response. He exchanged a confused look with Mat. "No… I'm telling the truth," he said, hesitantly.

"Oh, my goodness! Carter will be so excited when I tell him! Sorry, yes, I'm Joanne Williams. My son, Carter, is a massive fan of your YouTube channel. He's fourteen years old, so I watched some videos with him to make sure it was suitable viewing, and I thought they were brilliant! We watch every video together as a family now."

Mat and Charlie grinned at each other. Even though they knew there were over a hundred thousand people who watched their videos, it was always very strange to have an actual conversation with one of those people. It wasn't something they had experienced very often, and they certainly weren't used to it.

"Thank you! That really means a lot," Charlie said, beginning to feel a bit shy, which was very unlike him.

Mat beamed widely but stayed quiet.

Joanne continued excitedly. "Are you phoning to ask about Great Aunt Pearl? Carter has always hoped you would come and investigate the case. I told him it was very unlikely, but I secretly hoped you would, too. I think if anybody was going to be able to prove that her death wasn't an accident, it would be you two."

"Yes, that's why we called," Charlie said. "We've been investigating your great aunt Pearl's house, and we found some new evidence that we think might be useful for solving the case. We were wondering if there's any chance we'd be able to speak to your grandmother. We think she might be able to help us work out what it means. Do you think that would be possible?"

Joanne hesitated. "Grandma doesn't normally do interviews… but, she might make an exception if I explain the situation to her."

"That would be amazing," Charlie said, breathing a sigh of relief.

"I can't make any promises though. When do you want to meet with her?"

Charlie exchanged a look with Mat, who mouthed, "This afternoon?"

Charlie nodded. "This afternoon would be best, if that's possible?"

"I'll see what I can do. Is there any chance I could bring my son over to meet you? Just to have a picture with you and get something signed, we won't take up too much of your time."

"Of course! We'd be honoured," Charlie said.

"Oh, thank you! Carter will be over the moon! I'll let you know if I can arrange a meeting as soon as I've spoken to my grandma."

"Thank you so much, Joanne. We can't wait to meet you. Bye!" Charlie ended the call and turned to Mat with a gleeful expression. "That couldn't have gone any better!"

Mat nodded and grinned back. "I know! What are the odds of Rose's granddaughter having heard of us? Hopefully she can convince Rose to meet with us."

"Fingers crossed."

Mat and Charlie lugged their equipment back to the car as they waited for a message from Joanne. Either way, they were going to have to leave the house for the afternoon, so it was better for them to be prepared to leave as soon as possible.

Just as they were sorting the last of their things into the car, Charlie received a text from Joanne. "She's replied!" he called to Mat.

They gathered in the living room, Mat holding the camera, so they could find out what she had said.

Charlie read the text aloud. " 'Mat and Charlie, I have spoken to my grandmother about meeting with you. She was averse to the idea to begin with, but once I explained to her who you are, and why you needed to speak with her, she began to come around. In the end, she agreed to meet with you at two p.m. this afternoon. Carter and I will come along too. He is very excited to meet you both,' and then she's sent Rose's address."

Mat cheered. "So, the meetings on!"

"Yep. We might have to leave now if we still wanna drop off the film at the photography place first. We can think about what we wanna ask her when we're in the car. I might do some research on ciphers as well if I have time, see if I can jog my memory."

Mat nodded firmly. "Let's go!"

They headed out to the car and began the hour and a half long journey to Cambridge, Mat driving and Charlie giving directions using Mat's phone.

When they were around halfway there, Charlie looked up from his phone, where he had been researching ciphers. He turned on the camera and started speaking. "I was just thinking–"

"Don't think too hard, you might hurt yourself."

Charlie hid a grin as he glared at Mat, before continuing. "I've been thinking about Pearl, and how she worked away from home, and there wasn't anything specific written about her job, just, 'clerical work.' And then I thought about the notebook being written in code. What was a big thing during World War Two? Codebreaking. I don't know why I didn't think of it earlier. Do you think Pearl could've been employed at Bletchley Park?"

Mat's eyes widened, but he kept them fixed on the road. "Oh my god. You could be right!"

Charlie turned to the camera. "For those who don't know, Bletchley Park was the centre of the World War Two codebreaking operation here in Great Britain, where they managed to break the ciphers used by the German, Italian and Japanese forces. It was so top secret, that even the people who worked there didn't know the full extent of what they were doing. It was kept completely under wraps until the seventies, I think, *way* after the war ended. It was a really important part of the war effort, and it's supposed to have shortened the war by up to two years, or something like that. It really is amazing what the Bletchley Park codebreakers achieved." He turned back to Mat. "Do you think Pearl could've been one of them? It makes sense, doesn't it?"

Mat nodded enthusiastically. "It all adds up. But we could just be putting two and two together and making five. We'll have to ask Rose about it when we talk to her later."

"Yeah, definitely. Although, she might not know anything about it. They weren't allowed to tell their families what they were doing."

Mat frowned. "But wouldn't it be public knowledge now, anyway?"

"Not necessarily. They've managed to name most of the people who worked there, but there were around ten thousand employees at one point, so they haven't been able to list them all yet. And since Pearl died so long ago, it might be more difficult for them to identify her." Charlie shrugged. "I don't know for sure, though. It's just a theory."

"Well, if you're right, hopefully we can prove she worked there. It would be great if we could get her some recognition for her work."

Charlie agreed, then turned back to his research. They drove the rest of the way in silence, broken only by the music coming from the radio. When they arrived in Cambridge, Charlie directed Mat to a car park near the photography shop.

"I'm starving! I think I'm gonna pass out any minute now," Mat said, putting a hand to his rumbling stomach as they walked out of the car park and across the road.

Charlie laughed. "You're so dramatic! We'll get something to eat after we've sorted this out."

"I'm not sure I'll last that long. There's gotta be a Greggs around here somewhere," Mat said, looking around desperately for any sign of the popular bakery chain. He sighed in frustration when he couldn't see one. "There's a Greggs on every corner in Newcastle. You can hardly get moved for sausage rolls!"

Just at that moment, Charlie's stomach rumbled loudly. "Quit it! You're making me hungry now."

Mat laughed. "Sorry. I'll shut up about it," he said, but only a moment later, he gasped and pointed to the other side of the road excitedly. "I can see a Greggs!"

Charlie turned to look where Mat was pointing. "Perfect! It's only a few shops down from the photography place. We can go there straight after."

A bell tinkled as they entered the photography shop and a young man behind the counter looked up at them. He smiled. "Hi there, what can I do for you?"

"Hi, I think I spoke to you on the phone this morning?" Charlie said.

"Ah, about the old camera film?"

"Yeah. Do you mind if we film in here for our YouTube channel?"

The shop assistant looked surprised. "Uh, yeah, sure." He immediately reached up to fix his hair.

"Great, thanks. What's your name?" Charlie asked, as Mat turned on the camera.

"Uh, Mike." Mike glanced over at the camera awkwardly, obviously not used to being recorded.

Charlie smiled. "Nice to meet you, Mike. I'm Charlie, and this is Mat."

Mat smiled and nodded his head as a greeting.

"We were wondering if you could have a look at this." Charlie retrieved the roll of film from a pocket in his bomber jacket and handed it over to Mike.

Mike inspected it closely, looking much more relaxed now. "It doesn't look too bad, actually, but we won't know for sure until it's been developed. My guess is it'll develop alright, but it might be a bit grainy."

"Hopefully that's the case, then. Just as long as we can make out what's in the pictures," Charlie said, exchanging a relieved look with Mat.

"I can start developing the film now and the photos should be ready for you to pick up later today. I'll just need some information and I'll drop you a text when they're done."

Mike handed a form over for Charlie to fill out, and it wasn't long before they were ready to leave.

"Thanks, Mike!" Charlie called behind him as they exited the shop, the bell tinkling again as they opened the door.

"No problem."

"Well, that was nice and easy!" Charlie said, as they walked back along the path. "Now we just need to get something to eat before we meet Rose."

"Greggs?" Mat asked.

"Greggs," Charlie agreed.

CHAPTER TWENTY-TWO

Mat and Charlie arrived outside a quaint bungalow in a picturesque street, just outside of the hustle and bustle of Cambridge city centre. Mat parked partially on the curb, being careful not to block off any of the surrounding driveways. He turned off the engine and let out a low whistle. "I wouldn't mind living somewhere like this when I'm ninety-one."

"Me too," Charlie agreed, looking around at the charming houses which lined the cul-de-sac.

They gathered their things together before vacating the car and making their way up to the front door. The path had been gritted to cover the thin layer of ice that coated it, making it easy to walk on.

Charlie rang the doorbell, then they both stood back and waited. They heard some movement behind the door and then it opened, revealing a smiling woman with tan skin, dark curly hair and green eyes.

"Hi! I'm Joanne. It's lovely to meet you," she said, reaching forward to shake both of their hands. "Come on in! She's just in the living room."

Mat and Charlie entered the house and followed Joanne, managing to squeeze in a 'hello' when she stopped to take a breath.

"It's just Grandma and I in the house at the moment. My husband and son have taken Grandpa out to do a bit of shopping. He insists on doing it himself, you see, but he can't really drive anymore. They should be back before you leave."

They entered the living room and immediately stopped in their tracks, taken aback. The room was decorated with neutral furniture that contrasted dramatically with a display of vibrant art covering all four walls. There were all sorts of different pieces scattered around, and one wall was painted with a mural. In the bay window there was a Christmas tree filled from top to bottom with an array of multicoloured baubles and homemade tree decorations, adding to the homely feel of the room.

"Wow," Mat whispered, looking around at the artwork in awe.

Joanne smiled at him. "I know, she's very talented, isn't she?"

"Is this all Rose's artwork?" Mat asked, his eyes widening as he carried on gawping at every piece in turn.

"Not all of it," came a voice from the corner of the room, "I have a special section dedicated to art made by my grandchildren and great-grandchildren. There's one made by Joanne somewhere."

Mat and Charlie whipped around to find the source of the voice. An old woman with wispy white curly hair was sitting in an armchair, her green eyes sparkling as she smiled at them. She was wearing an orange blouse tucked into black flowy trousers, and there was a sketchbook resting on her knee. Mat and Charlie had been so preoccupied by taking in the artwork around the room, that they hadn't noticed her sitting there and watching them.

"Don't bother looking for my drawing, it isn't very good," Joanne said, before turning to her grandmother. "Grandma, these are the young men I was telling you about."

"Hi, Mrs Carter. I'm Charlie and this is my friend Mat," Charlie said, smiling at Rose as he moved further into the room.

Rose put her sketchbook aside and placed her pencil behind her ear. "Hello, dears. Call me Rose."

Charlie nodded. "It's lovely to meet you, Rose. We run a YouTube channel together called *The Paranormal*

Detectives, where we investigate haunted sites and look for proof of paranormal activity. We've been investigating the house where your sister passed away, and we found some new evidence that we thought you might be able to help with. Do you mind if we film our chat and post it online, as part of our video about the investigation?"

Rose nodded. "Yes, go ahead, dear."

Mat began to set up the camera on its tripod in the middle of the room, and Charlie sat down on the settee.

"Would anybody like tea or coffee?" Joanne asked, starting to make her way to the kitchen.

"Yes, please. A cup of tea would be lovely," Charlie said.

Mat looked up from the camera and smiled. "Tea for me too, please."

"Milk and sugar?"

"We both have milk and one sugar," Charlie told her.

Joanne nodded and left the room, leaving Mat and Charlie alone with Rose. Mat finished setting up the camera, then sat on the settee next to Charlie.

"Thank you for agreeing to meet with us, Rose," Charlie said.

Rose smiled. "I wouldn't normally do something like this, but Joanne assures me you have the best of intentions."

Charlie nodded. "Yes, we do. The reason we decided to look into this particular case is because I lived in the house when I was younger. I used to hear bangs and crashes and it was a really scary time for me, so I wanted to come back to check it out as an adult. But since we've been here, and we've learned more about Pearl, we've come to realise that the conclusion the police came to doesn't really make much sense. We want to find out the truth of what really happened that day."

"We want to help bring justice for Pearl," Mat added.

Rose smiled at them both fondly. "Thank you, boys, that's very good of you. I agree with you, I think the police were entirely wrong. All they cared about was closing the case as quickly as possible, so they didn't look into it properly, and they ignored many of the clues. I tried to tell them I thought they were mistaken, but they weren't about to take any notice of a grieving, fifteen-year-old girl – especially not back then. So, eventually I had to give in and carry on with my life, knowing that justice hadn't been served. I told myself I would find the truth one day, but unfortunately I've never been able to."

"I'm very sorry, Rose, it must've been really difficult for you. But don't give up hope yet; there's still time," Charlie said, giving Rose a smile of encouragement. "What was it that made you so sure it wasn't an accident?"

"There were a few things. The day it happened, Pearl had insisted I go with our grandmother to buy some new clothes. She said she had some work to take care of, but she would meet us later in the day. When it got to late afternoon and she still hadn't arrived, Grandma walked me back to the house. The door was unlocked when we got there, so Grandma told me to wait outside for a moment… I can still hear her scream when she entered the house. I tried to follow her in, but she stopped me; I'm glad she did.

"When I was recounting what had happened to the police later on, I told them it just didn't seem right to me that the front door was unlocked. Pearl *always* kept it locked. Of course, the police dismissed this and said she must have unlocked it ready to leave the house. But she had been acting quite strange for the few days before she died. She acted as if everything was fine, but I could tell she was distracted. There was something on her mind. She seemed… frightened, almost. It was as if she was carrying the weight of the world on her shoulders. We had a wonderful few days overall, but there was definitely something bothering her.

"Another thing I found very unusual happened at her funeral. I overheard her friends talking about a mystery boyfriend, and how they thought he might make an appearance, so they were on the lookout for him. I asked them about it and they didn't say much. I don't think they really knew anything more. But I don't understand why she wouldn't have mentioned him to me."

Charlie frowned. "That is very strange." He noticed that Rose was holding onto a dainty gold necklace that hung around her neck as she spoke. There was something about it that seemed very familiar to him, but he wasn't sure why. "That's a beautiful necklace," he said, pointing to it.

Rose glanced down, as if she had forgotten that she was wearing one. "Oh, thank you, dear. Pearl gave it to me for my tenth birthday. It has an angel wing pendant hanging from it. Pearl had a matching one, with the left wing while I have the right. They connected together, you see. We had this little ritual where we would connect the pendants and say, 'No matter how far apart we are, as long as we have our angel wings we will always be connected.' It was rather silly, really, but it always helped when I was at school and we were apart for a long time. Now, whenever I miss her, I close my eyes and think of her while I hold it. I know she is thinking of me too, wherever she is." There was a pause as she smiled and held the necklace, then her face creased into a frown. "The strange thing was, Pearl wasn't wearing her necklace when we found her. I thought this was very out of the ordinary, because we never took our necklaces off. I looked everywhere for it, but it was nowhere to be seen."

At that moment, Joanne entered the room carrying a tray with four mugs balanced on it. "Sorry to interrupt," she said, walking around and passing a mug to each of them in turn. They all thanked her, and she made her way out of view of the camera, sitting down in the second armchair. "Just pretend I'm not here."

Charlie grinned at her, then continued with his questioning. "Have you ever been back to visit the house?"

Rose sighed deeply. "No, I've never been able to bring myself to go back there. When I heard of all this nonsense about her haunting the house, I thought people must be making it up. Trying to get their fifteen minutes of fame. Of course, I've always wondered about it, but I'm not sure I'd want to communicate with her even if it were true. I like to remember her as I knew her in life."

"That's understandable," Charlie said. "What are your favourite memories of Pearl?"

Rose smiled. "Oh, where to start… Some of my happiest memories with Pearl are of us dancing together in the living room. We used to play music on the gramophone, or listen to the wireless – the radio, that is – and we'd dance and sing for hours. We would listen to Gracie Fields, Vera Lynn, Bing Crosby. Our favourite song was *White Christmas*; I always think of Pearl when I listen to it."

Mat and Charlie exchanged a look at the mention of *White Christmas,* but they stayed quiet, feeling it would be inappropriate for them to interrupt.

Rose continued, her eyes glazed over as she reminisced on her childhood. "We used to go to the pictures together when we could, and it was always a big event. We would get dressed in our finest clothes and make an evening of it. Pearl would always buy a chocolate bar for each of us as a treat, and we would eat it as we watched the film. My favourite was Dairy Milk, but Pearl always preferred a KitKat." She faltered for a moment, sadness crossing over her face. "During the war, it was difficult to come across some confectionary, due to rationing and whatnot. Pearl always said that she couldn't wait to buy herself a KitKat once they were back in the shops. But sadly, she died before she got her wish." There was another pause, and the room was now so silent, they would have been able to hear a pin drop. "Every year on her birthday, I listen to the music we used to listen to together, and I have a KitKat in her honour. It's become a little tradition of mine. I like to think she's there with me, dancing the night away." She smiled at the floor, before looking up at Mat and Charlie. "I have a picture of us together that I can show you, if you would like to see it?"

"Yeah, we'd love to see it," Charlie replied, and Mat nodded.

Rose reached to the side of her chair and picked up her handbag. She rooted around for her purse, then pulled out a small black-and-white photograph from inside it, handing it over to Charlie.

Mat picked up the handheld camera to film the photograph up close. It showed a young woman with curly hair and a bright smile, sitting next to a teenager who looked like a younger version of the same person.

"You were so alike!" Charlie said, grinning at the photograph.

Rose smiled, taking the photograph back from them and putting it away safely in her purse. "We were more alike in looks than in personality, although I aspired to be just like her."

"What was she like as a person?" Mat asked, putting the camera back down.

"Oh, she was wonderful. I always looked up to her, she was a brilliant role model. She was strong-minded, determined, independent, stubborn. She knew what she wanted, and she wouldn't give up until she got it. But, she was also kind and loyal, and she put everybody she cared about before herself. She was my hero, I thought the world of her; I still do.

"During our last week together, I painted a portrait of her. I think looking at it might be the best way to get across what sort of person she was. Follow me through to the dining room and I'll show you."

Rose heaved herself out of her armchair and began to shuffle towards the door, her back hunched over. Mat grabbed the handheld camera again and turned it on, then he and Charlie stood up to follow Rose, who was now holding onto Joanne for support as she walked.

As soon as Mat and Charlie entered the dining room, their jaws dropped for the second time during their visit. The walls were just as covered by artwork as the living room had been, but their eyes were drawn to a painting which took pride of place in the centre of the room.

The painting showed a woman with flaming red curls and startling green eyes, who Mat and Charlie both recognised from the black-and-white picture of Pearl. She was sitting in an armchair, wearing a white blouse tucked into a long purple skirt, and holding a teacup and saucer in her hands in a very elegant and sophisticated manner. She had a very warm smile and looked as if she would be an extremely kind and trustworthy person. There was a glowing fire in the background, and books piled at her feet.

Charlie frowned. The vividness of Pearl's hair and eyes seemed so familiar to him, and he couldn't help but feel like there was something he was forgetting as he looked at the painting. He quickly shook the idea away, marking it down as another case of déjà vu. He had only ever seen a black-and-white photo of Pearl, so there was no way he could have seen her in colour before.

"Wow," Mat said, walking towards the painting to film it up close. "You painted this when you were only fifteen years old?"

Rose's eyes crinkled as she smiled. "Yes, I did."

"I told you she was talented," Joanne commented, smiling at her grandmother.

"You can say that again," Mat said, taking in every inch of the painting.

"Thank you, dear. Pearl was always happiest when she was sitting in her favourite armchair next to the crackling fire, with a good book in her hands and drinking a cup of tea. So, I decided to try and capture those qualities of her in the painting."

"Well, you've definitely achieved that," Charlie said, joining Mat in front of the painting. "And that's coming from an art novice. This is more Mat's area of expertise."

"Oh, are you interested in art?" Rose asked, her eyes lighting up. When Mat nodded, she asked, "Do you do any art yourself?"

Mat shuffled his feet awkwardly. "I do a bit of art, yeah. It's nowhere near the level of the kind of art you do, though," he said, feeling embarrassed and staring at the ground.

Charlie jumped in. "He's just being modest. His art is really good."

Rose nodded. "I'm sure your friend is right. Art is very subjective. There is no bad art, it's all just a matter of personal opinion. As long as you're creating something you love, that's all that matters. What type of art do you like to create?"

Mat swallowed nervously. He hated being the centre of attention and was hoping profusely for an opportunity to change the subject as soon as possible. "I like doing cartoonish illustrations mostly, and I make short comic strips and that sort of thing."

"He animates some of his illustrations to add into our YouTube videos as well. He'll be doing some for this video," Charlie added.

"Oh, that sounds lovely! I can't wait to see your work when I watch the video," Rose said brightly.

Mat smiled, then shot a furtive look at Charlie, trying to convey how badly he wanted the conversation to move on to a different topic.

Taking the hint, Charlie changed the subject. "Anyway, speaking of the video, should we head back through to the living room and continue with our interview?"

"Yes, of course," Rose said.

Mat breathed a sigh of relief, and they made their way back through. As soon as he sat down, Mat picked up his cup of tea and began to sip at it quietly.

Charlie glanced over at him. "Oh, is the tea ready to drink?" he asked, reaching over to the coffee table to pick up his own mug.

Once they were all sitting comfortably again, sipping their tea, Rose continued. "Pearl was always my biggest supporter when it came to my artwork. She told me never to give up on my dreams. One day, I would have my own exhibition in an art gallery. I just needed to believe in myself, first. Of course, she was right, as she always was. I named my first exhibition *Pearls of Wisdom* in homage to her, the wisest person I've ever known. I know she would have been so proud of me for pursuing my dreams and achieving them.

"For Pearl, her dream was always mathematics. Women weren't able to get full degrees back in those days, but she went as far as she possibly could. She attended Newnham College, which was the women's college associated with Cambridge University. She was brilliant, she really was. Such a clever woman. She would have excelled in the field, I'm sure. Unfortunately, she never got a chance to pursue a career in mathematics, as she was recruited to the war effort as soon as she finished her education."

Mat and Charlie exchanged a look of mild confusion with each other. They were both quite surprised that there hadn't been anything written about Pearl's education in any of the extensive research Charlie had done about the case.

Mat sipped his tea. "Do you know anything about what Pearl's job entailed?" he asked, leaning forward keenly.

"No, not much at all. She was always quite private about it. All I knew was that she had to work away and do clerical work. It all sounded like a bit of a bore to me, to be quite frank, so I didn't probe any further. I was just pleased that she seemed to be safe wherever she was."

Mat and Charlie shared another look with each other, excitement evident on their faces as the same thought crossed their minds. They couldn't help but wonder if Charlie's theory had been correct, and Pearl had managed to pursue her mathematical career further than Rose realised.

Deciding the moment had arrived, Charlie placed his now empty mug back on the coffee table and reached into his backpack, pulling out Pearl's notebook. "When we were investigating the house last night, we came across this notebook. Have you seen it before?"

"It does look familiar," Rose said, frowning as she looked at it. She gasped. "Oh, yes, I remember! It was a birthday present for Pearl from our father, on her last birthday before his passing. Pearl always said she was keeping it for a special occasion, but I assumed she never wrote in it. Is it blank?"

"No, a few pages have been written on. But we don't know what it says, as it appears to be written in code." Charlie passed the notebook to Rose, so she could take a closer look. "Do you know if Pearl knew anything about cryptography?"

Rose flicked through the notebook, her look of puzzlement slowly melting into a wistful smile as she looked fondly through the pages of neat capital letters. "I'm not sure. She might have studied it, but I've never really been one for maths, so I didn't understand anything she learned about. It all looked the same to me, just letters and numbers. But one thing I can say for certain, is this is definitely Pearl's handwriting." She stroked the pages of the notebook as she spoke.

Charlie glanced at Mat, then thought carefully about how to phrase his next question. "Do you think it could've been possible for Pearl to have been recruited to work as a codebreaker at Bletchley Park?"

Rose frowned. "I don't think…" She trailed off, her frown deepening as she gazed down at the notebook in her hands. Her expression changed to one of shock as she thought it over. She turned to look at her granddaughter. "Do you think she could have…? I never even considered…"

Joanne looked just as shocked. "Well, we didn't have any reason to consider it before. But the notebook…" She looked at Charlie. "I think you could be right."

"I think the only way to find out for sure is to decipher the notebook," Mat said, turning to Charlie.

Charlie nodded in agreement. "Do you know anything Pearl might've used as a key for the code in the notebook?" he asked Rose.

Rose looked unsure. "What is a key, if you don't mind me asking? I'm sorry, I don't know anything about coded messages or how they work."

Charlie paused for a moment, trying to think of the best way to describe the process to someone who knew absolutely nothing about cryptography. It was made more difficult by the fact that he wasn't exactly an expert on the subject himself; it had been months since he had studied it at university. "Uh, when someone wants to send a message, but they don't want it to be read by anyone other than the intended recipient, they might send a coded version of that message. They decide on a key – which could be a word, or a phrase, or even just a bunch of random letters, as long as it's memorable. They use this key as part of a method which changes the message to an unreadable string of letters, called ciphertext. That's what's written in the notebook. To be able to read the message, the recipient must know the key, so they can use a kind of reverse method to work out the original plaintext. There *are* ways of cracking the code without the key, but it would be a lot quicker and easier if we knew what the key was. Did Pearl mention anything to you that could've been at all related?"

Rose thought this over for a moment. "No, I don't remember her mentioning anything to me. It was a long time ago, so I might have forgotten. I'm sorry. But if what you say is correct, then she could have used anything as the key. It might not have any meaning at all."

Charlie sighed. "It was worth a try." He shrugged. "Thank you so much for talking to us, Rose. You've been a great help."

"We promise we'll do everything we can to solve the mystery and find out what really happened to Pearl," Mat added.

"Thank you, boys. It means so much to me that you care about getting justice for my sister, even after all this time."

Joanne stood up and walked over to Mat and Charlie as they began to sort their things away. "Thank you so much. I'll let you know if we have any brainwaves about the key."

"Thank you. Charlie's gonna try his best to crack the code, so we'll let you know of any progress," Mat said, turning off the camera and beginning to pack it away.

At that moment, they heard the front door open. "Honey, I'm home!" came an old man's voice from the hallway.

Rose smiled widely, the corners of her eyes crinkling. "Right on cue."

An old man with dark skin and short grey curly hair hobbled into the room carrying a small bag of shopping. "Hello, darling."

"Bernard, these are the boys Joanne was telling us about! They're going to help us find out the truth about what happened to Pearl. Isn't that wonderful?"

"Is that right?" Bernard beamed at Mat and Charlie. He put his shopping bag down on the floor and tottered over to them, extending a hand. "Bernard. How do you do?"

"Hi. I'm Charlie, and this is Mat," Charlie said, as Bernard shook each of their hands in turn.

"It's nice to meet you," Mat said.

"Likewise," Bernard replied. "Thank you for doing this. It's nice to have a glimmer of hope after all these years. I hope you have more luck than we did."

"We're gonna try our best," Charlie promised.

A man walked through the living room door, followed by a teenage boy who was looking quite nervous.

Joanne smiled and walked over to them, putting her arm around the boy's shoulders. "Mat, Charlie. This is my husband, Nathan, and my son, Carter."

"Mat and Charlie! This is a bit surreal," Nathan said, smiling at them both.

"Hi," Carter said timidly.

Charlie smiled. "Hi, it's lovely to meet you both." He walked forward and shook both of their hands.

Mat followed his lead. "Hi. Nice top," he said, nodding at Carter's NASA t-shirt.

"Thanks." Carter suddenly looked like he might burst with excitement. "I love your videos! I've seen every single one!" he said breathlessly.

Mat grinned. "Wow, really? That's amazing."

"Thank you, Carter. That means a lot," Charlie said, beaming at Carter. "Right, how about we take some pictures?"

CHAPTER TWENTY-THREE

"Bye, thanks for having us!" Charlie called behind him, as he and Mat walked down the path and towards the car.

"Thank you, boys. Goodbye!" They heard the door close behind them and continued in silence until they reached the car.

Mat closed the car door and let out a long sigh. "Well, that was eventful," he said.

Charlie nodded. "It was. We learned a lot," he said, closing his eyes and leaning his head back on the headrest.

"But we're still no further forward on figuring out the notebook, so that's annoying."

Charlie shrugged. "You never know, there may be a hidden gem from our conversation. We just need to watch it back and see if we can make any connections."

"True," Mat said. "Have you heard anything back about the photos yet?"

"I'm not sure. I'll have a look." Charlie got his phone from his pocket and scrolled through his notifications. There was a recent text message from a number he didn't recognise, so he clicked on it to open it up. "I've got a text! The photos are ready to collect."

"Perfect! We'll go straight there to pick them up, then we can plan our next steps."

"Sounds good to me," Charlie said, putting his seatbelt on.

They drove back along the same route they'd taken earlier and parked in the car park near the photography shop. The sun had begun to set by now, and the temperature seemed to have dropped by several degrees.

Charlie shivered as he stepped out the car. "It's freezing!" he exclaimed.

Mat nodded, his teeth chattering. "We should've brought bigger coats."

They shoved their hands into their pockets and walked as quickly as they could, the bell announcing their presence as they burst through the shop door and shut it behind them.

The shop assistant, Mike, looked up. "Ah, you're back! Two seconds," he said, before walking out of sight.

Mat and Charlie walked up to the counter and waited for him to return, which he did only a moment later, a large envelope visible in his hands.

"This was a really fun project for me. I love when people bring unusual stuff into the shop." He smiled and handed the envelope over to Charlie. "Here you go. They all turned out pretty much perfect!"

Charlie beamed. "That's great, thank you!"

"Do you want to have a quick look at them before you go, just to make sure you're happy with how they turned out?" Mike asked.

Charlie shook his head. "It's okay. We were gonna have a look at them when we get back to the car. Right, Mat?"

"Yeah." Mat smiled and nodded.

"Okay, that's fine. Don't hesitate to get in touch if you find there's anything wrong with them," Mike said.

"Okay, thanks a lot. Bye!"

After another brisk walk, Mat and Charlie were back in the car, both rubbing their hands together to warm them up. Mat switched on the car's interior light, so they could see what they were doing.

Charlie placed the handheld camera on the dashboard in front of them. "It's time," he said, holding the envelope up to the camera. He turned to Mat and asked, "Are you ready?"

Mat nodded. "It's the moment of truth," he said, with a dramatic look to the camera.

"Okay, here goes," Charlie said, excitement building as he pulled out the black-and-white photographs from the envelope and held them in his right hand, so he and Mat could look through them together. They were slightly fuzzy and blurred, but clear enough to make out what was happening in them.

They looked at each photograph one by one, noticing that they seemed to tell a story: there was a man sat on a park bench with a briefcase by his feet, his face hidden by a newspaper; he was joined by a tall white man, wearing a trench coat, fedora and sunglasses, who sat down and placed a briefcase on the floor next to the one already there; the second man reached into his trench coat and pulled out a paper bag, which turned out to contain some sort of food, possibly a sandwich; there were a few photos where the second man ate his sandwich, while the first man read his newspaper; the second man finished eating and stood up, picking up the briefcase furthest away from him before walking away; the first man put away his newspaper, revealing his face to the camera as he picked up the briefcase and looked inside; he was white, with dark slicked back hair and the last photos showed him standing up from the bench and walking forwards.

"Ah, the old briefcase switcheroo," Mat said, leaning closer to see the grainy photos more clearly.

Charlie laughed and turned to look at him. "The old briefcase switcheroo? Is that the technical term for it?"

Mat grinned. "Yep, it is."

Charlie quickly flicked through the pictures again, trying to take them all in. "Should I show them to the camera?" he asked Mat.

Mat shook his head, staring intensely at the photos. "I'll just add them into the video in the edit."

There was a moment of silence, before Charlie said, "I dunno what to make of this."

Mat sighed. "Me neither."

"Right, let's theorise," Charlie said. "Get your thinking cap on."

Mat grabbed his beanie from the door pocket and pulled it on over his curls. "Done. Where's yours?"

Charlie let out a snort of laughter and pulled an imaginary hat onto his own head. "Okay, so this first man must be the one Pearl was trailing 'cause he's in all the photos. The other man just showed up."

"Yep." Mat nodded. He began to fidget with his ring as he thought. "And it's obvious there's something dodgy going on. If Pearl really did work at Bletchley Park, then this could be… big."

"That's a bit of an understatement," Charlie said, running a hand through his hair nervously. "We need to find out the identities of these men."

"Definitely," Mat agreed. "Do you think the first man could be the same person that wrote the 'Friday, three p.m.' note?"

Charlie raised his eyebrows and nodded. "It would make sense. Maybe that's when these photos were taken?" he suggested.

"They could've been. I think we need to try and figure out what the notebook says."

"Agreed. Let's go."

Mat started to put his seatbelt on, then stopped. "Wait, where are we gonna go? We can't go to the house yet 'cause Mrs Harris will still be doing her ghost tours when we get back."

"Oh, yeah. I almost forgot." Charlie thought for a moment. "Why don't we find a café to sit in? It'll be more comfortable than sitting in the car, at least."

Mat nodded and reached up to turn off the interior light. "Are there any cafes in Teaburn?" he asked.

"I'm pretty sure there's at least one. We can head off now and I'll Google it on the way." Charlie put the camera away and began to look up the address of the café on his phone.

"Sounds good to me. Get your seatbelt on," Mat said, starting the engine.

Charlie quickly fastened his seatbelt. "Sorry, got distracted."

They set off on the drive back, and an hour and a half later they arrived in Teaburn, having narrowly avoided getting lost only once, when Mat had almost missed their exit on the motorway. There had been a lot of panicked shouting (mostly from Charlie) and some swearing (mostly from Mat) and they hadn't spoken to each other for a good few minutes afterwards, until Mat had cracked a joke to release the tension. They were now driving through the streets of Teaburn, trying to locate the café Charlie had found online.

Charlie leant forward in his seat and craned his neck as he searched through the darkness that now engulfed their surroundings. "It's gotta be around here somewhe– that's it, there!" He pointed to a turning on their left.

Mat pulled off the road and into a tiny car park outside a little café. They quickly made their way inside the building and chose a table in the far corner which looked like it had comfortable seats, since they knew they would be there a while.

"I'll go and order," Charlie said, placing his backpack on one of the seats as Mat sat down. "What do you want?"

"Medium caramel latte, please," Mat replied, starting to unpack their equipment onto the table.

"Anything else? It looks like they've got millionaires shortbread."

Mat's eyes lit up and he squinted at the counter in the distance. "Ooh, have they? I'll have some of that as well, then, if you don't mind. Gotta keep ourselves fuelled up, or we won't be able to unravel this mystery."

Charlie grinned and made his way over to the counter. While he was gone, Mat set up the camera on the table next to theirs, hoping that nobody would try to sit at that table while they were there.

It wasn't long before Charlie had returned, delicately carrying a tray full of treats. "I asked at the counter, and apparently they're open till ten p.m. today, so that's handy. Ooh, are we doing artistic shots now?" he said, nodding at the positioning of the camera as he balanced the tray on the edge of the table.

Mat looked up from his laptop and grinned. "I thought I'd try to up our game for this video. I'm gonna do a time lapse of us figuring out the notebook," he said, moving the drinks onto the table.

"No pressure, then." Charlie settled down in the seat opposite Mat and retrieved Pearl's notebook from his bag. He sighed as he stared at the front cover.

Mat watched Charlie as he began to flick through the notebook. "Do you have any idea where to start with it?" he asked.

Charlie put the notebook down on the table. "Well, I think I have an idea of which cipher she might've used. It's only an educated guess, but judging by the look of the ciphertext, and the fact she would've been doing it all by hand, I think it's most likely that she would've used the Vigenère cipher. The Vigenère cipher actually works on the same principle as the German Enigma machines did in World War Two, where the formula used to encrypt the plaintext is changed for every letter. Obviously, it's a *lot* simpler than the Enigma machine, though. But that's another connection with Bletchley Park, albeit a very loose connection."

"Is that one of the ciphers you learnt about at uni?"

Charlie nodded. "Uh-huh. It was one of my favourites, as well. I used to do it just for fun sometimes."

Mat laughed. "We're really gonna be exposing just how nerdy we actually are to our viewers in this video."

Charlie snorted. "I'm pretty sure they're aware of it by now."

"So, do you know how to decrypt it without the key?"

Charlie sighed. "There are ways to do that, but it would be much easier if we could just figure out the key. I think we should start with trial and error."

Mat nodded. "Well, I think Pearl would've used a key that meant something, not just a string of random letters."

"I agree. She would've had to use something memorable, so she could encrypt her writing whenever she needed to. I think we're looking for a short phrase."

They sat in silence for a couple of minutes, racking their brains for ideas.

"Her sister's name?" Mat suggested eventually.

Charlie thought about it. "We may as well give it a shot. I'll try it out on the first sentence and see if we get anything that resembles English." He slid a notepad and pen in front of him and picked up his calculator, then flicked to the first page of the notebook. Just as he was about to start writing out the first line of ciphertext into his notepad, he noticed something on the page which caused him to stop abruptly. His brain ticked over as he stared at the notebook, his pen hovering in mid-air above the paper.

"What's wrong?" Mat asked.

"I think… I think I might know what the key is…" Charlie replied, slowly turning to look at Mat.

"Really? What are you thinking?" Mat asked excitedly.

Charlie picked up the notebook and passed it to Mat, pointing to a tiny musical note which had been drawn next to the first line of text.

Mat's eyes widened as realisation dawned on him. "You don't think…?"

"What did Rose tell us used to be Pearl's favourite song? And which song's been heard playing in the Carter house randomly over the years?"

"*White Christmas*!" they said in unison.

"She's been giving us clues all along!" Charlie said excitedly. He copied out the first line of ciphertext into his notepad.

LYWIITAPWXIQAJHJIKXGY

Mat watched as Charlie scribbled lines and lines of letters and numbers, furiously tapping buttons on his calculator and looking increasingly enthusiastic the more he wrote down. Within a few minutes, he was practically fizzing with excitement. He put his pen down on the table and thrust the notebook into Mat's hands.

"Look!" he said eagerly.

Mat scanned the lines of workings out until his eyes fell on the plaintext, which Charlie had written in capitals at the bottom of the page.

PROPERTYOFPEARLCARTER

"Property of Pearl Carter," Mat read out. He turned to look at Charlie excitedly and exclaimed, "You've done it! You've cracked the code!"

A couple who were sat a few tables across from theirs looked over in their direction curiously.

Mat sank down in his chair uncomfortably and lowered his voice. "What now?" he asked.

"Now I need to do the same for the rest of the notebook," Charlie replied. He drained what was left of his mocha latte. "But first, I think I'm gonna need some more coffee."

CHAPTER TWENTY-FOUR

While Charlie worked on decrypting the notebook, Mat decided to make himself useful by reviewing footage from the night before and listening back to the audio that had been captured on the EVP recorders they had been wearing on their wrists. Normally, this would be Charlie's job, as Mat was no use when it came to identifying spirit voices or anything of the like. He found it all too easy to think of a rational explanation for each and every unusual noise, and Charlie was much better at picking out words and phrases in the sounds. However, this time Mat was trying to keep an open mind as he approached the task.

He plugged his earphones into the laptop, so as not to disturb Charlie, and sorted through the footage and audio clips he planned on reviewing. He started by watching back through the footage the night vision cameras had recorded as they slept, all the while asking himself, "What would Charlie make of this?"

They sat in quiet concentration for a while, both absorbed in their respective tasks, until Mat frowned and interrupted the silence.

"Huh, that's weird," he said, rewinding the footage he was watching and playing it again.

His interest piqued, Charlie peeked out from behind Pearl's notebook, his pen hovering over the notepad on the table. "What's weird?" he asked.

"Have a look at this," Mat said, unplugging his earphones and turning the laptop around to show Charlie the video he was reviewing.

The footage was slightly grainy and in black and white, since it had been taken on the night vision camera. It showed Mat and Charlie lying in their sleeping bags on the living room floor, fast asleep. Charlie put his pen down on the table and scooted his chair over to get a better view of the video. Nothing happened for a couple of seconds, and then all of a sudden, the footage went fuzzy and a static noise erupted from the laptop, the kind that you would expect from an old VHS tape, but not from a modern night vision camera. It happened so suddenly that it made Charlie jump, as he hadn't been expecting it. It was as if there was some sort of interference that was stopping the camera from recording anything. Then, as quickly as it had started, it stopped, and the footage was back to normal. Mat and Charlie were still dead to the world, and everything was calm around them.

Charlie frowned and turned to look at Mat. "That *was* weird. I wonder what caused the interference?"

Mat paused the video and shrugged. "Your guess is as good as mine. I might have to do some research to see if this is something that commonly happens with night vision cameras. But have you noticed what's missing?"

"No," Charlie replied, turning back to the laptop to have another look.

"Here, watch it again." Mat rewound the video to before the interference. "And pay attention to our shoes."

Charlie looked around the room. He could see that both pairs of shoes were still lying next to their sleeping bags, exactly where they had left them when they had gone to bed the night before. The static started again out of nowhere, and Charlie jumped slightly, even though he knew it was coming this time. When the video returned, Charlie scanned the room again, but this time he noticed what was different. Both pairs of shoes were no longer where they had left them on the floor. In fact, they were nowhere to be seen, but Charlie thought he could take a pretty good guess at where they had ended up. He gasped and looked up at Mat, his eyes wide in shock.

Mat raised his eyebrows. "I know," he said, before Charlie could say anything. "Keep watching, there's more."

Charlie turned back to the video, and as he did he heard a distant bang. He watched himself sit up abruptly in his sleeping bag and grope around the floor for his glasses, before turning to Mat and starting to shake him.

Mat paused the video. "And we know what happened after that."

Charlie turned to Mat with a smug expression. "I *told* you there was a bang, and you wouldn't believe me!" he said, raising his eyebrows and folding his arms.

Mat rolled his eyes. "Yeah, I know. You were right. I was wrong. I'm sorry I didn't believe you. I'll never doubt you again. Blah-blah-blah. Are you happy now?"

Charlie grinned. "Yes, thank you." He let out a satisfied sigh, stretching his arms back and linking his hands behind his head. "It feels good to be right."

Amused, Mat shook his head at the camera, which was still sitting undisturbed on the table next to theirs. "*Anyway,*" he said pointedly, "I wonder what that was all about? The interference. The bangs. What caused them?"

"It was Pearl, I'm telling you!" Charlie insisted.

Mat ignored him. "Do you think there's any way that someone could mess with the camera from outside? I'm gonna Google it." He opened up the browser on his laptop.

"Mat, you literally *just* said that you were never gonna doubt me again."

Mat shrugged. "I was exaggerating," he said, staring at his laptop as he typed into the search bar.

Charlie pursed his lips. "Can't you just humour me for one second?"

Mat looked up and sighed. "Okay. I'll hear you out." He sat back and folded his arms. "Go on."

"Thank you," Charlie said, hiding his surprise that Mat had actually agreed to listen to what he had to say. "It doesn't make sense to me that anyone would do this on purpose. Even if it was a publicity stunt, why go to all that effort? I'm sure there's much easier ways to fake paranormal activity than interfering with a camera and moving shoes around the house. And then, the shoes led us up to the loft, where we found Pearl's notebook! No one could've known that was there."

Mat nodded. "Yes, I see your point. But have you considered: it could've just been a coincidence."

Charlie rolled his eyes. "It would've been a hell of a lucky coincidence to accidentally lead us to Pearl's old notebook, hidden away secretly in the loft. There's no way anyone could've known its whereabouts already; it was obvious it hadn't seen the light of day in years. The only explanation is that Pearl was the one who led us there."

Mat considered this. "I will say, it is very weird, and it's probably the most compelling evidence I've seen so far," he admitted. "But we'll have to just wait and see what happens when we go back tonight."

"Speaking of, I'd better carry on working on this, or we'll never get away tonight!" Charlie said, picking up his calculator and turning back to the notebook.

Mat stood up. "I'll go and order us another coffee. Do you want anything else? It's way past when we would usually have tea. My stomach's rumbling again."

"Yeah, please. I think I need something with a bit more substance to it than cakes or biscuits, though. I'm pretty sure I saw pizza on the menu board when I was up there earlier, so I'll have some of that if they have any left. If not, I'll have a teacake or something."

Mat nodded and made his way over to the counter, where he found that they did, in fact, have pizza. Once he had returned with the coffee and pizza, he set to work on listening back to the audio from the EVP recorders. He made sure to save each unusual sound that had been picked up by the recorders and decided to run them all past Charlie later on. To him it all just sounded like noise, but he was sure Charlie would be able to hear something interesting hidden in amongst the racket.

They carried on working like this in silence, Mat getting up every so often to keep them supplied with coffee and cakes. Other customers came and went, and the sky outside gradually became even darker than it had been when they had arrived at the café, until nothing could be seen through the windows at all.

Mat finished reviewing the footage and audio a long time before Charlie was finished decrypting the notebook, as the latter was such a massive undertaking. Charlie found that the more letters he worked out, the faster he became at decrypting them, as the process was very repetitive. But even so, it still seemed to be taking an eternity, and he felt himself flagging.

"Is there anything I can do to help?" Mat asked, when he had been sitting there for a while, twiddling his thumbs and feeling like a spare part, as he watched Charlie working tirelessly to decrypt the notebook.

"You could write up the plaintext for me?" Charlie suggested, without looking up.

"Sure," Mat said, relieved to have something to do. He slid over the pile of paper that Charlie had stacked in front of him on the table. The sheets contained all of Charlie's workings out for each letter, with an arrow pointing to a new letter at the end of each line. Mat found a fresh sheet of paper and began to transcribe the plaintext into legible paragraphs. He paused after having only written out one sentence and let out a low whistle as he stared at the paper. "Chaz, I don't wanna distract you, but I have to let you know that this is… well, let's just say, it answers a *lot* of questions."

Charlie looked up excitedly. "Really?"

Mat nodded. "Wait until you're finished to have a look, though. You'll be too stressed to finish decrypting it if you look now."

"Mat, you're already making me stressed by saying that!" Charlie exclaimed.

However, Mat's remarks seemed to give him the boost of motivation he needed, as from that moment on he worked even faster, his hand a blur as it moved across the page.

It wasn't much longer until he was writing out the final letter on the page and passing the sheet of paper over to Mat triumphantly. He yawned and massaged his hand as he waited for Mat to finish writing out the transcript of the plaintext.

Mat put the last full stop on the paper and sighed, then picked up the sheets and shuffled them on the table, as if he were a news reader. "Okay, this is it. Do you wanna do the honours or should I?" he asked.

"You can. I think I'm too tired to read after all that. I haven't done that much maths in one sitting since exam season at uni," Charlie replied, covering his mouth as he yawned again.

"Okay. Strap yourself in, it starts off strong," Mat warned. He cleared his throat. " 'Monday the eleventh of December nineteen-forty-four. To whoever is reading this journal, I work at Bletchley Park and I have reason to believe there is something suspicious going on there involving one of my colleagues.' "

CHAPTER TWENTY-FIVE

Charlie stared at Mat, all trace of tiredness gone as his brain ticked over, trying to process the words Mat had just read out to him. "So, we were right?" he asked slowly, as they began to sink in.

Mat shook his head. "*You* were right," he corrected. "It was nothing to do with me. I'm just the sidekick in this investigation." He held his hands up.

Charlie grinned. "Oh, shut up! As if! We wouldn't even be here investigating this case if it weren't for you. You kickstarted the whole thing! We're a *team*."

"Yeah, yeah," Mat said, waving away Charlie's reassurances, but secretly feeling very chuffed.

"Anyway, I can't believe we've got actual proof that Pearl worked at Bletchley Park! I can't wait to show this to Rose."

"I know. But it gets better – or worse, depending on how you look at it."

Intrigued, Charlie sat back and made himself comfortable. "Start from the top. I won't interrupt this time."

"Okay." Mat turned back to the transcript in his hands. " 'Monday the eleventh of December nineteen-forty-four. To whoever is reading this journal, I work at Bletchley Park and I have reason to believe there is something suspicious going on there involving one of my colleagues. The employee in question is Kenneth Johnson, and I am writing this to keep a record of his activities. There is evidence to suggest he is involved in something, but I do not know what. We work together in Hut Six. We have been romantically involved for several months now, but in secret at his request. He has no inkling of my suspicions at present.

" 'Earlier today I caught him smuggling a top-secret document from the building, inside his suit jacket. He does not know that I saw this.

" 'Later on, when I was over at his house for dinner, I took the opportunity to discreetly look around. I discovered a roll of camera film in a blank envelope. There is no way of knowing what the film held, as there was no label, so this could be innocent and unconnected.

" 'Later, he took a telephone call and I listened in. He didn't seem too pleased to be speaking to the mystery caller. He arranged to meet with them and wrote down a meeting time. He removed the paper from the pad, but I took the paper from below when he wasn't looking. It had impressions from the pen, as I had hoped, and I coloured over it with a pencil. It said 'Friday, three p.m.' but there was no location. I am going to question him about it. The note is in a pocket at the back of this notebook. If compared with samples of his writing, it will be evident that he wrote it.

" 'If I see anything else unusual, I will write it in here. I hope this is my last and only entry.

" 'Tuesday the twelfth of December nineteen-forty-four. I spoke to Kenny today and asked him what his plans were for Friday afternoon. He said he would be running errands, but he was not convincing. I am going to trail him from his house. Now it is a waiting game until Friday. I will report back afterwards.

" 'Friday the fifteenth of December nineteen-forty-four. Today was very eventful. I followed Kenny to an open area surrounded by shops. He sat at a park bench and read a newspaper. A strange man joined him on the bench and ate a sandwich. I couldn't see his face as he wore a fedora and dark glasses. Very unusual, as there was no sun. When he left, he took Kenny's briefcase, leaving an identical one in its place. Kenny looked inside and didn't show any surprise. I do not want to believe it, but I think he must be a spy. I do not have any evidence of what the briefcase contained, but I believe it must have been the secret files I caught him smuggling. I took photographs of the whole affair, but I do not know what to do with the film. I will hide it with the notebook for now. I am going home for Christmas tomorrow, so I will have to leave my investigation alone for the time being.

" 'Thursday the twenty-first of December nineteen-forty-four. I am home, and I am keeping this notebook and the roll of film in a hiding place my father made in the loft. It was the safest place I could think of. I have been trying to forget about Kenny for the holidays, but I cannot live with the knowledge that he is spreading government secrets, without doing something about it. I have arranged for him to meet me at the house tomorrow at ten a.m., and I have a plan to make sure Rose is out of the house. I am going to confront him about what he has done. I hope he will be remorseful and hand himself in. If what I know about him is true, then this will be the resolution. Otherwise, I will have to hand him over to the authorities myself. I cannot let this carry on. It is not right. I will report back tomorrow after my meeting with Kenny, and hopefully that will signal the end of the whole ordeal.' " There was silence as Mat placed the transcript down on the table and looked up at Charlie. "And that's the last entry..." He paused, then asked tentatively, "What date did Pearl die?"

"Friday the twenty-second of December nineteen-forty-four," Charlie replied instantly.

Mat sighed. "Well, I think it's suffice to say we've found our killer, then. She must've confronted him the next day like it says, and then he killed her to stop her from telling anyone about his little secret."

Charlie nodded glumly. "It seems like it."

"It's even worse that it wasn't just some randomer, it was someone she trusted. She must've felt so betrayed."

Charlie nodded again. He paused for a moment, before saying, "This is ridiculous! I thought I'd be happy when we found out the truth, but I feel rubbish. It's awful." Frustrated, he ran a hand through his hair.

"I know, it's such a bummer," Mat agreed, placing an elbow on the table and resting his chin in his hand. "That poor woman. The worst part is, we're gonna have to be the ones to tell her sister what happened to her."

Charlie groaned. "You're right. I'm not as excited to show her the transcript of the notebook now."

"I suppose we have to think of it as bringing Pearl to justice by discovering what actually happened to her, no matter how awful it is. And Rose will be relieved to finally find out the truth after all these years of not knowing."

"You're right. And there's no point in us sitting here sulking about it when we still have more work to do," Charlie said, sitting forward in his seat and sliding the transcript towards him. "At least we know who wrote the note now. And we know the identity of one of the men in the photos."

"Yep, Kenneth Johnson," Mat said, his voice laced with bitterness as he said the name. "I wonder what became of him?"

"Me too. I hope he came to a sticky end," Charlie said, then added, "No offence."

Mat laughed. "Should I look him up? There might be something about him online. Fingers crossed there is, anyway."

"Yeah, sure," Charlie said, as he began to scan through the transcript again. He sighed and put it to the side, then rooted around in his bag for the envelope containing the photographs Pearl had taken. He found the photo with the clearest image of Kenneth Johnson's face and stared at him. It was hard to believe that this man had caused so much sorrow, for so many people. Did he realise at this point just how much damage he was going to cause? Charlie didn't think it could have been his plan from the beginning, but rather his reaction when presented with an unexpected obstacle blocking his path. He thought it was a pretty scary notion that someone could have chosen to resolve the situation in such a horrible way.

Mat gasped, pulling Charlie out of his thoughts. "I've found an article about him!"

Charlie widened his eyes. "Have you? What does it say?"

"Well, it's not an article about *him* specifically, but there's a paragraph about him. It's an article about spies in the Cold War. It says, 'In nineteen-fifty-five, Kenneth Johnson was interviewed under suspicion of using his position at Bletchley Park, and later in MI6, to pass classified documents to the Soviets during World War Two and the Cold War. Johnson admitted to the charge of espionage and gave a written confession detailing all of his offences throughout his career. He was recruited during his time at Oxford University but refused to give up the names of any other spies he was aware of, even when presented with the chance of a reduced sentence. Johnson appeared to show remorse for his time spent as a Soviet spy, although he was always firm in the stance that he had never knowingly passed over any information that would be damaging to Great Britain. He was forced to resign from the Intelligence Service immediately and was later sentenced to nine years in prison for his crimes against Great Britain. Three years into his prison sentence, Johnson was found dead in his cell. His death is believed to have been self-inflicted.' "

"Oh." Charlie cringed. "I feel bad for wishing he'd met a sticky end now. But either way, it doesn't detract from the fact he was a bad person."

Mat nodded. "I wonder if he really felt remorse for his spying days, or if it was actually because he was secretly a murderer," he pondered.

"I'm leaning towards the second option right now."

"Me too," Mat agreed. He looked back at the laptop, then gasped. "I've just remembered! I was gonna show you what I found from listening to the audio we recorded last night. I don't think there's anything exciting, but then again, that's coming from me. I thought you might have more luck."

"Sure," Charlie said, moving to sit next to Mat and taking the earphone he was being offered. "There could be some hidden gems in there, and we need as much help as we can get before we head back to the house."

Mat began to play the unusual noises captured by their EVP recorders, and Charlie listened out for anything that sounded like human speech or sounds.

After a few minutes of listening intently to various snippets of audio, Charlie frowned. "Play that one again," he said, closing his eyes so he could concentrate better. Mat replayed the audio clip, and Charlie gasped. "That sounded like she said necklace!" he exclaimed.

"Really? I thought it sounded like hissing, like if wind rushed past a crack in the window or something. Or maybe the radiator turning on?"

"No, listen! It sounds like a female voice. You can clearly hear two syllables, and there's definitely a 'nuh,' 'kuh' and 'sss' sound in there."

Mat listened again. "I suppose it does sound a bit like necklace, if I concentrate really hard…"

Charlie turned to Mat excitedly. "When we were talking to Rose, she told us about their matching angel wing necklaces, do you remember? And she mentioned that Pearl's necklace was lost. What if Pearl is trying to tell us that it's still somewhere in the house? Where were we when this audio was captured?"

Mat turned back to the laptop and checked. "I'm not sure, but from the time it was taken, I think we were in the hallway."

"So, maybe her necklace is in the hallway somewhere?" Charlie suggested. "We're gonna have to look for it, at least. It would be amazing if we could find it for Rose."

Mat nodded. "Yeah, that would be great. It sounds like it means a lot to her."

"Hi," a soft voice interrupted, making Mat and Charlie jump. There was a young woman standing next to their table, smiling down at them. They recognised her as one of the people who worked in the café. "Just to let you know, we're going to be closing in around ten minutes' time."

Charlie checked his watch. "Oh, sorry. Is that the time already? We'll head off now." He and Mat began to pack their things away into their bags.

"No rush, I just wanted to make sure you were aware." The waitress smiled and began to clear their table.

Mat and Charlie both thanked her, then continued to collect their things together as quickly as they could. A couple of minutes later they opened the door of the café and were blasted with the cold night air. They hurried to the car and Mat put the heating on full blast to warm them up.

"Right," Charlie began, "it's nearly ten p.m.; we've spoken to Rose and found out some new stuff about Pearl; we've managed to decipher Pearl's notebook, and we kinda know what happened to her, but not fully; we know what happened to the man who is now the main suspect in her death. I think the only thing left to do is return to the house and see if Pearl can help us tie up any loose ends."

Mat rolled his eyes. "I don't know if *Pearl* will be any help, but going back to the house will be useful."

Charlie grinned. "So, we can agree on something then?" he asked.

"It appears so." Mat smirked. "Ready?"

"Yep, let's go."

They pulled out of the car park and headed towards the Carter house, determined to find the answers they sought before the night was over and learn the full truth of what happened to Pearl Carter.

CHAPTER TWENTY-SIX

Mat and Charlie pulled up outside the Carter house for the second night in a row and made their way inside, lugging all of their equipment with them. Once they had set everything down in the living room, Mat turned on the camera and pointed it towards himself, so both he and Charlie were in frame.

"So, here we are again, back at the Carter house. I'm starting to think we should just move in, we're here so often. I'm growing quite attached to the place," Mat said, turning to look at Charlie.

Charlie looked around the room and began to chew on his bottom lip. "Yeah, I'm not feeling the same way. I'm still *very* stressed. And that fireplace is freaking me out again. There's just something not right about it." He glared in the direction of the fireplace.

"Oh, that's a shame," Mat said, shaking his head sadly. "I'm sure Pearl would've loved having us as her new roomies; we're just starting to become good mates."

Charlie laughed. "Just because I'm feeling more comfortable around her now, doesn't mean I wanna move back in with her. My short stint when I was younger was enough for me," he said, before quickly adding, "No offence, Pearl."

"Right, where do you wanna start?"

Charlie breathed out slowly. "I dunno. We've got a lot we still need to figure out."

"Well, I think we should start with the most important thing first," Mat said, marching out through the living room door.

"What?" Charlie asked, following Mat through the hallway and into the kitchen.

Mat put the camera down on the bench and opened the cupboard doors. He pulled a packet of biscuits out and held them up to Charlie with a gleeful expression. "Mrs Harris hasn't disappointed, she's left us some custard creams this time! She's almost as bad a feeder as my *abuela*."

Charlie laughed. "Which is quite the statement, 'cause no one could beat Gloria in a feeding contest."

"Exactly! I'm surprised I don't gain fifty stone every time I visit her. Do you want a cuppa?"

"Yeah, please," Charlie said, pulling up a chair at the kitchen table. "It might help us focus while we draw up a plan of action."

"Of course it will. Tea solves everything – that's my life motto." Mat set to making their cups of tea, calling out into the air, "Bear with us, Pearl. We'll be with you soon to share our findings, but if you wouldn't mind waiting out in the hall until we're ready, it would be much appreciated."

Charlie laughed. "You're an idiot."

It wasn't long before they were both sat at the kitchen table in front of the camera, eating custard creams and poring over their findings. Charlie was writing down everything they knew, and what they still needed to find out.

Mat fiddled with his ring as he stared at the wall, deep in thought. "We still have no idea what actually happened on the day Pearl died. How did the situation escalate to her lying dead at the bottom of the stairs? We *think* we've worked out the why and the who, but we still don't know the how."

Charlie yawned and wiped the sleep out of his eyes. "My brain is too fried to make sense of anything."

"Same here, and I haven't just spent hours deciphering coded messages," Mat said, patting Charlie on the back sympathetically. "Look, we're never gonna know exactly what happened, 'cause there's no way for

Pearl to tell us now. But if we analyse all the information we've gathered, we might be able to take a good guess at something close to the truth."

"Yeah, you're right. Why don't we go and have a look around the hallway now? See if we can put ourselves in her shoes."

Mat sat back and folded his arms. "Wow, you must be tired. You didn't come out with some crazy idea of getting your little radio out and asking Pearl what happened. I had a snarky comment prepared and everything."

"Well, it'll be easier for us to say what we think happened, and Pearl can tell us if we get anything wrong. She's not exactly gonna come out with a full-blown monologue explaining the exact course of events, is she? That's just silly." Charlie threw his head back and guffawed at the thought of it.

Mat stared at him. "Yeah, that's the silly part." He widened his eyes at the camera and twisted his left index finger in circles by his temple, implying that he thought Charlie was losing his marbles.

"Ahh, imagine." Charlie wiped his eyes as he continued chuckling. "Right, should we go through to the hallway?"

"Yes, I think that would be best."

They drained the rest of their tea and made their way through to the hallway. Mat stood the camera on the phone table and he and Charlie began to look around, taking in the space around them as their brains whirred trying to fill in the missing pieces from the puzzle.

"Okay," Charlie said, moving over to stand by the stairs, "let's recap what we know for sure about the events of the twenty-second of December nineteen-forty-four. So, we know from Pearl's notebook that she had arranged to meet with Kenneth Johnson at ten a.m. that morning, at this address. She was planning to confront him about what she'd seen and accuse him of being a spy. We know from our conversation with Rose that this must've gone ahead as planned, since Pearl had arranged for her to spend the morning with their grandma. After this, everything becomes a bit hazy, until the afternoon, when Rose and Dorothy found Pearl dead, right here at the bottom of the stairs. Now, we need to figure out what happened in the meantime." Charlie started to pace around the hallway, biting his nails with a frown etched upon his face.

"What do we know about the crime scene? We might be able to use that to connect the dots."

"Good idea." Charlie got his notes and flicked through them until he found the part describing the crime scene. "Pearl had two head injuries, one on the back of her head and one on her forehead… they found her handbag lying on its side at the top of the stairs – that's why they thought she must've tripped over it…

they found blood on the edge of the phone table, which was never explained. There's no way she could've hit her head there if she'd fallen down the stairs… the blood pattern on the stairs was random and didn't match their conclusion either… and the front door was unlocked."

Mat frowned. "Well, I think what we can take from that is she didn't fall down the stairs, and she wasn't pushed either. That must've been set up after she was already dead."

Charlie nodded. "I agree. It was probably just to throw the police off the scent and make it look like an acci–" A floorboard creaked in the hallway, and he stopped talking. "What was that?" he said tensely.

"I dunno. Maybe it was one of us moving?"

Charlie shook his head. "It came from over there," he said, pointing next to the stairs. He walked over to inspect the floor.

"It was probably nothing to worry about. It's a very old house. Maybe there's a family of rats living here?" Mat said, walking over to pick up the camera.

"That doesn't make me feel any better, Mat!" Charlie knelt down and inspected the floor. Just as he was about to stand back up, the floorboard right in front of him shook slightly. He shrieked and jumped away from it, falling backwards and banging his elbows on the floor.

"Are you alright?" Mat asked, rushing over to help him to his feet. "What happened?"

"The floorboard moved!" Charlie said in disbelief, staring wild-eyed at the place he had just been kneeling on the floor.

"Are you sure?" Mat asked incredulously. He reached forward and put a hand on Charlie's forehead.

"What are you doing?"

"I'm just checking your temperature. Making sure you're not having fever hallucinations."

Charlie rolled his eyes. "I swear it moved! I'm not seeing things."

Mat nodded his head. "Of course you aren't, Chaz," he said kindly. "Maybe you should go and have a sit down for a bit. It's been a long day."

"Mat." Charlie glared at him. "I haven't gone mad. Do you think you might've caught it on camera?"

"I don't think so. I hadn't followed you over yet, I was just picking up the camera from the phone table."

"Typical!" Charlie scowled before walking back over to look at the floorboard. "Do you think it could be another hiding place?"

"Surely they wouldn't have used *another* floorboard as a hiding place. One is enough. Anyway, Pearl didn't mention anything about a second hiding place in the notebook."

"Good point… I think we should open it up anyway, though."

Mat shook his head frantically. "Charlie! We can't just go around prising up floorboards willy-nilly! Mrs Harris won't be very happy with us if we start pulling her house apart."

"Come on, we have to check it out," Charlie said. "We can just have a quick peek inside! It could be something important."

Mat narrowed his eyes and stared at him. "Okay," he said eventually, before adding, "But be careful!"

Charlie grinned, then felt around the edges of the floorboard. "How do you prise up a floorboard? This one doesn't seem to be loose. There's a gap on one side, though; that could come in handy."

"Well, I would've said to use a crowbar, but we don't have one of those with us."

"Do you think there's a possibility we have one stashed in the car boot that we don't know about?" Charlie asked hopefully.

Mat laughed. "I think we would've noticed by now, the amount of times we've had to go in there over the past couple of days."

"True." Charlie sighed. "Let's look around the house and see if there's anything we can use."

They began to wander around the downstairs of the house, scrutinising every object to see if any of them looked like they could fit in the gap next to the floorboard. Charlie searched the kitchen first, hoping to come across some sort of cooking utensil they could use. Meanwhile, Mat searched the living room. He scanned the room as he walked around, until his eyes fell on the set of fire pokers next to the fireplace. He picked one out with a somewhat flat but curved end and turned it over in his hands. "Chaz, I think I've got something!" he called, making his way back into the hallway.

Charlie hurried out of the kitchen with a beaming smile on his face, which slipped away when he saw what Mat was holding. "We can't use that!"

"Why not?"

"Because... we can't!" Charlie said, struggling to think of a valid reason.

"Is this because of the 'bad vibes' you keep going on about?" Mat asked, raising his eyebrows.

"Maybe..." Charlie said sheepishly.

"Charlie, it's just a fire poker. I'll do it though, if you want."

"I'd prefer that, thanks," Charlie said, stepping out of the way.

Mat passed the camera to Charlie and walked over to the floorboard. He put his hands on his hips as he inspected it. "If this goes wrong, the new floorboards are coming out of your pay check," he joked, shooting Charlie a look of disapproval.

Charlie laughed. "That's fine by me."

Mat pushed the end of the fire poker down into the gap and began to lever it upwards slowly. The floorboard began to lift as Mat pushed down on it, until it had fully lifted away from the floor.

"Yes! It worked. And not a scratch on it," Charlie said, bending down to move the floorboard out of the way.

He looked inside the gap and saw a glint of gold in amongst the dust. He reached in and pulled out the small object, then held it up to the light.

It was a delicate gold necklace, with a beautiful angel wing pendant hanging from it, just like the one belonging to Rose.

CHAPTER TWENTY-SEVEN

Charlie held up the dainty gold necklace to the camera, feeling so stunned that all he was able to do was look at Mat, a wide grin spreading over his face.

"We've found it!" Mat said, reaching down to take the necklace from Charlie and lifting his glasses as he squinted at it.

"I can't believe that's been down there this whole time!"

"I know! How has nobody ever come across it before?"

"Well, it was covered by a carpet for a lot of years, and I suppose the boards mustn't have needed to be taken up or replaced when they were removed."

"Rose is gonna be so chuffed when we give this to her!"

"She is." Charlie grinned. "I wonder how it got there?"

"I dunno..."

Charlie looked up from his vantage point where he was kneeling on the floor, and noticed he could see the stairs through the spindles that made up the bannister. He frowned and looked back down at the gap in the floor. "I wonder..."

"What are you thinking?" Mat asked, as Charlie passed the camera back to him and replaced the floorboard over the hole in the floor, as it had been before they had touched it.

"Aha!" Charlie said, pointing at the slight gap between the floorboards. "If Pearl's necklace came off on the stairs, it could've slipped through the bannister and onto the floor, then slipped through this gap!"

Mat followed the route with his eyes, analysing whether he thought it would work. He nodded. "Yeah, that seems plausible. But you would think she would've noticed it coming off and tried to get it back, or at least mentioned it to Rose."

"Maybe it happened when she was already dead," Charlie said darkly.

Mat's eyes widened. "Oh... you mean when Kenneth was setting up the 'accident'?" He grimaced.

Charlie nodded. He stood up and ran a hand through his hair, frowning. "But how did it get to that point?" He exchanged a blank look with Mat.

"Why don't we run it through from Kenneth's arrival, and see if we can deduce what might've happened?" Mat suggested.

Charlie shrugged. "It's worth a shot." He took the necklace from Mat and tucked it away safely in his backpack.

Mat walked over to stand by the front door and pointed the camera in front of him, the fire poker still hanging loosely by his side. "Okay… so, let's say, Kenneth turns up at the house at their agreed meeting time. Do they go through to the living room, or does the confrontation happen right here?"

"She was nervous, so I think they would've sat down first, so she could build up to it," Charlie said, walking through to the living room.

Mat followed him through and they sat down on the armchairs. "They probably had a bit of small talk, then she hit him with the real reason she'd invited him that day," Mat offered.

"Yep, she confronted him and told him what she knew. We can't know what was said, but I think it's safe to say he didn't like it. Maybe he got angry, or scared. Either way, he obviously didn't want anyone else to find out. Feel free to jump in and correct us, Pearl, if we get anything wrong."

"Pearl said in her last entry that she wanted the whole thing to be over and done with, whether that meant she had to hand Kenneth in herself or not – I might be paraphrasing there. Maybe she told him the same thing and he panicked."

Charlie nodded and stood up. "He would've known how stubborn Pearl was. There was no way he'd be able to change her mind once she'd decided she was gonna hand him in."

"He would've been scared that his little side venture was gonna be cut short. Maybe he lashed out. Hit her with something. That's what made the injury on the back of her head."

Charlie gasped. "Oh my god! The blood on the phone table!" He rushed into the hallway to check where the phone table was in relation to the living room door. "This phone table has been positioned in the same place as the original. The blood was on the corner closest to the living room door. What if, he hit her on the back of the head and she fell forward, banging her forehead on the corner of the phone table. That explains both of her injuries. So, she had to have been walking away from him when it happened."

"Yes!" Mat said, following Charlie into the hallway. "That would make sense. Maybe she was leaving to tell someone. Or she was gonna use the phone?"

"Yeah, exactly! I dunno what he would've hit her with, though. It must've been something within arm's reach, 'cause I don't think it was premeditated. It was a heat of the moment thing."

"*Ay*!" Mat exclaimed suddenly, dropping the fire poker he was still carrying around with him and cursing in Spanish. "What the hell?"

"What happened?" Charlie asked, staring at Mat with wide eyes.

"It burned me!" Mat replied, shaking his sore hand and frowning at the fire poker.

"You're not joking around?" Charlie asked tentatively.

"No! I'm being serious. I swear on my life," Mat persisted, putting the camera down on the phone table so he could massage his hand. "It might've been really cold actually, rather than hot, 'cause that can feel similar when it comes as a shock."

"Wait," Charlie said, a look of understanding washing over his face, "what if that was Pearl trying to point us towards the murder weapon?"

"What do you mean?" Mat asked, still sulking over his sore hand.

"What if Kenneth picked up the closest thing he could find… and that thing was a fire poker? That would explain why I always get such bad vibes from the fireplace. Pearl was trying to tell me all along."

Mat gave Charlie a sceptical look, then walked through to the living room and had a look around. After a moment, he turned around and nodded, looking impressed. "I'm not sure about the way you came to the conclusion, but I think you could be right about the fire poker. They're right there, easy to grab in the heat of the moment. They're made of iron, by the looks of it, so they could do some damage in the wrong hands."

"My exact thoughts," Charlie said, nodding his head. "Then, Kenneth must've panicked and tried to cover up what he'd done. He obviously cleaned up the crime scene as much as he could, but he missed that one patch of blood on the phone table. Then he dragged her up the stairs and threw her down, and that must be when Pearl lost her necklace."

"And he must've put her handbag at the top of the stairs to support the idea of it being a tragic accident."

"Yeah, he really thought it all through. But Pearl was one step ahead of him. If only the notebook had been found sooner."

"So, if we're right, then he didn't actually mean to kill her – but that's no excuse."

They stood in silence for a few moments, the significance of what they had discovered beginning to dawn on them. Knowing what had happened there so many years ago seemed to taint the innocence of the place, making it seem duller than it did before.

Charlie cleared his throat. "Pearl," he said softly, "if you're here with us, there's a few things we need to let you know. First of all, Rose is okay. We went to visit her earlier today. She misses you, but she's doing well. She's married to a man called Bernard Lawson, and they have a beautiful family. She became an artist, and she told us it's all because of the encouragement you gave her. We'll make sure we return the necklace to her as soon as we can, and we'll tell her the truth of what happened."

Mat stood back quietly as Charlie spoke. Even though he didn't believe that Pearl was listening, he thought this was something Charlie needed to do to be able to move on. For this reason, he listened without interruption, and when Charlie glanced over, he gave him a smile of encouragement.

"Secondly, we know that you worked at Bletchley Park. When you died, the codebreaking operation was still top secret, so you won't have ever found out what you helped to achieve during the war. You were a vital part of the war effort, and you helped to stop a number of serious incidents, saving the lives of millions of people over the course of the war. You should be so proud of yourself, Pearl. What you all did there was *amazing*, and I've always been so fascinated by it all. You and all the other codebreakers of Bletchley Park are my heroes, you really are. Thank you for everything you did. We're gonna make sure you're added to the list of people who worked there, because you deserve to be recognised for your work.

"And last of all, Kenneth Johnson. We looked up his name and found out what happened to him, and I think you have a right to know. I'm sorry to say, he continued working as a Soviet spy until nineteen-fifty-five, when he was found out by the government. He confessed to espionage and was sentenced to nine years in prison. If it's any consolation, he apparently showed remorse for what he did. But, he died three years into his prison sentence… and it looks like he killed himself. We couldn't find out any more than that.

"I'm really sorry for everything you've been through, Pearl, but know that we're gonna make sure your story is heard. You died because you were fighting for what's right, which is very noble, but also *extremely* unfair. I hope you can rest now, knowing that justice has been served – as much as it can be, at least."

The hallway became silent again, and Mat and Charlie shared a look of relief with each other, knowing they had done everything they could.

Mat patted Charlie on the back. "Good job, mate."

Charlie smiled, but before he could reply, the front door burst open and a fierce wind rushed past them, chilling the hallway instantly.

Mat rushed to the door and forced it shut, pushing against the wind, then locked it just to make sure it couldn't fly open again. "Oh my god! The wind's *really* strong tonight! I've never seen anything like it. What's up with that?" he said, breathing heavily.

Charlie ran a hand through his hair, the colour draining from his face. "I don't think that was just the wind, Mat. I think it was Pearl. She must finally be free."

Mat twisted his face and opened his mouth to retort, but then thought better of it and closed it again. He sighed and forced a smile. "Yeah, sure. Y'know what? That's actually a really nice way to look at it, Chaz. I hope she's happy now."

Charlie smiled, grateful that Mat was letting him have his moment to digest what had happened. The adrenaline from their investigation began to wear off all of a sudden, and his eyes began to droop. He yawned loudly and realised that his legs were starting to feel shaky.

Mat yawned too, the tiredness becoming contagious. "Come on," he said, "let's get some sleep. I feel like a zombie."

Charlie nodded, too tired to respond, and they made their way through to the living room. Luckily, they had already carried the sleeping bags in from the car, so all they had to do was roll them out and grab their pillows.

"Night, Mat."

"Night, Chaz."

They each got into their sleeping bags without even bothering to get changed, and within moments they were both fast asleep.

CHAPTER TWENTY-EIGHT

Charlie held up a hand to block out the bright light that was interrupting his deep sleep, scrunching up his eyes and trying to ignore it. As he was trying to force himself back to sleep, he suddenly realised he could hear birds tweeting merrily and water flowing in the distance. He frowned and opened his eyes to find that he was standing in the middle of a luscious green forest. Confused about how he had ended up there, he began to turn around slowly and take in his surroundings.

There were brightly coloured flowers scattered all around the forest floor, at the base of the trees which formed a canopy above his head. The blinding sun had managed to squeeze its way through the gaps in the trees, forming random patches of light on the forest floor.

Charlie felt as if he recognised the place and tried to force his brain to think of where he could have seen it before. The answer was on the tip of his tongue, but he couldn't quite reach it, no matter how hard he tried. He sighed deeply and began to explore the forest, feeling as if he were floating rather than walking.

As he reached an opening in the trees, he inhaled sharply. He remembered where he had seen the forest before. He smacked a hand to his forehead, wondering how he could possibly have forgotten about the dream. It all came flooding back to him at once.

The forest. The meadow. The stream. And Pearl, in full colour and pleading for his help.

He ran through the opening in the trees and across the colourful meadow grass, stopping at the stream and looking both ways. He spotted Pearl standing further along the bank to his right and began to walk briskly towards her.

"Pearl!" he called out, as he got closer. He quickened his pace into a jog, so he could reach her more quickly.

Pearl beamed at him as he joined her. "Charlie, I cannot thank you enough," she said, tears forming in her eyes. "I've been in that house for seventy-six years, waiting for someone to come along who would be able to help me. I was starting to think it would never happen! It gets rather lonely after a while, trapped in those four walls. I hope whatever is waiting for me next is better. I might get to see my mother and father again."

Charlie grinned. "I'm sure you will. And at some point, in the future, you'll be reunited with Rose!"

Pearl smiled brightly. "I cannot wait for that day – although, I hope it's a while before that happens." She bit her lip and moved her hand up to her necklace. "Please, Charlie, if it isn't too much to ask, could you take my necklace to Rose and let her know that our tradition still applies. No matter how far apart we are, as long as we have our angel wings we will always be connected."

Charlie nodded. "Of course. We're gonna go there first thing tomorrow, so we can explain everything to her. We wanted to show her your notebook before we hand it in to the police. Don't worry, we've got it all covered. We're gonna sort everything out as best as we can. It's important that people know about your sacrifice."

Pearl smiled and wiped away her tears, then stepped forward to hug Charlie tightly. "Thank you so much, dear. And tell your friend that I'm very thankful for his help, as well," she said thickly, before pulling away from him and stepping back.

"I will, but I can't promise it'll mean anything to him," Charlie said honestly.

"That's alright. I think somewhere deep down inside he believes more than he thinks he does."

Charlie grinned. "I like your enthusiasm, but I'm not so sure about that."

"I completely understand his scepticism, however. I wouldn't believe in ghosts if I wasn't one myself!" Pearl said, and Charlie laughed. She paused and looked over her shoulder. A wooden door had appeared in the thick trunk of one of the trees closest to them, and a soft white glow was emanating from behind it. "I think it might be time for me to depart now."

Charlie nodded. "Can I just ask you a quick question before you go?"

"Of course."

"How did you know Mat's full name is Mateo? It kinda freaked me out a bit last night, because we hadn't used that name in the house. Was it just a lucky guess?"

"I read his name over your shoulder yesterday evening, when you were making that short film for… oh, what did you call it?" Pearl paused and furrowed her brow as she tried to remember. "Instant stories?"

"Oh! You mean the video I posted on my Instagram story?"

"Yes! That was it! I was looking over your shoulder and I saw you write down the name Mateo Jones, so I just assumed that was his name. I'm sorry, I wasn't trying to frighten you!"

"So, you knew Mat's full name is Mateo because you saw me tag him on my Insta story," Charlie said slowly, starting to laugh. "I can't imagine the kind of sarcastic comment Mat will come out with when I tell him that. I can hear him laughing already."

Pearl smiled, her eyes twinkling. She glanced behind her and saw that the light coming out from behind the door seemed to be glowing brighter by the second. "Right, I'd best be on my way; I don't know how long the door will wait for me! Charlie, I cannot thank you and Mateo enough for helping me."

"It was our pleasure," Charlie said, smiling warmly.

Pearl returned the smile and turned around, beginning to walk towards the tree that held the wooden door.

Charlie watched from the edge of the stream as Pearl approached the door and tentatively reached her hand out to the handle. As she opened the door, the white glow streamed outwards, even brighter than before. Pearl walked into the light, and as she did so the light glowed even more intensely, stretching out from the tree and up to where Charlie stood. He squinted and covered his eyes, and soon everything around him was engulfed in the bright, white light.

Charlie blinked rapidly as he woke up to sunlight streaming in through the window. It took him a couple of seconds to process what had happened, then he smiled to himself and whispered, "Goodbye, Pearl."

Turning over in his sleeping bag, he saw that Mat was still fast asleep, curled up in his own sleeping bag.

After their hectic couple of days, Charlie thought they deserved a lie in.

He closed his eyes and drifted back to sleep.

EPILOGUE

It had been a few weeks since Mat and Charlie had returned home from their eventful trip to the Carter house. Christmas and New Year had been and gone, and Charlie's birthday was fast approaching. Every spare moment in their busy schedule had been dedicated to working on perfecting the video of their investigation, which turned out to be so long that they had decided to split it into a three-part mini-series.

One afternoon, when they were almost ready to start sharing the series on their YouTube channel, they took some time to sit down in the living room of their flat and film a conclusion.

"So… that was eventful," Charlie said to the camera, which was set up in front of the settee, where they were sitting.

Mat laughed. "No kidding!"

"In the last clip you saw, we had just figured out what really happened to Pearl Carter. Well, we're back home now, and we've had some time to digest what happened. We went to visit Rose the day after to give her back Pearl's necklace. We didn't film anything, because it was quite a private moment."

"She was over the moon, as you can imagine. She didn't think she'd ever see that necklace again," Mat said.

"Yeah, it was quite emotional, actually. We explained everything to her and she was sad, obviously, but she was also relieved to finally know the truth. We asked if it would still be okay for us to share everything we'd filmed online."

"We didn't wanna just put it out there for everyone to see, if she wasn't comfortable with that. Obviously, she agreed, otherwise you wouldn't be watching this video."

Charlie nodded. "Like us, she wanted Pearl's story to be heard, so we promised we would do everything we could to make sure that happened. We handed the notebook in to the police, and they said they're gonna look into it and make some enquiries."

"It might be a little while before anything happens, unfortunately, with it being an old case. But like we said, the most important thing is to get the story out there. So please, if you could share this series as far and wide as you can, that would be amazing. We want it to reach as many people as possible."

"Please do." Charlie nodded, before exhaling slowly. "So... final thoughts. The Carter house – haunted or not haunted? I'm saying *definitely* haunted. Although, it might not be anymore."

Mat paused and twisted his face. "I dunno."

Charlie turned to stare at him. "What do you mean, you don't know?"

"I just dunno..." Mat shrugged. "While it was happening, I have to admit, I felt a little freaked out."

Charlie grinned, his eyes sparkling. "Did you?"

"*But,*" Mat continued quickly, "since then, I've taken a step back and thought about it all properly, from a scientific point of view. I have to be honest, I think there's a logical explanation for most of the things that happened during the investigation."

Charlie's face dropped. "Seriously?"

"I mean, don't get me wrong, I'm happy we managed to solve the mystery of what really happened to Pearl. I'm just not sure it was because her ghost was still roaming the house. One thing I will say, is that if anywhere we've visited was gonna be haunted, it would be that place. The evidence was the most compelling I've seen so far. There were some big coincidences that led to us finding some pretty significant things. But there wasn't anything concrete, y'know?"

Charlie snorted. "You mean, Pearl didn't appear in front of you and strangle you to death?"

"Look, all I want is a scratch, or a ghostly hand print, or a bruise – any sort of physical proof that I'm in the presence of something paranormal. Is that too much to ask?"

Charlie let out an exasperated sigh and ran a hand through his hair. "I should've known you were gonna somehow explain it all away. I bet you've been sitting up all night, every night since we got home, coming up with theories and plotting how you're gonna get out of this one."

Mat laughed. "How did you know? Have you been spying on me?"

"I'm gonna get you to admit that ghosts are real one day, I swear!"

Mat sat back and crossed his arms, an amused expression on his face. "Good luck with that."

Charlie laughed. "Right, let's end this video before we have a falling out."

"Good idea." Mat turned to look at the camera. "Let us know down in the comment section if there's anywhere in particular you'd like us to investigate in future videos."

"Yeah, and follow us on our social media accounts, which we'll link to in the description box below. Tag us in your Instagram posts and tweet us with any of your theories that we might not've considered."

"Please send me any paranormal evidence you're unsure of. I'll happily refute it all."

Charlie laughed. "Check out our second channel, *More Paranormal Detectives*, for any unseen footage and extra videos, and we'll see you all soon on this channel, where we'll be investigating another haunted location. But in the meantime, stay curious."

"Stay *realistic*."

"Stay Paranormal Detecting!" they said together. "Bye!"

"I still feel like an absolute lemon doing that outro," Mat said as he stood up.

Charlie let out a snort of laughter. "Oh, shut up! You love it really. Anyway, you're the one who came up with it in the first place!"

"Yeah, but I didn't think we'd actually use it!" Mat replied, hiding a smirk as he turned off the camera. "So, where do you think we should investigate next?"

"I dunno… I'm thinking that maybe we should check out the American ghosts. See how they match up to the ones we have over here."

"I mean, they don't have much competition, to be fair."

Charlie ignored Mat's comment. "And while we're there, I think it's about time I fulfilled my end of the deal."

Mat frowned. "What do you mean?"

"When you agreed to go ghost hunting for the first time, you said that the only condition was that we went to the Kennedy Space Center at some point. It's been a couple of years now; I think it's about time we organised that trip."

Mat's eyes lit up. "Oh my god! I'd completely forgotten about that. I'm gonna start looking at holidays right now." He pulled his laptop over and opened it up, his fingers typing furiously. "When do you wanna go? I'm thinking maybe April or May, so the weather's getting warmer, but it's not too hot."

Charlie laughed. "Woah, Mat, let's not get ahead of ourselves. We'll have to do some research first and decide which haunted sites we wanna visit. We may as well do a few while we're over there."

Mat stopped typing and looked over at Charlie. "Yeah, you're right. I'm just excited."

"It's normally me who has to be reined in!"

"Yeah, but this is the *Kennedy Space Center*. I've wanted to go there my whole life!"

"I know. I'll tell you what, I'll start researching right away, so we can get it all organised as soon as possible," Charlie said, standing up from the settee. "But first, I'm gonna make a cup of tea. Do you want one?"

Mat grinned. "Is the Moon the fifth largest natural satellite in our solar system?"

Charlie hesitated. "I'm not sure."

"Yes, Chaz." Mat nodded solemnly. "The answer is always yes."

ABOUT THE AUTHOR

Emily Grace is a young author from the North East of England, where she lives with her parents and older sister. When she isn't writing, she enjoys reading, playing board games, watching murder mystery shows, hanging out with her best friend, and has a keen interest in mathematics. While this is her first published novel, she plans to share more of Mat and Charlie's adventures, and write many more books beyond!

Follow Emily on Instagram: ***@booksbyemilygrace***

Check out her website for updates on future releases: ***booksbyemilygrace.wordpress.com***

Printed in Great Britain
by Amazon

63532221R00206